THE WRATH
OF THE
RAINFOREST

Encounters with the supernatural, based on actual events

GUENTER MEMMERT

Copyright © 2013 Dr. Guenter Memmert
E-mail: wrath.rainforest@gmail.com
All rights reserved.

ISBN: 0615775780
ISBN-13: 9780615775784
Library of Congress Control Number: 2013904001
Guenter\Memmert

To Karin

PREFACE

It is the year 1888. A physics professor at the Karlsruher Politechnikum (Technical School of Karlsruhe) enters the classroom. Under each arm he carries a simple device made up of two metal balls each and a few wires. He puts one of these identical devices on the left side of a table and the other device a little distance away, maybe three to four feet, on the other side of the table. When the professor begins to feed one of these simple contraptions with electricity, as expected, sparks are generated in the gap between two wire ends, rapidly oscillating electric sparks.

To the utter surprise of his students, the device at the other end of the table responds with oscillating sparks as well.

With this simple experiment, Heinrich Hertz proves that the theory of the Scottish physicist James Clerk Maxwell is correct. Electromagnetic or radio waves do exist and can travel with the speed of light from one point to another without the help of a wire.

Heinrich Hertz was the first man who sent and received radio waves. His students were awed. When they wanted to know what use might be made of this astounding phenomenon, Heinrich Hertz replied:

"It is of no use whatsoever."

How utterly wrong he was!

A young, spoiled tinkerer, the son of a wealthy landowner, who just turned twenty-one, Guglielmo Marconi read about Heinrich Hertz's experiment and instantaneously recognized a practical application.

"It should be possible to use Heinrich Hertz's oscillators to send signals, yes, not only signals, even messages without the need for wires," Marconi mused in the attic of his parents' villa.

He set about to rebuild and improve on Heinrich Hertz's machines and was soon able to send a signal over a distance of a mile and a half. A year later he demonstrated to the British Post Office his system on Salisbury Plain and even across the Bristol Channel. In 1899 he established a wireless communication between France and England across the English Channel. Encouraged by his success, he dared to try the unimaginable. In 1901 he transmitted the first wireless signals all the way across the Atlantic between Cornwall and Newfoundland, a distance of 2,100 miles.

With his experiments based on Hertz's classroom demonstration, young Marconi flung the barn doors wide open, allowing a bright and vivid new reality to flood into our world, a real world that not even the wildest futurists could have imagined. From sending telegraphic messages, the development rapidly moved on to transmitting radio shows. And it was not too long before television established itself in our living rooms. Today the cellular phone is as common and ubiquitous as the food we eat and the clothes we wear.

At any given moment we are surrounded by billions of conversations and hundreds and thousands of colorful, living pictures, expectations, arguments, fantasies, and emotions. For us the presence of radio, television, cell pones, GPS, Wi-Fi, and Bluetooth has become such a reality that our lives are not imaginable without them anymore. They are as real as the things we can touch with our fingers, smell with our noses, taste with our tongues, see with our eyes, and hear with our ears. Yet, we neither see, hear, smell, taste, nor feel these sounds and pictures that are all around us. Our biological senses do not grant us access to this world.

We need a portal into this parallel world of ours, a rather simple device that grants us access. These devices are nothing else but some silicone, the most abundant material of our tangible world, some copper wires, and a little plastic. If we put these basic things together in the right way and feed them with energy and electricity, then bam—the portal springs wide open, and we walk through into this Garden of Eden.

With the myriad of information all around us, one would expect that stepping through the portal would drown us in a bottomless sea of chaos, of billions of voices in Babylonian language confusion storming in on us like a typhoon, of millions of colorful pictures blending together into one swirling vortex of color. But with our little devices, we can filter from this gargantuan hotchpotch exactly the information we want, undisturbed by everything else around it. From our patio in a suburb of Los Angeles, we can talk to our son who is riding a cab in England on his way to Heathrow Airport; we can talk to him as if he were sitting across from us at the round patio table. The GPS in our car tells us within feet where we are on this planet of ours. While our daughter watches via satellite dish a love story on her TV set in her room, we follow live a football game brought to our living room from the same satellite dish. No confusion, no chaos, no hotchpotch. And we take this all for granted as if it were the most natural phenomenon on earth. And yes, from today's knowledge it is, and it is all explainable and comprehensible.

Let us turn the time back a mere one hundred years. Thanks to modern medicine, many people still live who were born about a hundred years ago. When they were young and somebody had told them about our world today, they would not have believed him one word. Humbug, phantasm would they have called it. Jules Verne's futuristic books are naïve compared to today's reality, a reality to which they did not have the key, the necessary receptors yet.

Who dares to say that there is not so much more around us in this very nature of which we have no knowledge yet? Who can claim with certainty that we know it all, that there are no other parallel worlds, that there are no spirits, no ghosts, and that they are not as much part of our world, our nature, our reality as we are? It might well be that we are just lacking the sensory organs to acknowledge their existence and their presence. Ghosts and spirits might be as real and natural as we are, and one day we might be able to communicate with them at ease. Actually many cultures and nations do already. Can we dare to look down on them, the people of Indonesia, Thailand, Malaysia, Singapore, China, the Philippines, India, and many more? The countries of the Far East, especially Southeast Asia, are developing faster than the West. Their economies are more energetic than those of Western Europe and even North America. Singapore is an international high-tech center, India is leading in software development, Shanghai eclipses New York, and some of the world's top hotels can be found in Bangkok and in Manila. The Far East is modern, high tech, highly advanced, well educated, and full of energy and drive. Nevertheless spirits and ghosts are an integral part of everyday life in these countries; they form part of nature as much as plants, animals, and we humans do.

Maybe we should heed William Shakespeare's advice in *Hamlet*:

> There are more things in heaven and earth, Horatio,
> Than are dreamt of in your philosophy.

PROLOGUE

PRAMBANAN

Once upon a time, a time long gone, there lived two kings on an island far, far away from our shores, an island floating in the tropical sea under the Southern Cross. King Prabu was a wise man whose kingdom was flourishing and prosperous. The other kingdom was ruled by a cruel man-eating giant, Boko. This giant became jealous of the prosperity of King Prabu's people and decided to attack his neighbor. King Prabu's people were no match for the giant's cohorts, and Boko's henchmen killed many of Prabu's soldiers in a bloody battle and then set about to devastate Prabu's land. In despair Prabu sent his own son into battle. Prabu's son, Bandung, was in unison with nature and respected and honored by the animals of the forests and the spirits of the earth, the fire, the water, and the air. With their help Bandung defeated Boko in a furious battle and killed him. Bandung marched on into Boko's kingdom, where he met

Boko's daughter Loro Jonggrang. He was overwhelmed by her beauty and grace and proposed to marry her.

Loro Jonggrang, however, was repelled by the prince because in her eyes he was the murderer of her father. To deter the prince from his desire to marry her, she set him a task, a task so insurmountable that she could be certain he would not be able to accomplish it. She declared that she would marry him if he could build a temple with a thousand statues in one night. The prince took on the challenge. With the help of the spirits of the island, he began to build, and built and built through the night. The morning was still far away when he had almost completed the monumental task. The princess panicked and in her despair asked the women of the villages to come to her aid. The women were only too glad to give her their support in defeating the prince. In a feverish effort, they piled up huge stacks of hay to the east and set them on fire to make the prince believe that the sun was about to rise. The women also pounded rice as if the day's work had begun. They even fooled the roosters into crowing.

The spirits fled in terror of what they took for the sunlight. Feverishly the prince counted the statues he had built during the night with his helpers: nine hundred ninety-seven, nine hundred ninety-eight, nine hundred ninety-nine... He was one statue short. He was ready to admit his defeat, when he realized the trick Loro Jonggrang had played on him. In his rage he furiously cursed her into a stone statue, the final touch in his nightly work, and thus he finished the temple.

"Loro Jonggrang, there was only one statue left. Let you be the one to make the temple complete."

Then his heart broke and he died at the feet of the statue, the most beautiful of all the thousand statues of the temple.

Because of this tragedy, nobody dared to go near the sprawling temple, and the spirits of the forest and the earth lay claim to what they had built in one night. With their green fingers, they reached out for their masterpiece and day by day took over a little more of the vast temple. Soon the temple disappeared in a thick jungle and was eventually completely hidden from human eyes although it was not more than three hundred feet away from a busy country road. Travelers passing by every day were unaware of the beauty not more than a stone's throw from their route.

There the temple slept its sleeping beauty sleep until early into the twentieth century, when a scientist set out to kiss the temple of Prambanan awake. He was convinced that if the epic saga of Troy had turned out to be true, why not should the Indonesian legend of Prambanan be true as well in some way or another?

Some ten miles northeast of Yogyakarta on the island of Java in the Valley of Kings, the scientist lifted the green veil from the Prambanan temple complex. Today when you travel by air from Bali to Yogyakarta in Central Java, you will inevitably see the massive Hindu temple complex of Prambanan. If you travel by road from an easterly direction to the city of Yogyakarta, you cannot miss it. Prambanan is only the length of a football field off the road. Whichever means of travel you take, when you become aware of this massive temple complex, you will be overwhelmed and spellbound by its beauty. Its towering temple structures are awe-inspiring, and its beauty is breathtaking. The temple compound has a square inner court surrounded by a wall. Outside are scattered ancient ruins all over the Valley of Kings. Within the walled square are eight shrines. The three main temples are dedicated to the Hindu trinity of Shiva, Vishnu, and Brahma.

The three temples bring to mind stalagmites as formed by dripping water in limestone caves reaching up to the sky. Their exterior walls are as intricate and multifaceted as those of stalagmites. When the visitor looks closer, he will be astounded to realize that what seem to be water drops frozen to stone turn out to be stone carvings of celestial beings and mystical animals, pictures from the classical Indian dance manual of *Natyasastra*, and, foremost, scenes from the Ramayana—a thousand sculptures as demanded by Loro Jonggrang from the prince.

The temple appears to be blackened as if it had been burnt by fire a long time ago. The visitor who knows the old legend cannot escape a shiver crawling down his spine.

As if by magic, the complex draws its visitor into the largest of the eight temples, the temple of Shiva. It is a towering forty-seven meters high. And there, in the northern room of the Temple of Shiva, can be found on a pedestal against the wall, what the locals call the "Cursed Maiden," the statue of Loro Jonggrang. The statue exudes a strong sexuality. Only a thin transparent veil is wrapped around her voluptuous hips. Her tiny waist and her firm and perky breasts are uncovered. She wears royal headgear and jewelry around her ankles. Her breasts and her stomach are shiny black from fond caresses of hundreds and thousands of her followers who make a pilgrimage to her statue. Loro Jonggrang is the highlight of Prambanan, adored by many, but at the same time a most disturbing presence, and old villagers still believe that dating couples who enter Prambanan temple will break up.

CHAPTER I

BRANDY'S MEMORIES

"The truck has arrived, Brandy...Brandy, where are you?" Since the janitor could not see Brandy, he waved the truck driver to stop and wait and then rushed into the school office looking for Brandy. "Brandy, the truck is here!"

"What truck?" She looked up from the papers that she had been studying and that had absorbed her attention.

"The truck with the supplies for the next school year," explained Sam, the janitor, a little peeved about Brandy's absentmindedness. "The driver is waiting for you outside."

"Ah, thank you, Sam. With all that paperwork, I completely forgot that he would come today." Brandy Beck stood up from her swivel chair and followed Sam outside to the truck into the gleaming sunlight of Southern California.

1

Halfway to the truck, she stopped and said, "Oh, I left the keys in the office!" She turned around, went back to her office to pick up the keys to the shack where they kept their supplies, and hurried back to the truck.

The truck was parked already in front of the little storage shack at the back of the school grounds. The driver had started unloading five heavy wooden crates with his forklift.

Brandy Beck said a quick hello, signed the papers, and then asked the driver if he could haul the heavy crates into their supply shack since they did not have a forklift.

"Sure, madam!"

Brandy unlocked the double door and swung both sides wide open. The driver lifted the crates with his forklift up one by one and drove them through the double door into the dark storage room, where he stacked them against the wall.

The crates were marked: "Product of Indonesia."

"Oh my God, Indonesia," flashed through Brandy's mind, and she asked the janitor, "Sam, could you please open one of the crates for me?"

"There are only pencils in these crates; you know it, Brandy. Let's wait until the beginning of the new school term."

But she had a strong urge to see the contents. She did not care about the pencils, but the origin of the crates had aroused her curiosity.

"I would like to make certain that the contents agrees with the papers," insisted Brandy. She appeared very determined when she said this.

"No problem." Sam shrugged. "Women…Don't argue with them," he thought. "If she really wants to check the crates, it is fine with me, but why didn't she say so earlier?"

The driver had left already. Brandy had signed the papers.

"Why didn't she check the crates while he was still here?" Sam thought. "And since she signed and the driver is gone, what difference does it make whether to open the crates now or wait until the pencils are needed?"

But something in Brandy's body language told Sam that she was serious. She was determined to inspect the contents now. So, if that was what she wanted to do, he would not stand in her way. He walked in an ostensive slough over to his toolbox, took out the cat's paw and his hammer, and began to pull the nails out of one of the crates. He took his time; one by one, deliberately he pulled the nails and put them in his toolbox.

"For later use. You never know," he said. Brandy could have strangled him.

The school had ordered these pencils from an American pencil manufacturer in Van Nuys, a suburb of Los Angeles not far from the school. When Brandy had written out the purchase order, she did not spend a single thought on the origin of the pencils. They were probably manufactured right here in Los Angeles. What difference did it make anyhow? But when she saw the crates and the imprint "Product of Indonesia," it was as if she had touched a live wire and an electric shock went through her body.

Sam cranked the planks from the top of one of the crates, and she looked inside. There were neatly stacked rows of rows and layers of layers of cardboard boxes, each of them containing one gross of pencils, twelve boxes of a dozen pencils each.

Sam did not care. "Is it OK if I leave now? I would like to fix the leak in the boys' bathroom."

"Oh yes, Sam, please go. I do not need you anymore."

Brandy was glad to finally get rid of him. She took one of the boxes out of the crate, opened it, pulled a dozen-box out, and opened it. The sweet, morbid fragrance of the tropics faintly rose from the box and met her nose. With her thumb and her index finger, she pulled one of the pencils from the box. A tiny, little gold imprint on the pencil read: "Made in Indonesia. Jelutong Wood." The wood was soft, so soft. She could easily scratch it with her fingernails. And the wood had the telltale marks of jelutong wood, a myriad of miniature holes like freckles. She lifted the pencil to her nose and drew in the odor that oozed from the pencil. She scratched the tip with her thumbnail to enhance the fragrance.

Oh, how familiar this fragrance was: "Kretek!"

The pencil smelled like kreteks, the cigarettes Indonesians love to smoke. They mix tobacco with clover leaves and roll the mix loosely in cigarette paper. Kreteks look and smell very much like marijuana cigarettes and to a certain degree have a similar effect, just lighter and gentler. In Indonesia the scent of kretek cigarettes seems to hover everywhere in the air and blend with the unmistakable fragrance of the tropics into a scent that is unique to Indonesia. It is pleasant and seductive, calming and mysterious; it reminds one of tropical flowers and of dream dust, of desire and indifference all at the same time. When the international traveler arrives at Soekarno-Hatta Jakarta International Airport and steps from his plane, the scent of kretek instantly welcomes him to the Orient, to, what used to be called, the Spice Islands. He steps from his superficial world driven by greed and ambition into a realm of legends, mysteries, and sagas.

The morbid, sweet scent meandered from the pencil boxes through the warm California air into Brandy's nostrils and from there found its way into her brain. The scent was so rich and strong that Brandy expected to see fumes curl like cigarette smoke from the tip of the pencil upward in spirals toward her face.

Brandy began to feel slightly dizzy. At first a thin, then gradually a denser and denser veil settled tenderly over her eyes. Her breathing became slower, and her knees, softer.

As she gently sank to the ground, her mind drifted into a sweet slumber. She felt a light draft that became stronger and stronger, and when she looked up, she saw a huge, colorful bird hovering over her, flapping its enormous wings. Oddly enough she was not afraid of the creature. Moving its wings up and down in a controlled and deliberate manner, the bird slowly descended on her. It opened its talons. Brandy watched wide-eyed yet calmly and with confidence and trust in the exotic animal. The bird wrapped its talons delicately around Brandy's body, picked her up as if she were weightless, and carried her high up into the clouds and beyond, taking her on a journey back to the country she loved so much, an enchanted country. A country so unreal as if it were from a storybook, a country where ghosts and spirits were real and an integral part of the daily life, a life so full of color and history, a life where the boundaries of our world and the worlds of fairy tales, sagas, and imagination were blurry. A country were these worlds merged into one reality, Indonesia.

Brandy slowly sank down to her knees. She began to lean to her side, more...and more...and more...and then with a slight thump fell down on the ground. Lying curled up on the warm gravel in front of the storage shack, Brandy embarked again on the journey she had traveled with her husband, Eric, and Charlie Wong, the Chinese from Singapore. The journey that had begun almost four years ago, a journey full of wonders and happiness, a journey of pain and suffering, a journey of hopes, love, and despair, of promises and broken vows, a journey that she had thought lay behind her, that had become nothing but memories that, however, was about to be resumed at this very moment thousands of miles away from Indonesia, in the schoolyard of a private school nestled against the foot of Griffith Park in Los Angeles.

THE JOB OFFER

On a Tuesday afternoon about four years ago in a low-income neighborhood on Lankershim Boulevard a few miles north of Universal Studios, Brandy was preparing lunch for herself and Eric. She was not aware that Eric had pulled his beat-up Chevy into the driveway and was now racing up the flight of iron stairs that led outside the building to the hallway door on the second floor. The security door to the hallway was always open. Nobody bothered to shut and lock it. While Eric passed through the doorway, he fingered in his pocket for the apartment keys and found them the instant when he reached the door to his apartment down the hallway on the right side. His hands were shaking, but he managed to get the key into the lock. He flung the door open to their little one-bedroom apartment. He did not even bother to take the key out of the door lock. The knob on the inside of the door hit the wall and knocked a hole into it. Eric did not notice it. He raced toward Brandy, his cheeks gleaming with excitement. Brandy had turned her back to the entrance door and was just about to shove a frozen pizza from Vons into the gas oven. At the sudden loud bang of the door, she jumped and turned around, dropping the pizza onto the open oven door, where it hung in limbo ready to drop to the floor any moment.

"Eric, are you crazy to scare me so—" But then she stopped in the middle of her scolding when she saw the excitement on Eric's face.

"Yes, yes, yes! Brandy, I got it! I got the job! I am the new factory manager for that pencil factory in Indonesia! Can you imagine? Just out of college and bingo—factory manager," shouted Eric while storming across the little living room into the open kitchen area. He grabbed Brandy, lifted her up, and spun her around, kissing and hugging and pressing her against his body.

Her dark eyes wide open, her cheeks glowing with excitement, she kicked her legs in the air. "Tell me. Tell me, what happened?"

"You know, The Ziegler Pencil Company over in Van Nuys is building a new pencil factory in Jakarta with some Chinese partner. And they hired me, me, me, me, the college graduate, the rookie, as their engineer and factory manager. I can build the factory from scrap and then run it."

After the first rush of excitement, she could not help being concerned about such an immense challenge and responsibility. She put her feet back down on the ground resolutely. "Eric, isn't the job too big for you? You are just out of college." Then a frown threw a dark shadow on her otherwise joyous face. "Eric, tell me, is there something wrong with the job?"

"No, no. It is only a small factory, a pencil factory. And they already have a general manager, a young Chinese from Singapore. He will take care of everything, like marketing, sales, personnel, government relations, and whatnot. My job is only to run the machines, keep them up, and repair them. Actually, I had the same concern as you, and I was honest about it. This is what got me the job. They said they liked my enthusiasm and honesty…well, you know, besides my excellent grades."

Wide-eyed she looked him in the face, admiring and loving him. She drank his words from his lips.

"Oh, those big eyes and long black, curved lashes, and these glowing cheeks. What a beauty is my Brandy," flashed through his mind, and he uttered, "Brandy, I love you so much." Squeezing her, he continued, "They wanted somebody young and adventurous. You realize, we will have to move to Indonesia. Not everybody is ready to take such a challenge!"

Brandy and Eric had known each other since junior high school; they had been high school sweethearts and had gone together to their prom. Afterward Eric had studied mechanical engineering at ITT Tech, which was very expensive. Their parents did not have the means to pay for Eric's tuition; therefore Brandy had decided to work as a secretary to support both of them. She was more gifted than he, but she sacrificed her education for their love. Her income and a student loan paid for Eric's college and allowed them a small one-bedroom apartment in a sixty-year-old building in North Hollywood. Downstairs were a bakery and a shoemaker, and upstairs were four apartments. Their apartment was spacious and the rent low. It did not matter to them that it showed its age. Despite their little means, Brandy had managed to turn their apartment into a charming little home with character.

She had stripped the horrific oil paint off the floor and revealed beautiful oak hardwood planks, which she stained and sealed with varnish. She patched the myriad of nail holes in the walls and washed the walls in fresh spring colors. On the old-fashioned windowsills, she put flowerpots filled with geraniums cascading down the walls below the window. It took her days to scrub the burnt-in grease and crummy old food from the stove and oven, and she even managed to regrout the shower all by herself.

Right after Eric had passed his final exam, they went to Las Vegas to get married. A big wedding was out of the question. To celebrate they stayed a few days over at the Excalibur. They did not gamble, nor did they go to a show. They were happy spending the afternoons at the poolside and strolling through the lobbies of the hotels on the Strip in the evening. They ate from the buffet after their nightly walks because at night the buffet was dirt cheap. Back to Los Angeles they took a Greyhound Bus that dropped them off at the bus terminal on Cahuenga Boulevard in Hollywood. During the bus ride, they slept most of the time, her head leaning against his shoulder. An elderly woman across the aisle smiled and said, "Like lovebirds."

From Hollywood Brandy and Eric had ridden the MTA subway to Universal Studios. The last leg of their trip was another short bus ride to their apartment. The bus stopped right in front of the driveway to their apartment building. Eric took a deep breath and carried his newly wed wife all the way up the metal stairs, down the short hallway, and across the threshold into their apartment.

Then reality had kicked in again. Eric had to find a job and rummaged the *LA Times* and the *Daily News* every day for something suitable, and he checked out the new Craigslist website on the Internet. At first the going was slow. Brandy wrote his job applications and mailed them. He went to the interviews. Sometimes Brandy felt it would be better if she would go to the interviews with him, since she was more eloquent and all together brighter, but this was not possible.

The offer from The Ziegler Pencil Company had come completely unexpected. Eric had gone to the interview with no hopes to get the job. The job was probably too big for him, but since they offered him an interview, he accepted. What could he loose? To his utter surprise, they offered him the job then and there at the first and only interview.

The Ziegler Company was planning a joint venture with some Indonesian partner in Jakarta and desperately needed a factory manager, somebody with engineering background who was prepared to move into the unknown for several years. Most people had no idea where Indonesia was. They thought, somewhere in the South Sea. Some better-educated job applicants somehow connected the name with the Spice Islands, which brought to mind dark-skinned beauties in Hawaiian hula skirts, pirates, and tall ships. But to all of the job applicants, Indonesia had been a great enigma, and fear of the unknown kept them from accepting Ziegler's job offer. Therefore Ziegler's management was very happy to have found in Eric somebody who did not ask too many questions and who was ready to accept the challenge. Bingo, he got the job.

For the next four weeks Eric had to prepare himself for his new responsibility. He spent all day long at the factory in Van Nuys, tinkering with pencil-making machines and studying the production process.

ꙮ

The very next day, after Eric had come home with the good news, Brandy went to Barnes & Noble's flagship store in Westwood during an extended lunch break and rummaged the store for anything she could find on Indonesia. There was not much. At first she came across a small Berlitz booklet, *Indonesia for Tourists*. She flicked through it and liked it. It contained some colorful pictures, short descriptions of the important sightseeing spots, and, best of all, some important phrases in Indonesian that would be handy for tourists. She would buy it. But it was not enough for her voracious appetite. She wanted more, something she could immerse herself in, something with more depth on the history, the culture, the people, and the land. After a while she dug out an *All-Asia Guide to Indonesia*. As so often happens, somebody had put it back in the wrong place among books on India. Maybe whoever that was thought this was the same or close enough. Whatever! It did not matter. The *All-Asia Guide* turned out to be a real treasure trove. In contrast to most travel guides, this book afforded Brandy an in-depth picture of Indonesia's history and culture. It went far beyond a superficial description of the sightseeing spots and landmarks; it brought the country, its people, their religion, culture, and history to life. Brandy started reading the *All-Asia Guide* while walking to the check-out register. The book drew her in and took her on a magical journey. She bumped into several other shoppers, murmured some automatic apologetic words, and stumbled on. The clerk behind the counter scanned the small and the big book and asked for some thirty dollars, which brought Brandy back to reality. Full of expectations and excitement, she left Barnes & Noble.

While Eric studied maintenance manuals and assembly plans for machines, Brandy was completely absorbed by the *All-Asia Guide*. Although physically sitting on the worn-out living room sofa next to him, in her mind she was far, far away, sometimes only in miles, sometimes in miles and years.

Most Indonesians are Muslims; however Indonesia's culture is heavily influenced by Hinduism and also to a degree by Buddhism. The Indian epic drama, the *Ramayana* is woven into the fabric of everyday life and the mindset and thinking of the Indonesians. Scenes from the *Ramayana* are printed on batik shirts for men, batik skirts for women, and batik pictures in the living rooms of Indonesians. In the villages scenes from the *Ramayana* are performed with filigree leather puppets at the wayang, the traditional puppet theatre. The puppets are painted in bright colors, but the audience only sees their shadows against a white bedsheet spread out between two bamboo poles and lit from the back by a lamp.

Borobudur, the single most visited tourist attraction in Indonesia, is a Buddhist temple. And although Indonesia is dominated today by Islam, Borobudur is still a place of worship and pilgrimages. An astounding two million Indonesians visit Borobudur every year. Wesak, the day dedicated to commemorate Buddha's birth, death, and wisdom, is in Indonesia a national holiday on which many Indonesians flock to Borobudur to worship Buddha.

Prambanan is one of the largest Hindu temples, with very typical Hindu architecture. It was declared an UNESCO World Heritage Site. At the full moon, the Indonesians perform a ballet in the temple, telling stories from Indian legends.

Borobudur and Prambanan are both located in Central Java near the metropolitan city of Yogyakarta, near the foot of the towering volcano

Merapi, a volcano as beautiful and impressive as Mount Fuji in Japan or the Etna in Sicily.

Brandy was overwhelmed by the cultural and historic richness of Indonesia. Before devouring her two books, she had had no idea about this fascinating country at all. She could not wait to go there as soon as possible. She wanted to submerge herself in all that Indonesia had to offer. She knew it would make an immense difference if she could speak the language to fully appreciate her soon-to-be new home. She did not have much she could go by, a few words scattered throughout her *All-Asia Guide* and one chapter in her little Berlitz book. This chapter contained important words for tourists and some key phrases. Like a dry sponge, Brandy absorbed them all.

She was convinced that in order to make a good factory manager, Eric had to know at the very least some basic Indonesian. She tried to teach him some of the words and phrases that she had learned, but his mind was filled with machines, operating manuals, tools, logistics problems, and what was completely new to him: tropical wood species.

Brandy read to him from her Berlitz book. "*Selamat datang* means good day or hello in Bahasa Indonesia. Bahasa Indonesia, this is what the Indonesian language is called."

Eric was fidgeting with a seven-inch-long wooden board in his fingers, completely ignoring her little lecture. "This is what they make pencils out of. It is called a pencil slat. They grind grooves into it, then fill the grooves with lead slips and put another slat with such grooves on top of it. Now you have a wood sandwich with seven lead slips in it. Clever, don't you agree? The next step is they cut the sandwich into seven pencils."

"Interesting," remarked Brandy without registering what Eric had said and continued with her little language class. "Say, Eric, when you enter an office in Indonesia, how do you greet the person there?"

"See how soft the wood is?" He scratched it with a fingernail.

"Come on, Eric, you know the answer. I told you a dozen times."

"And it is very pale; we have to dye the wood. It has to be reddish like cedar. People expect pencils to be made of reddish wood. This wood is almost white."

He held the board up in front of Brandy, expecting her to be enthusiastic about his observation.

She tried something else to gain his attention. "Do you remember the name of the airport in Jakarta?"

"See these little holes all over the wood? When the locals harvest latex from the jelutong tree, the latex sap leaves these tiny holes behind in the wood. It is easy to recognize jelutong. Cedar does not have these holes. We will make our pencils of jelutong, not cedar like the manufacturers in America."

Brandy gave up. She got up from the sofa and went into the kitchen to prepare dinner.

With her cooking she had been more successful gaining his attention. Food had even a higher priority for Eric than these little wooden boards. For tonight she had decided to serve for dinner satay, little wooden skewers with pieces of chicken or beef. In two little bowls, she served peanut sauce and soy sauce. They were supposed to dip the sticks in the sauce and pull the meat with their teeth from the sticks. She had tried it in the kitchen, and it tasted heavenly.

For dessert she would surprise him with a durian fruit. None of the supermarkets in her area sold durian. She had to take the MTA Bus to Chinatown to get a durian fruit.

When she put the wooden skewers with the meat on the table, Eric sniffed skeptically. "You did not cook skunk tonight?"

She laughed. "No, what you smell is the dessert. We are going to have durian for desert; the entrees are beef and chicken."

He still looked quizzical.

"At least I got his attention," Brandy thought and went back into the kitchen to get the durian. She returned with a strange-looking fruit about the size of a melon and also dark green in color but with thorns spiked all around its husk. Instantaneously it became clear that this extraterrestrial something was the culprit of the strange odor that had been drifting from the kitchen to their dining table. Brandy walked upright like a queen, in a cloud of a strong and penetrating odor, certainly offensive to the nose, but not a stench, maybe even addictive, and most certainly unusual and strange for Western senses.

Smiling, Brandy introduced her prey, which had been so hard to find in Los Angeles. "May I present to you the King of Fruits? This is what it is called in Indonesia." She raised an index finger. "Its odor may be disagreeable to some people, but its flesh tastes like manna from heaven. A British scientist called its taste rich and highly flavored with almonds. Please try it at least."

Eric still was taken aback.

Brandy pushed on. "It is good for sex."

"OK, OK, I will, after dinner. In the meantime please take it back into the kitchen, and open the kitchen window."

The skewers dipped in peanut and soy sauce were delicious, the only problem being you could not stop eating; your taste buds wanted more every time you ate one. Once they had finished the very last morsel, Brandy got the durian from the kitchen and cut it open. The odor intensified instantaneously to an almost unbearable level.

"Definitely skunk spray," mocked Eric.

"Sure, sure. You are right. That is why durian, or raw durian at least, is forbidden in hotels, airports, and on public transportation in Southeast Asia. But come on, let's taste it!"

Eric carefully dipped his spoon into the smooth pulp and touched his tongue with the tip of his spoon. "Not bad." He ate a tiny little bit more. "Not bad at all!"

The stench was forgotten; the taste of the fruit was sensational.

"Yes, like custard with almonds, but I would say also raspberries or a hint of cream cheese. But, hey, whatever. It is good, damn good!"

Brandy laughed out loud. She enjoyed it as much. They agreed they had had the King of Fruits for dessert. And the durian had its promised effect. They had wild sex this night.

*

The days before their departure melted away with lightning speed.

When time came to leave Los Angeles, Eric and Brandy invited all their friends to a farewell dinner. She had decorated their little apartment with inflatable palm trees from Aahs and banana leaves from a Mexican market. On the walls were posters from Bali, The Thousand Islands, the Borobudur temple, and the Obelisk in Jakarta. She had managed to obtain these posters from Garuda Airlines, the national air carrier of Indonesia.

For dinner she had prepared water buffalo patties with potato salad. Since she could not get water buffalo meat at the market, she took regular beef and dressed it with an authentic peanut butter sauce. The patties tasted to their friends as authentic as real water buffalo. For dessert she surprised her friends with lychees, which she had found at Gelson's, an upscale supermarket. She served these white, little fruit balls floating in ice water.

The farewell party was such an overwhelming success that most of their friends wanted to drop everything and follow them to Indonesia. According to Brandy it was a hidden paradise, an archipelago of thousands of tropical islands with beautiful, soft, and gentle people, lush vegetation, fragrant flowers, and exotic fruits—some of which her guest had just sampled—live volcanoes in the distance, a fascinating history, and a highly developed culture rooted in Hinduism, Buddhism, and Islam.

CHAPTER II

ARRIVAL IN JAKARTA

Finally when the day of their departure arrived, Brandy and Eric stood in the endless line of passengers at the Bradley Terminal of LAX, Los Angeles International Airport, waiting to board the Singapore Airlines Boeing 747-400 from Los Angeles to Singapore. These modern air cruisers were able to cover the immense distance nonstop. Formerly at least one stop was required on Oahu to bridge the vast Pacific Ocean.

The public address system crackled and whistled and then a strange, very young-sounding female voice came out of the loud speakers. "Singapore Airlines flight fifty-nine is now ready for boarding. Please have your boarding passes ready. We are starting the boarding with our first class passengers, parents with children, and handicapped travelers!"

When it was Brandy and Eric's turn to board and they stepped across the little gap between the ramp and the plane into the Boeing 747, they stepped out of America and into the magic of the Orient. Two exotic air hostesses welcomed them and showed them to their seats: one of the stewardesses was a dark-skinned, slender Indian lady; the other one probably Malay, with milk-chocolate brown silken skin. They wore skintight ankle-length skirts and bodices snuggly wrapped around their upper bodies. Their dresses were colorful with big flowers and graphics on rich blue backgrounds. Other stewardesses, as beautifully dressed, from China, Japan, and the Philippines handed out newspapers and orange juice or champagne. The glasses were decorated with real orchids; most of the newspapers were written in characters that meant nothing to Brandy and Eric. The plane was brand new and immaculate. The passengers were a mix of all races and nationalities, many of them wearing barong tagalogs, richly embroidered shirts from the Philippines, or sarongs, colorful garments wrapped around the hips and legs, or veils, turbans, or round hats that looked like pillboxes.

Then came the announcement, first in English but afterward in a number of languages that sounded very strange to Brandy and Eric.

The Orient had embraced them.

The flight took much, much longer than they had expected. They knew the Pacific Ocean was vast, but to comprehend its true expand you had to cross it. Despite their excitement, the new environment, all the magazines, the movies they could watch, and the exquisite food that was offered, the flight seemed to stretch forever and ever.

Finally, after endless hours, the plane began its descent into Changi Airport, Singapore's international airport. Eric and Brandy had butterflies in their stomach, not so much because of the descent but because of their expectations. They held each other's hands tightly and pressed their noses, cheek on cheek, against the plastic window. When the wheels touched down on the tarmac with a slight thump, Eric put his arm around Brandy and squeezed her hard against his body.

Here in Singapore they had to change the airline. Garuda Airlines would take them from here to their destination, Jakarta. When they walked behind a long line of passengers from the plane, down the long ramp into the airport arrival hall, the sight that opened up to them took their breath away. They had never seen anything like the arrival and departure hall of Changi Airport. The hall seemed to have no end. They looked right; they looked left—the hall stretched into infinity. The wealth and luxury displayed at this airport was mind-boggling. Immaculate thick carpet and marble covered the floor. Soft music embraced them. Waterfalls all the way down the center decorated with live tropical plants soothed the stress away from weary travelers. And deluxe stores were everywhere gleaming with polished brass, shiny nickel, and sparkling glass. All the big fashion and luxury item names were present in these stores. Changi Airport, by far, eclipsed Rodeo Drive in Beverly Hills.

They had about two hours before their connecting flight left for Jakarta. Arm in arm they leisurely strolled along the endless display of the finest merchandise the world had to offer. Even in Eric's new position as factory manager, most of the goods were out of reach for them: jewelry, exquisite leather goods, rare whiskies, oriental artifacts, exorbitantly expensive perfumes, and so much more.

There in a little booth tucked away in a corner, they spotted affordable souvenirs from Singapore.

"Look, Eric! This cannot be!" Brandy pointed at a display with golden orchids at only fifteen dollars each. "The sign reads real orchids, twenty-four karat gold plated. The store must have forgotten two zeros on their price tag."

"No, madam," answered the storekeeper for Eric. "These are real orchids. We dip them in some secret alloy to give them strength and then cover them with a micro thin layer of twenty-four karat gold. Each brooch is unique—as unique as the orchid it are made off."

"May I?" Eric picked one of the orchids and put it in Brandy's dark hair. "Now you are a real princess." And he kissed her. They were in heaven.

⸙

The onward flight on Garuda Airlines brought them back into reality. What a difference! The little 727 was older than they were. It was crammed to the very last seat with Indonesians who had spent the day shopping in Singapore and were on their way home for the night. The carpet and the seats showed wear and tear, the overhead racks rattled at takeoff, and the whole plane smelled of something that reminded them of marijuana. Still it did not dampen their spirit; somehow the smell, the dark-skinned stewardesses, the colorful passengers, and the exotic food that was served raised their expectations. Brandy took the in-flight magazine out of the pocket of the backrest in front of her and read a little passage out of it explaining why Indonesia's airline was called Garuda Airlines.

The airline was called Garuda Airlines because the Garuda was the national symbol of Indonesia. Garuda statues can be found everywhere in the country and range in size from miniscule to gigantic, and they are mostly cut out of wood but may also be made of metal or chiseled from rock. The Garuda has its origin in Hindu mythology, where it is considered one of the three main animal deities together with the elephant-headed Ganesha and the monkey god. The Garuda is the king of birds. He has the head, wings, talons, and beak of an eagle and the body and limbs of a man. His face is white, his wings are red, and his body is golden. The Indonesian people admire him for his ethics and strength. He is depicted with serpents in his talons. Serpents symbolize evil and are thus the enemies of Garuda. He was hatched from an egg that his mother laid. When his mother was enslaved and guarded by serpents, Garuda bargained with the serpents that they would release his mother if he would deliver to them a cup of ambrosia, the celestial drink. The ambrosia was protected by two fire-spitting serpents. Garuda managed to extinguish their fire by flapping his wings. And with his wings he threw dirt into their eyes so that they could not see his attack. With his sharp beak, he cut them to pieces. When the other serpents, the prison guards of his mother, got the ambrosia, they released Garuda's mother. From then on Garuda, devouring all bad and evil, became the enemy not only of dangerous serpents but of all evil.

❧

After about a short hour, the 727 left its cruising altitude. Again Brandy and Eric pressed their noses full of expectations against the plane window to get a glimpse of Jakarta, their future home. After the landing in Singapore, they were completely surprised to notice that Jakarta was almost completely dark; hardly any street lights or lights from the windows of homes twinkled forlornly down below them. Only in the distance, what must have been downtown or the financial district, the streets and buildings were as illuminated as in America or Singapore. But everything else was dark. Jakarta was a metropolitan city of nine million inhabitants, but from above it looked like a tropical jungle with red-tiled roofs peeking out between the lush green foliage here and there in the dim moonlight.

Compared to Changi Airport, the airport of Jakarta was simple and old fashioned, a little bit like Burbank Airport back home in Los Angeles. The air in the arrival hall was heavy and moist and carried the same strange scent as the air in the plane. Immigration and customs procedures were awkward and time-consuming.

Once they were through immigration and customs and stepped through the automatic sliding doors into the welcome area, they spotted a young Chinese in khaki-colored cargo pants and an airy, short-sleeved batik shirt. He carried a big cardboard sign reading: "Welcome Mr. and Mrs. Beck from Ziegler." He recognized them immediately and approached them with a big smile. "I am Charlie Wong, and I welcome you most heartily to our Indonesia, your new home."

In America Charlie Wong would have introduced himself as Charlie. In the Far East, it was not customary at all to use first names upon first meeting somebody. A first name had to be earned through trust and respect. Brandy and Eric knew this already and were not surprised by the formal welcome. Mr. Wong was tall for a Chinese, rail thin, and he wore big spectacles. His eyes were sharp and intelligent. His nose reminded Brandy of the beak of a Garuda. He greeted them warmly and politely and expressed his joy that they had arrived safely. But he did not hug or kiss Brandy. This would have been extremely impolite and inappropriate. Charlie Wong helped them drag their luggage to the curb. They had taken as much as they could on the plane and had thrown everything else in the dumpster in front of their apartment building in North Hollywood.

Brandy whispered in Eric's ear, "I have such difficulties understanding Mr. Wong. He speaks so fast and with this staccato Singapore accent."

"Same here," whispered Eric back. "He speaks like a machine gun."

When they walked through the glass door, it was as if they hit a wall, the air was so thick, humid, and fragrant.

"Is it going to rain?" asked Eric.

"It rains here every day; we are just south of the equator," answered Mr. Wong. "It will not rain anymore today. It rains most of the time around noon. The air here is always like this, always; we have no winter or summer. It is always hot, and it is always humid, like in a greenhouse."

"But Singapore was so fresh and pleasant," interfered Eric.

"Oh no! You were not in Singapore. You were only in the arrival hall, all air-conditioned. When you step out of Changi Airport, it is not any different from here."

"What time is it? I thought it was only seven p.m., but it is already so dark," wondered Eric.

"Yes, Mr. Beck. It is seven p.m. As I said, we are at the equator. Sunrise and sunset are at six a.m. and six p.m. year-round."

Charlie offered for Brandy to sit in front in the passenger seat so that she had a better view. Brandy went to the right side of the car, and Charlie could not help laughing.

"Wrong side! Or do you want to drive? We here drive on the left side of the road."

With this they climbed into the Toyota Land Cruiser that had been waiting for them at the curb.

"This is much better!" Eric took a deep breath of the fresh, air-conditioned air in the car.

Brandy decided to sit in the back with Eric, and Charlie Wong took the passenger seat next to a young Indonesian since Brandy did not accept his offer to sit in front.

"Aren't you driving, Mr. Wong?" Eric inquired.

"Certainly not! Never, ever drive a car in Indonesia yourself. If you hit somebody, the crowd might lynch you if they notice that you are a foreigner. It is even more dangerous for us Chinese."

"Is Indonesia that dangerous?"

"Not at all! The people are actually extremely nice and friendly. You can move freely around wherever you want. Go to the local market, bet in a cock fight, and go for a hike up a mountain or whatever you like. Nothing will happen to you. But with car accidents, it is different. At least that's what everybody says. I really don't know whether it is true, but I don't want to take a chance either. And then a driver costs barely anything, two hundred to three hundred dollars a month. When he hits somebody, he is one of them. And then imagine the luxury of having a driver! Once you are used to it, you don't want to do without one anymore. You are not in America.

The driver is at your disposal day and night. When we go out for dinner, he sleeps in the car. Most hotels and restaurants have paging systems. You tell them to page your driver, and he comes rolling around the corner. You step in an air-conditioned car, and off you go."

Charlie Wong kept talking and talking like a waterfall. His English was immaculate, and he displayed an immense wealth of English words. But his accent was horrific. In the beginning Eric and Brandy had to concentrate in order not to lose him. It would take several weeks before they were used to this hard staccato accent. And on top of that, he talked so fast. His words were coming out of his mouth as if he were spitting out pebbles in an endless stream.

Brandy dared to ask Mr. Wong, and after all, her question was a compliment, "How come you speak such fantastic English?"

"I am from Singapore. Singapore had been a British colony until 1965. I attended an English school and an English college."

Again Brandy had opened up the floodgate, and Charlie Wong continued talking. "Malaya and Singapore were both British. Then in 1965 Malaya and Singapore became one country, hence Malaysia, a combination of both names. But Malaya is mainly made up by Malays and Singapore by Chinese. Therefore it was better for them to separate again, which was only two years after the merger. Although Singapore is predominantly Chinese, everybody speaks English in Singapore. And Singapore is a truly multiracial country, with Chinese, Indians, Malays, and Europeans. And there is absolutely no conflict between the different ethnic groups."

Charlie Wong did not stop talking until they arrived at their hotel, The Prambanan International. While they stood in line at the check-in counter, their eyes were wandering around, taking in the impressive lobby.

"The hotel is named after the Prambanan Temple, an old Hindu temple near Yogyakarta." That was about all Charlie Wong knew about the Prambanan. Yet, Charlie Wong knew a lot more about the hotel and continued, "The Prambanan Hotel is one of the finest hotels here in Jakarta. It is a five—what do I say—a six-star hotel. You will love their breakfast buffet: any imaginable tropical fruit, omelets cooked to your liking, Danish pastry, you name it. And after breakfast you can take a dip in the pool or stroll in the lush tropical garden." Charlie Wong read their sudden concern from their faces. "Don't worry; it is all paid for by the company. Just sign off whatever you order and enjoy the luxury. You will stay at this hotel as long as it takes to find you a nice house."

The hotel was an exotic dream. The walls were adorned with oriental temple carvings. In the center of the lobby set a dark brown man with crossed legs behind an instrument that looked like a xylophone. Soothing sounds from this strange instrument filled the air. Golden-brown girls with long black hair and tight, ankle-long batik skirts scurried through the lobby carrying colorful drinks on little rattan trays.

When they checked in, they had not the slightest idea that the temple that gave its name to the hotel would change the lives of all three of them.

After they had completed the check-in procedures, a bellboy guided them to the elevator and rode with them up to the fifth floor where their room was. Mr. Wong accompanied them down the long hallway. The ceiling of the hallway was carved from one end to the other in wood. The bellboy opened the door to their room, and Brandy screamed at the top of her lungs, grabbing Eric by the arm. With shaking fingers she pointed at the opposite wall. A green reptile, a dragon, was hanging from the top of the wall just below the ceiling and trained its big protruding eyes on the intruders. Brandy was convinced the creature would attack them any instant.

Charlie Wong had to hold his stomach; he laughed that hard. "It's a gecko. It is completely harmless. Actually it means good luck. Don't hurt it. And if you do not believe in this good luck thing, then it still eats all the insects, mosquitoes, spiders, flies, and so on in your room. So, you are lucky that you have one in your room—most rooms don't."

Brandy felt better but still did not quite trust this miniature dragon. She would leave it alone but would make sure that she did not come too close to this prehistoric-looking monster during their time at the Prambanan.

Once the bellboy had left the room and checked his tip walking back the hallway, Charlie Wong explained to the newcomers the plan for the next few days. "I will pick you up tomorrow morning at eleven, so that you have plenty of time to rest and recover from the long flight. Tomorrow I will show you Jakarta, and then the day after tomorrow we will meet Mr. Sura Baya, the Indonesian partner of The Ziegler Company. Mr. Sura Baya owns fifty-one percent of our factory, and Ziegler only forty-nine, because Indonesian law does not allow a foreigner to have the majority. So, he is the big boss. If you wake up early, enjoy the breakfast buffet and have a swim in the pool, or you can browse through the little boutiques in the lobby."

After a little pause, Charlie Wong raised his index finger as if to stress that he had something important to say. "You will find that everybody calls Mr. Sura Baya *Lee*. You should do the same. Lee is his Chinese and true name. In order to camouflage their Chinese ethnicity, most Chinese have adopted Indonesian names as their official names. Too many Indonesians are jealous of wealthy Chinese businessmen and carry a grudge against them. To avoid unnecessary conflict and to appear patriotic in government matters, Chinese people give themselves Indonesian names. Lee decided on Sura Baya for two reasons. Sura Baya is the capital of Sumatra, where Lee is from, and more important, the name means invincible power. Sura is the shark, and Baya the crocodile. How could you possibly pick a more impressive name?"

With that, Mr. Wong left them.

Brandy and Eric took a hot shower together and fell fast asleep right afterward. Brandy dreamt of being abducted by a huge dragon that carried her in his claws, high up to his nest on the side of a mountain cliff.

AT THE HOTEL

The next morning Eric and Brandy had breakfast on the patio by the pool. They had papaya juice and scrambled eggs with coffee—dark, extremely sweet Indonesian coffee—with French croissants and a basket full of exotic fruits they had not even seen at Gelson's back home in Los Angeles.

Brandy studied the menu. "Look, Eric, they serve wiener schnitzel with potato salad, and they even have sauerbraten with bread dumplings here in the tropics. The menu reads as if we were in Germany."

"Let me see. Yes, you are right."

After their breakfast they walked across the lobby to look around. They saw a man in a dark suit behind the assistant manager's desk shoveling some papers.

"C'mon let's ask him about the wiener schnitzel."

"Excuse me, sir, how come you are serving German food here at the equator?"

"Oh, yes, I have been asked this quite often," the man answered. "The explanation is very simple. Our chef is German, he is from Bavaria, and he is a fantastic cook. You should try his wiener schnitzel or his sauerbraten."

Eric looked quizzically at the person and asked, "It seems to me that you have an American accent. As a matter of fact, you might be from California."

"I sure am. I am from Van Nuys. This is a suburb of Los Angeles—"

Before he could continue, Brandy interrupted him. "This cannot be! We are both from North Hollywood. My husband was hired by a Van Nuys pencil maker as their production manager for Indonesia. What a small world!"

The man in the dark suit explained that he had been general manager of the Van Nuys Airport Hotel until he got the job as general manager of the Prambanan Hotel in Jakarta.

"Oh, you are the general manager! I am so sorry. I thought you were the assistant manager. You know, because of the sign on your desk!" exclaimed Brandy, and she apologized that they had bothered him.

"Don't worry. I am happy to meet some folks from back home down here. You know what? I would like to invite you for dinner. Let's have some Bavarian food under the Southern Cross. May I suggest that we meet at eight p.m. by the pool where you had breakfast and enjoy some hearty German fare? Oops, I almost forgot to introduce myself. I am Gus Waldheimer, or just Gus."

Eric and Brandy happily accepted the invitation.

Gus escorted them to the curb where Charlie Wong just arrived in a cab. The three took Charlie Wong's cab to Medan Merdeka, the Freedom Square, a vast parade ground surrounded by impressive-looking government buildings. Eric and Brandy had never seen a square of that size. From Mr. Wong they learned that it was something like a square kilometer in size. In its midst towered the National Monument, the Monumen Nasional, or Monas for short. This monument was a 450-feet tall obelisk or pinnacle with a golden flame on top.

"The Monumen stands for the fight for Indonesia's independence. The flame weighs almost fifteen tons and is covered with thirty-five kilos of solid gold," lectured Brandy, proud of her knowledge that she had acquired from her little Berlitz book.

"Here we call this obelisk 'Sukarno's last erection.' He was the first president after Indonesia became independent from Holland in 1949. He built this gigantic monument and the wide boulevards here in Jakarta, and yes, you will have guessed, he was a famous womanizer. In 1968 Sukarno was followed by Suharto," chuckled Wong in his shirtsleeved way.

When Brandy and Eric returned to their hotel shortly after eight p.m. after a long and interesting day, Gus, the hotel manager, was waiting for them by the bar at the poolside. He ordered a small selection of appetizers and three Singapore slings, a delicious concoction of grenadine syrup, gin, cherry brandy, and soda.

"Cheers, you guys. Enjoy your Singapore slings, the best cocktail in the world. People visit the Raffles Hotel in Singapore just to sip a Singapore sling in the place where it was invented." With that, Gus raised his glass to the two newcomers.

"Gus, this hotel is so beautiful. Did you build it?"

"No, no. This hotel is owned by a group of wealthy Chinese business-men. But they have an American hotel group to manage it. This is how I came here. I was transferred only a year ago. The manager in charge of building this hotel, or, to be more precise, of supervising the construction, was also an American. He was supposed to run it after its completion. But things turned out differently. It's a fascinating story, maybe even a little scary. It depends on what you believe."

Brandy was excited and wanted to know more about this story, but she was also a little confused.

"Look, they are serving our schnitzels. I will tell you the story while we eat." Gus showed them to their dining table.

The waiters put a serving table next to their table and began to deftly lay out their food. Finally they sprinkled a few orchids on the tablecloth and retreated, walking backward, bowing constantly, with folded hands in front of their chests.

Then Gus began his story. "Fred Fast was appointed to general man-ager of the future Prambanan Hotel. It was about two years ago when he came to Jakarta to supervise the construction of the hotel. From the very beginning, numerous accidents happened. At first small ones, of which nobody took notice. But as the construction project progressed, the accidents became more serious. A worker fell off a scaffolding, another worker got his hands in the gear wheels of a concrete mixer, and so on and so forth. Fred Fast blamed the accidents on the stupidity and lack of education of the construction workers. The workers saw it very differently. They were convinced that a spirit lived at the construction site and took revenge for the disturbance. They approached Fred Fast and asked him whether they could build a shrine for the spirit to gain his forgiveness. Fast had nothing better to do but to laugh at their request and throw the delegation out of his office.

"'You are not going to build a voodoo shrine on my property. This is an international luxury hotel and not a hick town country inn,' he grumbled. And Fast kept on ranting even after the delegation had left his office.

"The construction workers built the shrine anyway, without Fast's blessing. None of them would have dared to return to the construction site without a shrine pacifying the spirit. The shrine was hidden behind the pool house. The workers hoped that Fast would never venture there and that their shrine would therefore be safe. But it came about differently. Only a few days after they had completed their project, Fast was strolling around the grounds with nothing specific on his mind. When he came around the back corner of the pool house, he almost stumbled over the little shrine. The workers had lit red candles and put plates with bananas, oranges, star fruit, and fried chicken legs in front of the shrine.

"Fred Fast, a choleric, completely flipped out. Uncontrollable rage grabbed him, and he trampled the fruits and the other sacrifices to mush. He kicked the porcelain pieces of the broken plates and the red candles into the lawn. Then he stomped on the wooden roof of the little shrine so that it caved in, and he gutted the contents of the shrine with his feet. Only after he had completed his work of destruction did his rage subside. He took a deep breath and felt so much better.

"'They had it coming. If they think they will do it again, I will find the culprits and fire their sorry asses,' he belched out loud. Satisfied, he walked away. From a distance a gardener and his helper watched the onslaught in horror."

Brandy and Eric sat motionless, a shudder running down their spines. How could Fred Fast do something like this! How disrespectful!

Gus continued with his story and told them that Fast paid dearly for his sacrilege. Early the next morning after his rampage, he was found dead at the very spot where he had desecrated the little temple. His eyes were wide open, popping out from their sockets, his face was purple and bloated, and the tip his tongue had been bitten off in his death struggle. The cause of Fast's death was never determined. Somehow it seemed that the authorities had no interest in a thorough investigation. For the hotel employees, the ghost had made Fred Fast pay for his vandalism.

"After Fast's death the management transferred me from Van Nuys to Jakarta to take over Fast's position. The very first night when I arrived in Jakarta, I learned about Fast's story. Everybody was eager to let me know what had happened, because they were all convinced that the spirit had taken revenge for Fast's behavior. And to avoid further disasters, they wanted me to take immediate action.

"'Mister, sir, please let us rebuild the shrine. Please sir,' pleaded the assistant manager with me. I did. The next morning we rebuilt the shrine before tackling anything else. I also sent a boy to the market to buy with my own money fruit and vegetables, which I personally sacrificed to the spirit. From this day on we did not have one single accident anymore! The hotel was finished, as if by a miracle, in no time, and you are here to enjoy the result. All the locals are one hundred percent convinced that I managed to reconcile with the spirit. I was their immediate hero. The employees adore me and do whatever I want; they practically eat out of my hands. This actually, in my personal opinion, is one of the reasons why we did not have any accidents anymore, but please never ever tell anybody. Another definite reason is that I installed immediately upon my arrival strict safety procedures according to American OSHA standards. On a vacation to America, I consulted with a doctor at the forensic institute of UCLA. For him the cause of death was very obvious. Based on my report, it was death by choking. Probably somebody put a plastic bag over his head and removed it after Fred Fast had expired. It is up to you whom you want to believe: the American doctor or the locals."

For Eric, the mechanical engineer, it was no question at all. He did not believe in this witchcraft nonsense. Yet, he had no idea how close he was to his first encounter with a ghost.

Brandy kept her opinion to herself. She had no doubt. Fred Fast had played with fire and got badly burnt. He had dared to challenge a spirit and lost. Gus pacified the spirit and was successful irrespective of what he wanted them to believe.

THE LOT

While Brandy and Eric had dinner with Gus Waldheimer, Sura Baya, or simply Lee, as everybody called him, held an urgent management meeting with his executives in his office on Jalan Thamrin, Jakarta's main street, not far from the hotel. He had no formal board of directors; he owned everything outright himself. Nevertheless he had bestowed on all his managers and advisors the director title to give them more self-esteem and better standing in dealing with outsiders. He was a goodhearted and kind boss and treated his employees extremely well, which was very unusual for this part of the world. But he was also an astute and very smart businessman. Being aware that competitors might steal his managers from him, he had designed an ingenious scheme to assure their loyalty. Once he promoted one of his employees to director, he gave him as a dowry an expensive house. The house cost his directors nothing. Lee, however, carried a mortgage on the house for one hundred percent of its value. Each year his directors stayed in his employment, the mortgage reduced itself by five percent. Should a manager decide to leave him prematurely, the balance of the mortgage became due immediately.

❧

Lee had gathered with his managers in his board room behind the general office. They sat around an elaborate, hand-carved conference table with a glass top that protected the carvings but allowed the eye to enjoy the intricate details of the craftsmanship. Lee and his managers did not care. Their minds were on something else. Once in a while a young woman knocked hardly audibly on the door and came in, bowing all the way. She carried a tray with tiny teacups and a pot of steaming Chinese tea. The managers would take a new cup each and place the used cups on the tray.

The woman would fill the new cups with tea and then stoop back out of the room with delicate little steps. Her tight sarong did not allow her to move in any different way.

"Yesterday, our new factory manager arrived with his wife from the United States," said Lee, opening the meeting. "I will meet him the next few days. The machines for our factory have left the port of Los Angeles on a container ship. It is about time that we find a piece of land for the new factory."

"But isn't that the job of Mr. Wong or this Eric Beck?" interfered one of Lee's directors.

"In theory, yes, but they are both new to our country. How can they find something suitable and not be taken to the cleaners? It is our duty to find the land for the factory. What would you say, Mr. Woo?"

Woo, Lee's right hand and most trusted manager, stroked his chin and smiled fiendishly. "Well, then I think I have an idea. Why don't we sell them our Batavia lot, the lot down by the Old Dutch harbor? They will love this property. It is right by the harbor. It has a flat, useable five acres and there are unemployed workers all around. Charlie Wong and this American will think we found them the best lot in Jakarta and will be all happy."

The northern part of Jakarta that used to be dominated by the warehouses of the Dutch East India Company and called Batavia at that time, was now an incredibly crowded area with little wooden houses on stilts, hundreds and thousands of stores and warehouses, and some emerging factories. Some of the properties had been developed with permits, but most structures were completely illegal and a thorn in the eye of the city developers. The streets were muddy without asphalt, hardly any of the huts had running water, and only the old Dutch properties were connected to a faltering sewer system. Yet there was hardly any area in Indonesia that was as densely populated as the area around the old harbor of Batavia. Goats grazed on the roads and between the houses, and stray dogs rummaged through the garbage. Street vendors sold everything from pencils to knifes, from soft drinks to food, and the food was not chilled and hygienically doubtful, at the very least. Craftsmen, with their legs crossed, sat on wooden porches hammering magnificent works of art out of silver and leather. The few factories blew their smoke and soot happily and carelessly into the air. *Tutuks* and *Bemos*, tricycles and scooters with three wheels, dashed back and forth.

Trucks blew their horns, plowing their way through the throbbing crowd, careful not to hurt anybody. Some foreigners might have sniffed their nose and considered the area a slum, but it was life in its densest, most vibrant and dynamic form: from the little bacteria, to the powerful water buffalo, from the mischievous monkey, the shy dog, the crafty cat, to the chickens that plucked their feathers to stay cool, and last but not least, to the tens of thousands of humans, old and young, man and woman, arrogant and self-confident, submissive and polite, strong and healthy or struck with leprosy, with no face and fingers anymore.

Yet, in all this pandemonium and helter-skelter, there was one big lot—maybe five acres or so—that was completely deserted. Nothing on it! No hut, no food stall, no store, no shop, no nothing. No children played on it; no people walked on it. Nothing! As long as anybody could remember, nobody stepped across its boundaries despite the fact that the lot was not fenced in. Somehow even the animals picked up on the behavior of the humans and avoided the area. It was the property that was owned for generations by the Lee family. They did not try to get any use out of it. It is possible that they tried to sell it once or twice but could not find a buyer. When asked why they did not do anything with this property, they answered it was swamp and would not support any building. Since it had been for such a long time in the family, they simply let it be and did not care. Over the years thick undergrowth covered the lot. It attracted mosquitoes and snakes. Maybe this was the reason why all the animals stayed away from the lot. Or maybe the animals stayed away because humans did not go there, and thus there was no food to be found. And when you got stung by a mosquito, you might get malaria. All these reasons seemed to be a good explanation why everybody avoided this lot.

The locals, however, knew better. A spirit had lived on this property for as long as anybody could remember. And this spirit would destroy anybody who would dare to intrude into his home and disturb his peace. At certain nights when the moonlight was right, you could literally see the spirit rise from the ground and hover over the lot. Modern scientists might try to explain this with gases or vapor rising from the ground. Who knew? Who could tell who was right?

Woo continued with excitement, proud of his idea. "If we sell this lot by the harbor to our new joint venture, let us say for one million dollars, than in effect The Ziegler Company pays us five hundred thousand dollars for this worthless piece of property."

The Ziegler Pencil Company and Lee had each paid two million dollars into their new joint venture that they had named Ziegler Indonesia, taking advantage of the reputation of the Ziegler name. With these funds the new company would buy or lease some land and then build a factory on it. Most of the machines would be bought from Ziegler in Van Nuys, since Ziegler Van Nuys had the know-how and the connections to furnish the new factory. Lee and his management did not know anything about pencil making machines. Buying from their partner would make it foolproof for them to establish a factory without any know-how of their own. To guarantee that somebody would know how to run all these odd-looking machines, Ziegler Van Nuys would even provide the factory manager. Lee had no idea and did not even care that Ziegler hired a young man fresh out of college for this job. He trusted his partners in this respect. He also trusted that they would build some nice profit for themselves into the machines they supplied and thus get some of their investment back right from the start at his expense. But this was acceptable to him. He got a potent partner, and that was far more valuable to him. What alone counted was that their project became a success in the end.

On the other hand, Lee was also of irreplaceable value to the Americans. Not only did the law require an Indonesian partner, but Lee offered them government connections and his customer base. Everybody bribed everybody in Indonesia. Corruption was rampant in Indonesia; without a bribe, nothing happened. For this very reason alone the Americans needed a local partner. Without a local partner, they would also not stand a chance to smoke out local wholesalers. No matter how wealthy some of these wholesalers might be, as a precaution against extortion by some government officials, they made it a habit to hide their offices in shanty towns. What might appear from the outside to be a filthy tavern could be in realty the hub of a million-dollar wholesale operation.

"I don't know. I really don't know," doubted Lee. "I myself don't even dare to go near the property, least walk on it. And now you want me to start a factory on this lot?" On the other hand, Lee thought, "The Americans cheat us for sure with the pricing for the machines. Selling the land to them would get us even. And that up front! Hmm, we would actually be a step ahead of them."

"Look," Woo pressed on, "this humbug with a ghost. Charlie Wong and Eric Beck are modern people; they do not believe in such nonsense. Wong is from Singapore, educated in some English school, and Beck, from the United States. Even if they knew about the ghost, they would not care." Woo, the oldest of the group, had attended a Dutch school and college. This had influenced his thinking.

"It's better they don't learn about this ghost story," said Lee, who was slowly drawn into Woo's reasoning. He thought, "If anybody, anybody at all, could ever break the spell on the land, it would have to be a foreigner." Lee himself was unable to shake off his superstition. "But if they ever find out that we sold them a haunted piece of land..." he mulled.

"I would use a trustee, a stooge for the sale. They will never find out that the Batavia lot had belonged to you." The more Woo talked, the more he talked himself into the scheme.

It had its effect on Lee. "Let's do it!"

With this laconic conclusion, the official part of the meeting was over, and it was time to have some fun. Lee pressed a hidden button at the underside of the table, and the lady came back, her hands folded and bowing. Once she was through the doorway, she stopped and waited humbly for her instructions.

"The game and XO," commanded Lee.

She shuffled back and returned in an instant with the ivory mahjong game, the expensive cognac, and a tray full of kreteks, the Indonesian cigarettes. Lee took the case with the mahjong stones and emptied it on the big meeting table. Woo poured the Hennessy Cognac. While Lee shuffled the stones, some of his managers lit kreteks. Little smoke columns curled from the glowing tips of the cigarettes, spread out above their heads, and filled the room with the heavy aroma of smoldering clover leaves, sweet, aromatic, and beguiling.

THE PARTY IN SINGAPORE

The next day Charlie Wong took the two newcomers to the last landmark of their sightseeing tour, the great mosque of Jakarta, the Istiqlal Mosque, as grand and impressive as any cathedral in Europe.

Wong and Eric took their shoes off and were allowed into the grand main hall. The ceiling of the main prayer hall was a dome spanning forty-five meters to commemorate the independence revolution from Holland from 1945 to 1949. Brandy had to stay outside; she was only allowed to walk in the narrow hallway that circled the main hall. Through small portholes she could get an idea of the overwhelming size and volume of the main hall.

Afterward Mr. Wong took them back to the Prambanan Hotel. They decided to have dinner together. All three took showers in Brandy and Eric's room to wash off the sweat that drenched their bodies form the hot and humid air outside and to wash off the dust of the metropolis of nine million that stuck to their sweaty skin.

Eric gave Charlie Wong one of his polo shirts and, laughing, he commented, "We are brothers now. We share the same shower and the same shirts."

Mr. Wong took the cue and offered that they should call him Charlie; after all, they were in the same boat. Together they had to build a factory and develop a market from scratch. They did not even have a factory site yet, at least they thought so. And as Americans, Brandy and Eric preferred first names anyhow. It was Charlie Wong who had, despite his English education, difficulties clearing this hurdle. For him, offering his first name was a big step and an expression of trust and respect for his new friends. On and off he would fall back into addressing them more formally, even after several months.

The threesome decided to have dinner together by the poolside. Having sampled Indonesian food at little roadside food stalls during the day, the two Americans wanted some solid American food for tonight. This was fine with Charlie. They ordered hamburgers with fries and pickles and Tsingtau beer. Tsingtau beer was a Chinese beer that German brew masters had introduced to China and had become a favorite brew throughout Southeast Asia.

"Tell us, Charlie, do you know how this whole pencil factory project came about?" wondered Eric while munching on his burger.

Again it was as if Eric had opened up floodgates, as if Charlie had only waited for this cue. Sure he knew! He knew all about it. He was there from the very beginning when the decision was made. Charlie started his story, eating noisily and smacking his lips. Eric did not notice, but it took Brandy a while before she got over this Far Eastern habit. She had been raised to eat without making noises. But well, here in the Far East it was different.

"OK, it was a mere nine months ago," began Charlie Wong. "At this time I worked for Tom Toepfer Imports & Exports. Tom Toepfer is a Swiss businessman who represents, besides other companies, The Ziegler Company in Singapore, Malaysia, and Indonesia. I was Toepfer's pencils salesman, or you could say pencil peddler, for those countries. He gave me Indonesia because I speak Malay, and Malay and Bahasa Indonesia are very similar. Every other month I would travel to Indonesia to visit Lee. Lee, a typical entrepreneur, has his hands in everything. Besides lots of other businesses, he owns a chain of stationery stores. He buys stationery items from Toepfer and sells them in his own stores but also acts as a wholesaler.

"Anyhow, to celebrate his sixtieth birthday, Tom Toepfer invited all his major customers, his top employees, like me, and his major vendors to a big marketing conference. Ziegler in the United States sent Joe Manner, their vice president of sales, to the event.

"Toepfer made me the gofer for the event. 'Mr. Wong, could you please pick up Mr. so-and-so at the airport? Do all guests have their hotel rooms? Mrs. Henderson got sick and needs to see a doctor,' and so on.

"I booked the visitors from Asia into the Goodwood Hotel on Scotts Road, a first-class luxury hotel but not one of the very top hotels. For Joe Manner from Ziegler I picked the very best, the Shangri-La Hotel, with its stunning sky-high lobby in green marble and the tropical garden to which the deluxe rooms were facing. Toepfer thought I did this to honor Joe Manner since he came from far away and was very important to his company. I had a very different reason. I did this to make sure that Joe Manner felt in heaven during this conference, since I had planned to reel him in at the end of the conference. Even Tom Toepfer did not know of my scheme. I was in cahoots with Lee because on my last trip to Jakarta, Lee had come up with a proposal for me that I could not resist. This marketing conference was my chance in life.

"The Far East Marketing Conference became a great success. At the end of the conference, Tom Toepfer invited everybody to his birthday bash at the American Club in Singapore. At six in the evening, I picked up Joe Manner at the Shangri-La.

"'How come Toepfer celebrates at the American Club? I always thought he was Swiss?' Joe Manner wanted to know on the way to the party.

"'Anybody can become a member of the American Club. You do not have to be an American. The American Club is the sanctuary for many expatriates. You can eat there, they have a pool, you can get a massage, play tennis, and they even have a beauty salon just for little girls. You know, where they can get a manicure,' I answered him.

"Anyhow, we arrived at the club. Toepfer had rented the whole pool area and had it decorated with colorful lanterns and real torches. Waiters were dashing back and forth, offering champagne and little horse d'oeuvres; for dinner Toepfer had arranged an opulent buffet with Swiss and Malayan delicacies."

Charlie Wong sure liked to hear himself talk. His story was fascinating and interesting for Brandy and Eric, yet still they hoped he would come to the point, telling them how the joint venture between The Ziegler Company and Lee came about and how he got the job as president.

Charlie Wong continued, "Joe Manner enjoyed the tropical night, the food, and the music, and the elegant, slender ladies; he talked animatedly with a number of Toepfer's guests.

"Suddenly I realized it was high time to make my move. I had to introduce Joe Manner to Lee and his right hand, Woo. Besides those two, I was the only one who knew the true reason why Lee attended the marketing conference.

"'Mr. Manner, do you have a minute? I would like to introduce you to a very important dealer from Indonesia,' I asked Joe Manner when he was standing in line for a refill of his wineglass.

"'Sure.'

"We walked across the lawn to a quiet corner where Lee was talking to Woo. Somehow they seemed to be shy. It turned out that Lee hardly spoke any English. His director Woo, on the other hand, spoke not only English but also Dutch and German. Woo was maybe seventy years old and had attended a Dutch School in old Batavia, which is nowadays called Jakarta. While Indonesia was Dutch, the upper class and the upper middle class afforded their children a Dutch education and even spoke Dutch at home. Even after Indonesia gained independence, some members of the upper class preferred to continue speaking Dutch in private circles.

"Joe Manner and Lee liked each other at first sight. Joe Manner had never been to Indonesia and knew very little about this country.

"Lee and Woo knew how to wet Joe Manner's appetite for Indonesia. 'Mr. Manner, do you know that we are probably your biggest dealer in the Far East?'

"Joe Manner was perplexed. 'No way!'

"'You possibly could not know,' grinned Woo. 'Indonesia has insurmountable import restrictions. It is very difficult to import anything, anything at all, officially into Indonesia. This is why we never applied for an agency agreement with The Ziegler Company. It would have made no sense. In order to import into Indonesia, we need a potent partner in Singapore. This is Tom Toepfer. Tom Toepfer buys from you what we need and keeps our merchandise in a Singapore go-down, I mean warehouse. We have two channels to bring this merchandise into Indonesia. We have some of the customs officers under retainer.' He winked. 'When we know that they are on duty, we rush our shipment to Jakarta, and it clears customs completely uninspected and in no time. The second route into Indonesia is smuggling, plain and simple smuggling, by junks and sampans at night to Sumatra.'

"Joe Manner injected, 'Is that not way too far for these tiny, old-fashioned sailing and rowing boats?'

"'No, sir,' continued Woo, 'the Indonesian island of Sumatra is very, very close to Singapore. You can see the mountains of Sumatra from Singapore with your bare eyes. From Singapore to Sumatra is a very short boat ride. Many companies in Singapore live off the smuggling trade with Indonesia.'

"Now Woo was ready to lay his bait. 'Indonesia is the fifth most populous country in this world. Only China, India, Russia, and the United States have bigger populations. There live much more people in Indonesia than in Thailand, Malaysia, Singapore, and the Philippines combined.'

"Joe Manner had not been aware of this and kept shaking his head in disbelief while he listened intently.

"Woo went on. 'The country consists of about fourteen thousand islands. Anything you can imagine grows in Indonesia. Not without reason, these islands used to be called the Spice Islands. Because of our mountains, we have all kinds of different climatic zones, and the volcanoes, which are everywhere, provide rich volcanic soil. The whole country is one big garden. And then Indonesia is rich in oil, timber, and copper. It is maybe one of the richest countries on Earth.'

"'I never heard of it. Excuse me, but I always thought it is just another developing country,' interrupted Joe Manner.

"'Indonesia is certainly not as highly developed as the US, yet. But make no mistake. It is a sleeping giant of bottomless wealth. Indonesia was under Dutch ruling for, I don't know, some three hundred and fifty years and gained its independence only in the nineteen forties. It took our country a while to find itself. But right now we are at the threshold of enormous economic growth,' continued Woo.

"Joe Manner interrupted, 'How does this do us any good, if we cannot import because of all these restrictions?'

"'You are absolutely right; you can never develop and penetrate a market with smuggling and bribing. However, you can take advantage of the situation. Imagine that you had a factory inside this market, and then you had almost complete protection from competition. A gigantic market would all be yours, yours alone! The government is planning to hire 139,000 new—you hear me—new and additional teachers just this year. This number alone should tell you how big this market is already right now, and it is growing by leaps and bounds.'

"You could tell that Joe started to become excited.

"Woo continued, 'We are thinking of building a pencil factory in Indonesia, and we would like to have your company as a partner. You have the technical know-how, the quality, and the brand names. We know the market and have connections, and without the right connections, nothing happens in Indonesia. You need connections in the marketplace; you need connections with the government and with customs. Without the right connections, you will never get your factory approved. We have the connections; others don't. This gives us an immense advantage.'

"Joe Manner had tasted blood. This sounded almost too good to be true. He spent the rest of the evening with his two new friends in the quiet corner of the American Club, behind a huge hibiscus bush, listening to Woo's tale about this Atlantis, of which he had so far been completely ignorant."

Charlie Wong smiled broadly, for he was so proud of himself and his elaborate scheme.

"On our way back to the Shangri-La Hotel, Joe Manner enthusiastically tried to sell me the project. 'I am totally convinced that a pencil factory in

Indonesia will be an immense success. Look at the size of this market. And we will have almost a complete monopoly. If we let this opportunity pass by, Lee will start a joint venture with somebody else, maybe a German pencil maker from Nuremberg, and we will regret it forever. I am planning to write an extensive report on my conversation to the top management, and I know they will go for it.'

"Joe Manner did not have to convince me. I was on the bandwagon long before him. I had arranged the meeting with Lee. And now comes the best part. Lee had promised me already the position of president of the new factory.

"So, when Joe Manner asked me, 'Mr. Wong, how do you feel about a factory in Indonesia?' I dutifully answered, 'I think it is a great idea. I am all for it. But we still have to be prudent and move with caution. I suggest that I should go over to Indonesia and do some research for you, Mr. Manner, to make sure that they are not promising us a pie in the sky.'

"Joe Manner liked my suggestion. 'This is very prudent of you, Charlie. By all means, do so and report to me your findings.'

"Well, the rest is history. Joe Manner managed to convince his management back home in LA to invest in Indonesia and start a joint venture with Lee. Each partner would bring in the same amount of money, and with this equity they would buy the land and the machinery for the factory and construct a factory building. Working capital should be raised through financing by a local bank or a bank in Singapore."

*

While Charlie Wong gave his extensive lecture to Eric and Brandy, Lee and his team discussed their plan a second time in Lee's back-office to make sure that they did not make a mistake. They arrived at the same result as the day before and patted themselves on the backs for their shrewdness. They hardly paid any attention to their mahjong game that followed their discussion and which normally completely absorbed them and transferred them from their world of daily problems into a Shangri-La of joy and happiness.

"Oh yes, we can only win," mused Lee, unaware that he was chewing on a mahjong tile. "It has been agreed that Los Angeles will manage the new factory. Right! So, if something goes wrong because of the spirit, it is all the fault of the white devils." White or long-nosed devils were expressions that Chinese quite commonly used for Westerners.

"Yeah, if worst comes to worst, we can still look for a new piece of land. In the meantime we would have been able to sell our jinxed property for a handsome profit. If, on the other hand, no ghost appears and everything turns out fine, we made money on a worthless piece of land and know then in the end that it had never been jinxed. But believe me, my friends"—his eyes became wide open, and his face showed fear—"I will not go there for a long time, until I feel completely safe."

Lee's managers agreed with his plan and prepared an elaborate proposal for The Ziegler Company in Los Angeles. They wrote a report detailing why they felt that this lot was the ideal lot for the new joint venture; they added to it a zoning map and a site plan and even took some flattering photos. Nobody in LA knew really anything about Indonesia—even Joe Manner had never been there. The report looked good. Therefore LA approved of the site. The fledgling joint venture, Ziegler Indonesia, bought the property from somebody who appeared to be a complete stranger, and Lee had a major chunk of his investment back in his pocket.

PENCIL MAKING MACHINES

Thousands of miles away at the far shores of the Pacific, the thinking of Ziegler's management was not any different from that of Lee's team.

According to the joint venture agreement, The Ziegler Company had to ship new and modern pencil making machines to Jakarta. Although Ziegler had signed this agreement without blinking an eye, they had never ever planned to ship new machines to Indonesia. The joint venture in Jakarta was, for them, a once-in-a-lifetime opportunity to get rid of all their old junk at highly inflated prices.

For more than fifty years, Ziegler had kept all the old, out-of-service machines in the basement and the attic of their factory. These old machines were made of cast iron and steel and lasted forever; they would probably last as long as the pyramids in Egypt. Ziegler used these old, obsolete machines as quarry for spare parts or sometimes as backup if one of their new production lines was out of commission for a longer period of time because of some stupid computer glitch. And once in a while, Ziegler found a pencil maker in a Third World country that would buy some of their equipment.

Lee was not supposed to ever find out that Ziegler was going to ship him these old machines. The technical department replaced the old boiler plates with shiny new ones showing this year's production date. They sanded off the old oil paint and spray-painted the machines with new paint. They brushed off the rust and oiled all the moving parts. And ta-da—with their little magic they generated a brand new pencil making factory, which they shipped as such to Jakarta and for which their joint venture with Lee paid the price of a new factory. The plant had cost Ziegler literally nothing, and through this clever trick they had recovered a large chunk of their investment from the very beginning.

This was at least what the management of Ziegler thought. At the same time, Lee and his managers believed that they had a handsome part of their investment back right away by selling a haunted piece of land to Ziegler Indonesia. In effect both clever tricks leveled each other out more or less, and without their knowledge, justice was done to both parties.

THE PERMIT

Since Lee had the necessary connections, it was his job to obtain the building permit. Nothing in Indonesia worked without connections, and since Indonesia was firmly in the hands of the military, Lee had in his employment a retired general, Malik, who was Lee's trump card and secret weapon. His only responsibility in Lee's company was to maintain ties to the government. Malik never failed. On his next trip to Singapore, Lee bought at Larry's Jewelry Store a two karat diamond ring. Two karats he felt were enough. He did not want to spoil these government people too much. Otherwise they might become too greedy, and in the end you could never satisfy their appetite. The ring had some small inclusions, which was good so. It saved Lee quite some money, and with the bare eye the inclusions were undetectable anyhow.

Lee gave the ring to Malik, and Malik took care of the building permit. At a barbeque in his home, he sneaked the ring on the inspector's wife's finger, and the next day the inspector signed off the necessary papers for the factory. The people at The Ziegler Company could not believe how fast Lee was able to obtain the permit. They had been afraid that the process might take years. At least this was what they had learned from the American Indonesian Chamber of Commerce and what Joe Manner had read in the Asia edition of *The Wall Street Journal*.

The construction could begin. Charlie Wong and Eric Beck would supervise the project on the spot, and Joe Manner would come over once in a while to check on the progress.

THE DEEP SEA

O n one of Joe Manner's visits, Lee decided to give his guest of honor the royal treatment.

"Hey, guys, tonight we are going to have dinner at the Deep Sea," he announced, beaming mischievously from ear to ear about his great idea. From this moment on, his managers bounced around like children, smiled all the time, kidded each other, and conducted their work more lightheartedly than usual.

"What is so special about dinner at the Deep Sea? I guess it is just a seafood restaurant," wondered Eric.

"No, no, it is just a name. It's a Chinese restaurant where you can eat anything. What is special about it? Well, eh…I don't know. Nothing," ducked Charlie, answering Eric's question with a grin.

When night came, Lee, his confidante, Woo, his government liaison, Malik, Joe Manner, the guest from America, Charlie, and Eric rode in two chauffeur-driven cars to the Deep Sea.

A cavalcade of expensive cars was lined up at the entrance; wealthy Chinese businessmen and European bankers stepped out of the cars, and their chauffeurs drove on around the building to the parking lot. The entrance reminded one more of a movie theatre than a restaurant. Gaudy neon lights flashed, and all around the entryway were glass boxes with colorful posters.

A flight of stairs led up to the second floor where two ushers held the huge double door to the dining room open for the arriving guests. To Eric's surprise the dining room was pitch dark except for a well-lit stage in the back and, like fireflies, small flashlights held by waitresses dashed around the immense room. From time to time a match flared up, and the tip of a cigarette began to glimmer. Once Eric's eyes had adapted to the dark, he could make out round Chinese dining tables arranged throughout the vast room. An usher with a flashlight showed them the way to their table near the stage. This was better because the stage light took some of the darkness away.

They had hardly sat down at the table, when expensive French cognac was served. After a short while, Lee lit a match and lifted it above his head.

"We are ordering food now," explained Charlie.

"But how can I order when I can't even see the menu?" asked Eric.

"You will not get a menu, Eric. Mr. Lee orders for all of us whatever comes to his mind. They can prepare anything here. And don't worry; there will be something which you like, because we will get such a variety."

And so it happened. Waitresses scurried back and forth placing a myriad of little plates with delicacies on the large lazy Suzan in the middle of the table. While the party dug in and enjoyed the delicious foods, the show began on the stage: a series of rowdy sketches, all of them in Chinese or Bahasa Indonesia. Apart from Joe Manner and Eric, everybody in the room laughed and roared and slapped their thighs, munching, smacking their lips noisily, and slurping cognac at the same time.

"So, that's it—why they were so happy all day long. A stupid variety show over dinner. If only I could understand one damn word," grumbled Eric under his breath. "You cannot see anything, it is so dark. You do not understand a word of what happens on the stage. How funny!" He hoped that the show and this wonderful evening would be over soon and he could go home to his Brandy.

After the show, Lee stood up, patted his tummy, and proceeded to a small door to the left of the stage. His managers and the guests trailed after him. Eric had no choice but to join, carefully sloughing his feet over the floor so that he would not trip over anything.

"What is this going to be, now? Do they all go to the bathroom together?" he thought.

They walked through the narrow door into a brightly lit room. The strong light hurt the eyes at first. Eric blinked and then he was able to take in his new surroundings. The back wall of the room was all glass, like a big shop window. Behind the window were bleachers on which sat, chatting or beckoning to the visitors, maybe a hundred young women, all of them scantily clad and very good-looking.

"Oh, no!" shot through Eric's head. Whenever one of the managers pointed at one of the women, she smiled, stood up, and walked with swaying hips to a door through which she disappeared. The manager also left.

Soon everybody was gone; only Eric and Lee remained.

Lee poked Eric. "Come on, pick one!"

Eric had to think of Brandy. He could not do this. This would be like treason.

"OK, if you do not know which one, I'll pick one for you—the best, the most expensive one! I mean, the second best, because the best is for me. Ha, ha, ha...Take this one!" And with this, Lee pointed at a slender, tall Filipina, her dark hair cascading down to her waist, with long red nails, a glittering stone in her belly button, and green almond eyes. She must have been an Eurasian. Just the sensation of picking her for Eric stirred Lee's penis to life. The little guy pushed eagerly against his zipper, ready to come out and spring into action. The woman smiled, delicately stepped down the bleachers in her stilettos, and disappeared through the little door, her black thong accentuating her bare, well-rounded rear end.

"She is yours! Come with me." Lee led Eric through the door into a long hallway with doors on both sides. Eric felt awkward. He could never do this. He could not look Brandy in the eyes anymore. His love for Brandy was too strong to fool around.

The Filipina tenderly took Eric's hand and guided him into a small room behind one of the many doors. The room was neat and clean, with a sink, a chair, and a bed that reminded Eric of a hospital bed.

There they stood now, looking at each other. Eric had his thumbs in the pockets of his pants. She smiled, a friendly, girlish smile. Eric looked insecure.

With the long red nail of her index finger, she poked his chest. "C'mon. Don't be so shy. Please undress!" she coed.

42

Eric was frozen to ice. She unbuttoned his shirt, took it off, unzipped his pants, pushed them down to the floor, then his boxers. He let it happen. His penis was hanging lifelessly between his legs. Eric felt so guilty, so rotten. How could he get out of here?

She looked down at his penis. "No problem." With that she helped Eric on the bed that stood in the room. He did not resist. He moved like a zombie. "Many men problem. I help."

She rubbed his penis between her hands. Nothing, it remained lifeless. She scratched the underside of his penis with her sharp, long nails. Nothing. The more she tried, the less she achieved. Eric admitted to himself that she was very pretty, but he would never ever cheat on Brandy, not even with a prostitute. In a last effort, she slipped a condom over the soft penis. It took an effort. And then she took the penis in her mouth and sucked it and played with it with her tongue.

This was too much for Eric. He carefully pushed her away, sat up, and sadly looked her in the eyes. "You are beautiful, but I am married. I cannot do it. I love my wife, and I could never cheat on her. I am so sorry, but she is too important to me!"

She looked at him, not at all comprehending what he said to her. But be that as it may, she had been paid. And whatever he wanted was fine with her. Eric decided to wait a little bit before leaving his cabin. He dressed himself and sat on the bed staring, hoping to leave soon. Through the walls on either side, he heard the sounds of giggling, laughing, moaning, and squeaking.

After a while everybody gathered in the lobby downstairs. Happy and satisfied, they drove home. For Eric it had been the worst evening in his life. Yet he was proud of himself. He had remained loyal to Brandy. Lee had led him into temptation. He did not succumb; he had resisted.

THE CONSTRUCTION PHASE

Lee hired a contractor from some other part of Jakarta, who had no idea about the local people's superstition. This contractor hauled in his own construction crew on huge, big, beat-up open trucks. Charlie

Wong and Eric Beck were puzzled. Why did they have to bring in the construction workers from far away when all around the factory site young men were loitering around with no chance of finding employment in these slums? God knows what they lived off. When their Toyota Land Cruiser rattled down these pothole-infested dirt roads, through the overcrowded slums, they saw to the left and to the right, wherever they looked, young men in rags, half naked, squatting on the elevated wooden porches of their shanties, smoking kreteks and following with their eyes Wong's car.

"Odd. Why don't they come to us and try to get a job? Why do they not seem to be mad that we do not give them work?" wondered Charlie.

Eric did not know either. "You know Lee probably wants experienced construction workers and not these bums."

"Nah, this is not my point. I know they have no experience, and Lee may do whatever he wants. But, hey, when you build a factory, there are so many jobs for inexperienced people—you will see when they start building. We do it quite differently from you people in the United States. What I do not understand is that there is not a long line in front of our property. People should be begging us for jobs. They should grab us by our shirts and hold us back until we give them some sort of work, but nothing. Nobody seems to care. They observe us; they watch us. They seem to be very curious. It seems to me as if they are whispering all the time to each other. But none of them makes a move. It is as if we were lepers or a curse is following us."

Eric had a more Western approach. For him they were just lazy bums. In his opinion Lee had anticipated this and not bothered to hire local people.

Once their car had pulled into the factory site, Charlie and Eric got out of the vehicle and stilted around the ground in knee-high rubber boots, sinking into the soft soil up to their ankles.

"What are you going to do about the ground? It's all muddy and soft. This is swamp land; it will never support a factory slab unless you sink concrete pillars into the ground, which is very, very expensive," wondered Eric

"Wait and see. Maybe this is why Lee brought in people from far away. They are certainly specialists in marsh land," replied Wong, grinning.

To Eric's great surprise, the contractor did not haul in any heavy equipment but truckload after truckload of rail-thin workers. The trucks with the laborers were followed by an armada of trucks of all sizes and ages. They

44

were squeaking and rattling and moaning under their heavy load of bamboo sticks, thousands and many thousands of them. The laborers unloaded the myriad of sticks and scattered them all over the future factory site. Then they fetched hammers, mallets, and sledgehammers from the trucks and began to squat down all over, a certainly unusual if not embarrassing sight. But there was nothing embarrassing to it. With great dexterity and speed, the workers began to hammer the long bamboo sticks into the soft ground. More and more and more...

Some days later what had been a wobbly mud hole turned into a solid, strong, and level foundation.

"What do you say now?" gloated Charlie Wong.

Eric was still skeptical. "And this will hold up? We in Los Angeles, when we build on hillsides, use steel-reinforced concrete pillars that with the help of a helicopter are sunk into the ground."

"Sure," answered Charlie with confidence. "Don't you know that Venice in Italy is built on oak logs and they have been holding up for centuries? Bamboo is even stronger than oak and holds up longer."

Wong was not concerned about the quality of the foundation. He knew it was strong and durable. Something else bothered him. Why on earth did the contractor not use any local people in his workforce? To hammer the bamboo sticks into the ground might require some experience, but to unload a truck and schlep bamboo sticks around could not be so difficult that it could only be done by trained workers. Well, this would change when the building stood and they would recruit their factory hands. And yet, nobody came by to sell food or water, whereas all around the factory site food and water vendors peddled the neighborhood.

Once all the bamboo sticks were in place, finally a convoy of cement mixers lined up, and within one day they poured a concrete slab onto the bamboo foundation. This step of the construction process was one that Eric understood. It was not any different from the way it was done in America. The slab had to cure for several weeks before the walls of the factory could be erected. The brand new factory floor did not look different from any American factory floor: flat, level, and with a matte sheen. Beautiful! Eric's concerns about the foundation soon faded, and by the time the walls were tackled, his concerns had vanished.

WONG IN BED WITH JAUNDICE

To erect the building would not take long. It would be nothing but a huge, open-space hall with a corrugated metal roof. On one end of the hall they would put a wooden mezzanine for the few offices. A wooden staircase—more like a chicken ladder—would lead up to the offices: Wong's office, Eric's office, and a general office for a handful of women. Sales as well as imports would be handled by Lee's established organization. The new factory had no need for extravagant offices. These wooden boxes would do.

Wong and Eric decided it was time to hire their workforce. For most jobs uneducated hands were sufficient. After some training anybody should be able to do most of the jobs. Therefore Charlie Wong nailed together a little wooden hut at the entrance to the factory site. The front did not even have a wall. The hut actually served only as a shelter against the searing sun and the daily downpour. All around his hut Wong put up colorful posters in Bahasa Indonesia and English and in pictograms. And since most people in this area would not be able to read, Wong walked the dirt roads with a megaphone, advertising the new job opportunities. The newly formed Ziegler Indonesia Company offered unheard of wages of the equivalent of about five dollars per day. Five dollars a day would offer a comfortable life in this neighborhood.

Charlie Wong had no doubt that within a day hundreds if not thousands of job applicants would line up at their little job opportunity shack.

But not one single soul applied for the job, and Charlie Wong became nervous and concerned. When Charlie approached one or the other brown young man and tapped him on the shoulder to emphasize his great job offer, the young man would twitch and quickly move away from him with sloughed shoulders.

"Damn it, damn it, damn it. I sit here all day long, I walk around in this filth and heat with my stupid megaphone, and nothing, nothing, nothing! Gawkers, fucking rubbernecks! They prefer to starve instead of making good money. Eric, I don't know what is wrong; I have to find out. And believe me I will find out why nobody is applying for a job. Eric, you stay here; the villagers might not trust you. I will roam around, mingle with the people, buy some food at the food stalls, and talk to the people about why nobody applies!"

And Charlie Wong did as he had said. He chatted with peddlers and hawkers; he ate from food stalls that no Westerner would have dared to eat from, making conversation with the locals while munching *krupuks*, the delicious crab chips. He got his money's worth; he got even more than what he was after. The locals were only too happy to tell Charlie all they knew about the property. And although Charlie Wong did not believe in ghosts and "nonsense like this," the stories told so vividly by the villagers managed to run an icy chill down his spine. For his informants these ghost stories were no stories; they were hardcore reality. The more Charlie talked to the people around, the more their stories took him into their ban.

Eric laughed at Charlie and his sudden superstition, and he joked about Charlie's insecurity. Charlie did not know what to believe anymore. But Charlie brought home from one of his forays more than just ghost stories.

One afternoon, after having eaten some sweet and succulent pork, perched on a three-legged stool in front of a little nearby eatery, Charlie felt kind of woozy.

"Charlie, you are nuts. In this midday heat! How could you sit out there in the sun and get roasted!"

"Ah, this pork was so good. I think it was piglet; you know, all cut up in neat little pieces and served with rice and some vegetables. And, Eric, I drank plenty of water."

"You drank what? Water! Bad enough that you ate that food, and you drank water too!"

"Everybody drank it. I am sort of a local. Why couldn't I?"

Charlie had discarded all the precautions they had observed so far. Every day Brandy boiled for them two thermos bottles of water for a full twenty minutes, which they took to the factory. Charlie dangled a tea bag in his bottle for better taste, and Eric diluted some instant coffee in his bottle. Brandy also made sandwiches for Eric and Charlie and packed every day into their lunchboxes a surprise tropical fruit, such as a star fruit, papaya slices, or mango halves. She made sure that all meat was cooked thoroughly, and she washed with water that had been boiled all fruit that had no skin.

"Well, you probably got some minor food poisoning, and you deserve it," joked Eric.

How wrong they were—both of them.

About a week later, Eric noticed that Charlie looked somehow yellow.

"I am Chinese. We do look yellow!"

"No, you never looked yellow to me." Eric stepped up closer to Charlie and squinted at his eyes. "Your eyeballs are yellow. Charlie, you have jaundice!"

Charlie shook it off. "You old woman. I am fine."

That very night Charlie woke up feeling terribly sick. He staggered to the bathroom and made it just in time to vomit violently into the toilet bowl. He dragged himself back into his bedroom and called Eric on the phone.

By the time Eric and Brandy arrived, Charlie had passed out. They immediately called the paramedics, who took him to the Medistra Hospital, where Charlie learned the next day that he had a serious case of hepatitis A, an acute inflammation of his liver, probably contracted through contaminated food or water.

Charlie had to stay in the hospital for a full four weeks and could consider himself lucky that he did not need a liver transplant. From then on he had to be very careful of what he ate and would have to stay away from alcohol for the rest of his life. The doctors recommended that his diet should include a lot of papayas and long vegetables, such as asparagus, bamboo sprouts, leeks, and so on. In Southeast Asia, medics believed that all long and sleek vegetables clean the human body of poison.

The news of Charlie's hospitalization spread like a wildfire in the Batavia area. Charlie was the subject at all gatherings, be it at coffee shacks, at food stalls, around a water vendor with his metal tanks dangling from a bamboo stick, or at home at the stove. The foreigner from Singapore had challenged the ghost by building a factory on his home, and the ghost had punished Charlie for the sacrilege. The opinions were split whether Charlie would survive the strike or die.

After Charlie was released from the hospital, the villagers eyed him as if he were a leper. But oddly enough he had survived the attack. For the villagers that meant he had overcome his disease not because of the treatment at the Medistra Hospital but because the ghost had only given him a warning and did not want him dead yet. To Eric, who had gotten a gamma globulin shot to protect his liver before being transferred to Indonesia, Charlie had become careless and had therefore been risking his life.

THE WALL

While Charlie Wong was bedridden, curing his serious jaundice, the factory building took on shape and form. The contractor had erected the four walls towering like the walls of a cathedral amid the tiny wooden shacks all around. Only the roof rafters and the corrugated metal roof were missing.

When Charlie came back from the hospital, he looked a little thinner and paler, but he felt pretty perky and spirited. He asked Eric to take him to the factory. He was curious to see the progress.

"Impressive what has happened in these four weeks. Maybe I should play sick more often," Charlie was his old saucy self again. He stood with Eric in front of the new factory building and looked up at the wall. Then he and Eric turned around, and they looked out into the shanty town. Charlie shook his head. "It could all be that easy. But no, it isn't! Where on earth are we going to get our workforce from?"

"Maybe we will have to truck them in, every day," answered Eric solemnly.

"This will only work as long as they do not talk to these idiots around here."

On the dirt road in front of the factory, a peddler with his six-year-old son was passing by. The boy tugged at his father's T-shirt. "Daddy, look!" Thin curls of fume, almost invisible in the bright sunlight, where rising from the soil around the factory building. While they were rising, they diluted more and more and became invisible higher up.

"Boy, it's the ghost. Promise me to stay away from this factory." The father took his son by the wrist and pulled him down the street. Yes, so many people had seen the ghost; now he and his son had also seen him. The peddler shivered and dragged his son on.

While Eric Beck and Charlie Wong continued their talk about the problems they were having finding a workforce, the top of the wall seemed to sway in the sunlight, only so slightly. Or was it nothing but the movement of the air in the sizzling, humid noon heat? The wall began to imperceptibly lean against them. Almost motionless and completely soundless, the wall kept moving toward them. Now Charlie noticed a movement; instinctively he thought he was dizzy and reached for his forehead.

In this very instant, the wall came thundering down on Eric and Charlie and slammed to the ground, engulfing everything in a thick cloud of cinder blocks, concrete, dust, and dirt. The construction workers dropped their tools and stared, mouths wide open. They knew Eric and Wong had been standing there. Hundreds of local people came running and gathered outside the property.

They had always known a disaster would happen. The ghost had struck Charlie Wong once with a serious warning. Wong had survived but refused to heed the warning. And now the ghost struck a second time, this time with an all-out attack. And he got both intruders. They deserved it. Had they not be warned by their neighbors over and over again? Had not this Charlie kept pestering them with questions about this haunted property? And did they not tell him the truth? He had not taken their warnings seriously. He even had the audacity to ignore the massive warning the ghost gave him. Now, he got what he deserved. The factory venture was all over.

It took a little while for the dust to settle in the heavy and humid tropical air. And there they stood, like concrete statues, Eric Beck and Charlie Wong, covered in dust and dumbfounded. All around them were concrete blocks and twisted iron rebar.

Eric recovered first. He grabbed Charlie. "Charlie, heaven gave us a second life. Had we not stood in front of the main doorway, we'd be dead."

Charlie looked bleary eyed.

"Hey, Charlie, we are alive. It was the doorway that saved us."

Charlie regained his composure and jumped into the air.

"God, what luck, what an unbelievable luck! One step left or right, and we would have been pulverized."

The effect on the villagers was even more dramatic than on the two lucky survivors. The crowd outside the factory became bigger and bigger. What had been hundreds of people, turned within minutes into thousands. They all talked excitedly and pointed at Eric Beck and Charlie Wong. These two had no idea what the locals were whispering to each other.

"Have you seen this?"

"Yes, I stood right here, when the spirit pushed the wall. I even saw him. Believe me, I saw him rise up from the ground."

"My little boy saw him, and I did too, just before it happened."

"But how is it possible that he did not kill them?"

"These two are stronger than the spirit. He cannot harm them. Remember this Chinese guy"—one man in the crowd pointed at Charlie Wong—"he survived the first attack, and now both of them survived. They must have superhuman powers."

"Do you think they will take revenge on the spirit?"

"I don't think so; look at them. They were playing with him. The spirit has to serve them."

"Yes, they are his masters."

To Eric it was as if they had lived through an old Buster Keeton movie. The whole situation was so unreal. Saucy and feisty Charlie was still shaking. When his knees wanted to give, Eric supported him. Nobody noticed that in all the excitement.

Soon everybody in the neighborhood was convinced that Eric Beck and Charlie Wong were the new masters of the spirit, and he had to serve them. If this was the case, then everybody on Eric Beck and Charlie Wong's side would be protected by these two warlocks, and the spirit could not do any harm to them.

After some soul-searching, Eric decided he had to tell Brandy. She would find out anyhow. At first Brandy was very quiet, very, very quiet. She sat at the kitchen table and looked with big, watery eyes at Eric. When he smiled, she smiled too. She stood up, came over to his side, and squeezed him so hard, as if she wanted to crush his ribcage. He gave her a big hug. She dug her head into his shoulder and sobbed uncontrollably. He could not help it; he had to cry too. This night they were very tender to each other and slept cuddled together, holding each other tight. God, what would she do without Eric? How dearly she loved him!

The very next day, the factory was literally overrun by water vendors, food vendors, and throngs of young men and women who wanted to work for the factory.

Word came to Lee. The spirit had challenged the two and lost; the spell was broken. Eric Beck and Charlie Wong strutted around as proud as peacocks, both of them convinced that they had defeated the mighty spirit.

The wall was reerected and this time Eric, the engineer, made sure that it would not come down a second time. After that it took a short week, and the roof crowned their factory.

Although they were still waiting for the pencil making machines from America, the place was now vibrant with life. The newly hired workers did not care that they could not commence with their jobs yet. In anticipation they milled happily about the yard and in the factory building. They brought live chickens and goats and dogs and cats. The factory site turned into a village of its own. The chickens provided eggs, the goats milk, and the cats took care of the rats, and the dogs of the garbage that the workers carelessly dropped everywhere. Nobody needed a refrigerator. Their meat ran around alive until its time came to be eaten.

What had been a desolate island in a sea of life turned into the throbbing heart and center of the shanty town. The contractor was not needed anymore. The locals built the offices; they hung the doors and windows as skillfully and expertly as any master craftsman and tied all the other loose ends together.

VISIT TO PRAMBANAN

To celebrate the completion of the factory and the gift of their life, Brandy and Eric invited Charlie to their home, where Brandy had prepared a dinner for the three of them. Whereas Brandy and Eric enjoyed steaks and French red wine, Charlie had to content himself with papaya, mangoes, and fruit juices. For dessert Brandy served bananas that she had fried in a skillet with candied sugar. Eric ate so many of the bananas that his stomach began to hurt.

"Eric, be careful; you might end up like me," teased Charlie.

"Sure, because you got your jaundice from overeating," replied Eric, rubbing his tummy.

After dinner the small party moved outside to the patio. Brandy had placed citronella candles all around the banister to keep the mosquitoes away. The candles and the busy music of the cicadas were soothing and pleasing to the senses. They generated a romantic atmosphere. The tropical sky with its myriads of stars and the perfumed air from the hibiscus bushes enchanted Brandy's little backyard garden.

After all that recent excitement, it was the first evening that the three could completely unwind. The pencil making machines would take a while before they arrived. Eric and Charlie had no work to do for now.

Brandy and Eric sat in the Hollywood swing and sipped heavy Java coffee, holding hands. Charlie had to be content with hot tea. Eric puffed an aromatic Philippine cigar that he took from a lacquered rosewood box with his name carved into the lid. Brandy had bought him this cigar box at the kiosk of the Prambanan Hotel. The storekeeper had Eric's name carved into the lid overnight. The three hardly talked at all. It was so pleasant to sit there saying nothing, watching the stars, listening to the nightly concert of the crickets and breathing the tropical air.

After an hour or so, Brandy got up, went inside, and came back with the *All-Asia Guide* that she had bought at Barnes & Noble in Los Angeles.

"I have an idea how we could celebrate that you two survived the collapse of the wall and that Charlie recovered from his hepatitis." Brandy opened the *All-Asia Guide*.

"How do you guys feel about visiting the Ramayana Ballet?"

Eric and Charlie were puzzled. The what did she say? The Ramasomething ballet did not mean anything to them. Eric would go there anyhow out of love for Brandy, no matter what it was. To Charlie the mere mention of ballet sounded terribly boring. Drinking a liter of castor oil would have been more pleasant to him than going to a ballet performance.

"You guys look perplexed. I will tell you what the Ramayana Ballet is all about. It is one of the most fabulous events our world has to offer, and the ballet is only held at the full moon, when the moon can serve as a lighting source. This weekend is full moon. Our timing is perfect. We could leave the day after tomorrow for Yogyakarta and then attend the ballet on Saturday."

Brandy was all excited. "The ballet is performed at the Prambanan Temple outside Yogyakarta, a Hindu temple complex that consists of eight major and two hundred and forty smaller temples. This temple complex alone is worth the trip. The ballet unites various Indonesian arts, such as dance, drama, and music. As its name says, it performs the ancient Indian *Ramayana* story, which originally was written in Sanskrit. This story is also engraved in the walls of the temple. The performance takes six hours."

Charlie swallowed and almost fell off his chair. "Six hours; I am going to die," he thought.

Brandy did not notice. "The story is presented by beautifully controlled dance movements performed by as many as two hundred dancers in exquisite costumes moving graciously on the stage. The dancers do not speak; instead a female singer tells the story, accompanied by gamelans."

Brandy lectured like a school teacher. Eric could not resist teasing her: "Gamelans is this something to eat?"

"Erica, you are funny! A gamelan is an Indonesian orchestra with xylophones, flutes, drums, gongs and string instruments. You have seen some of the instruments in the lobby of our hotel," answered Brandy and continued with her lecture: "The epic is performed against the backdrop of the temple. Heroics, tragedy, mayhem, and romance presented under the tropical moon will transfer us into medieval times."

"What do you say? Let's go to the ballet!" Brandy beamed, proud of her knowledge and excited about the prospect of attending the performance this weekend.

Charlie had to bite his tongue. He wished he could escape, but he was afraid he owed it to his friends to join them. He would survive. Most likely he would sleep through that spectacle.

Eric was more open to the proposal. It sounded interesting. He imagined Balinese temple dancers. Definitely eye candy! Why not? And Brandy was so enthusiastic about it. Why not?

"Brandy, did you say it is performed here in Jakarta?'

"No, Eric, not Jakarta. Yogyakarta. We will have to fly. We could take a train, but this would take too long, and it is too far to drive. I checked it out already. They have a five-star Sheraton there."

They decided that Brandy would make all the travel arrangements. She knew so much more about Indonesia than even Charlie.

The next morning Brandy made reservations at the Sheraton Mustika hotel in Yogyakarta. She told the two that she picked this hotel because it was close to Adisucipto Airport and because of its tropical gardens, in the center of which was a gigantic swimming pool. But Brandy had another reason for picking this hotel. She kept it to herself. The two guys would find out soon enough.

When they arrived at their rooms at the Sheraton Hotel two days later and opened the drapes to the huge picture windows, the view took their breath away. Even Charlie was overwhelmed. Straight ahead of them, so close that they felt they could touch it with their hands, rose the Merapi volcano from lush green rice fields, toward a blue sky with tiny, little white clouds sprinkled on it. Mount Merapi had the typical conical shape of a picture book volcano. It was velvety gray-blue against the much lighter blue sky. It seemed to reach all the way up to the sky. The Indonesians had baptized it Mountain of Fire, Mount Merapi, for a good reason. It was the most active volcano in Indonesia, a country abundant in volcanoes. The beauty of the volcano was acutely enhanced by the awareness that it might erupt any moment and spew fire and ashes from the middle of the earth. Even the tourists knew that an eruption could be so powerful that the embers might reach as far as Yogyakarta and burn you on the balcony of your hotel room.

The three decided to spend the day after the arrival at the poolside, slurping Singapore slings at the Tamansari Pool Bar; Charlie's Singapore sling had to be virgin. Eric got tipsy from all the sweet alcohol he sucked all day long. Brandy was more reasonable. She swam a lot and dozed in her lounge chair as much. She was going to be ready for the spectacular performance tonight.

When it was time to get dressed and board the shuttle bus to Prambanan, Eric staggered like an old sea bear. Charlie was ready to continue his nap. Only Brandy was as fresh as a daisy, alert and full of excitement.

Even Eric and Charlie could not escape the magic of Prambanan when they stepped from their bus at the entrance to the temple area. It was the time between sunset and the rising of the full moon. The last rays of the day surrendering to the cloak of the young and innocent night painted everything in magical, unreal colors: the dark fans of the tall palm trees against the even darker sky, the black carved lava temple structures with their myriad of ornaments and hundreds of figures, lifeless during the bright sunlight of the day but now, shortly after dusk, full of life. It seemed as if the figures moved in the alternating light and as if their big eyes followed every step of the visitors.

Brandy was in heaven. She leaned her head against Eric's shoulder; Eric put his arm around her. They felt each other's warmth, and Eric enjoyed

Brandy's softness. He kissed her on her forehead and squeezed her a little firmer. Brandy wiggled against him. Charlie let himself fall back a few steps. He did not want to disturb these two cooing doves. Watching these two lovers and the tenderness with which Eric treated Brandy was a heart-warming sight for Charlie. How sweet she was. Her delicate summer dress accentuated her slender figure, the reflection of her body on the fabric constantly changing and teasing Charlie as she walked.

"If only I could find a sweetheart like Brandy. If these two were not so much in love with each other, I would grab her and run away with her right now. After all, the trip to Yogyakarta is turning out to be quite enjoyable," he mused.

A young woman in a skintight ankle-length sarong guided them with a flashlight to their seats. The skirt was so tight that the little usher could only take tiny steps swaying her hips from side to side. Neither Charlie nor Eric had eyes for her. Brandy had booked first row center in the open air theater. The stage was integrated into the temple structure. They sat down in almost complete darkness. While they waited for the moon to rise on the horizon and the performance to begin, Eric wrapped himself and Brandy in a tartan blanket. Charlie fell asleep, dreaming a sweet dream in which Brandy plaid a major role.

After quite a while, Brandy and Eric noticed some shadowy movement on the stage. The tunes of the gamelan orchestra began to pearl over to them, and the moon rose over the silhouette of the tropical jungle. Brandy and Eric straightened up in expectation. There...the pale rays of the rising moon hit a small female statue on a pedestal in the back of the stage.

Eric was electrified as if he had touched a high-voltage wire. The shock ran from his head, down his throat. He swallowed. The shock passed his chest. Eric reached for his heart, and the sudden shock reaped havoc in his stomach, creating a burning sensation, as if he had a sudden ulcer. The feeling was warm, not hot, yet somehow pleasant and at the same time painful. He did not understand what was happening to him. The little statue stared at him with such intensity, as if it were alive. Her body radiated desire, sensuality, and an incredible demonic force.

Brandy noticed that Eric moved away from her and that his eyes were fixated on the little statue in the background.

"This is Loro Jonggrang, an ancient princess that was turned into stone by a prince who desired her but whom she rejected," lectured Brandy. She was pleased that Eric noticed the statue and thus showed some interest in the Indonesian culture. This little statue was without any doubt a beautiful and fascinating work of art. It managed to catch Eric's attention although it was so small and way back behind the stage.

"I will tell you tomorrow the story of this princess, but now let's watch the dance performance."

Dancers had filled the stage and began to tell the story of the contest in which Prabu Janaka determines who would be the husband of his daughter Shinta. Eric did not care about the story or the ballet anymore. He could not take his eyes off Loro Jonggrang. It was as if she beckoned him to get up on the stage and join her. Then she seemed to be talking to him. He could not understand what she said.

"Oh, my God, she is alive!" flashed through his mind. She was so real, so human, that he was afraid she might step down from her pedestal and leave. Her lips, yes, her lips pouted—or no, now they seemed to smile, the corners of her eyes moving imperceptibly upward. He completely forgot that Brandy was sitting next to him, squeezing his thigh and snuggling up to him under the blanket. His mind had left his body and was up there in the back of the stage.

When the performance was over, artificial lights came on so that the audience could safely find its way back to their buses and taxi cabs. The sudden change in the noise and the bright lights woke Charlie. He stretched his arms, yawned, shook his head, and needed a moment to realize where he was. He had slept through the whole spectacle.

Brandy blabbered and blabbered about the performance. She had never seen anything like this before. This performance could not be compared to anything else she had ever seen. It was somehow stilted, very stylized, stiff, and the performance of the dancers was very controlled and slow and yet fluid and full of life and energy. It was a mythological medieval performance but presented by young modern ladies and men. Outside their bus and the luxury hotel were waiting: a different time, a different world.

Eric kept praising the performance although he didn't understand it.

At home in their hotel room, Eric complained he had a bad ulcer attack and that now that they finally relaxed, the shock of the collapsed wall and the desperate search for factory workers in this heat had caught up with him. Brandy gave him Pepto-Bismol and a mild sleeping pill from the kiosk in the hotel lobby. Then she tucked him in. Somehow her love and attention left him cold. He fell asleep slightly curled up because of the pain in his stomach.

Brandy regretted that they had booked only one performance. She could have visited all four in a row, but, well, there would be another time.

ARRIVAL OF THE MACHINES

Back in Jakarta, Lee was furious. "Where is this damn Malik? Every time I need him, I cannot find him."

"Mr. Lee, you know it is Ramadan."

Lee had forgotten. He was Lutheran. Malik was Muslim and observed Ramadan. From sunrise to sunset, he would not eat, drink, or smoke.

Malik had no problem refraining from eating and drinking during the day. What made him grouchy and heavily affected his work ethic was that he did not smoke before sundown during Ramadan. This was not easy for him. But he was strict, and his surroundings had to suffer.

Malik had been a general, and Lee had hired him after he had retired because of his excellent connections. Now that the machines from the States had arrived, Lee needed Malik. He could make the impossible possible: only Malik could clear the machines through customs.

Some three years ago, a German manufacturer had shipped a plant for the production of glue sticks and adhesive tape to Jakarta, where the company had started a joint venture with an Indonesian partner. Neither the Germans nor their Indonesian partner managed to get the machines through customs in the harbor of Jakarta. Customs refused every effort to clear the machines. According to the investment laws in Indonesia for foreign joint ventures, only the most modern and technologically advanced machines were allowed. Now, who can tell and prove what is most modern and most advanced? The Indonesian customs simply did not believe the story the Germans told them. They kept finding a fly in the ointment whatever the Germans did. The Indonesians suspected that the Germans were dumping old machines on them. The Germans argued that the machines were brand new but admitted that they did not incorporate the most advanced technology. In the eyes of the Germans, this made absolute sense. Most advanced technology meant highly computerized. If something went wrong, nobody in Jakarta would be able to fix it. They would have to fly in a technician from Germany. This would lead to a standstill in production and would involve unnecessary costs. The Germans explained that it made a lot more sense to use mechanically modern machines but without the electronic gadgets. This would offer Indonesia the additional advantage that more people were required to run the machines. Thus they generated jobs in Jakarta, where poverty and unemployment were rampant.

The Indonesian officials had a very different point of view. For them the argumentation by the German company was nothing but a revitalization of the old imperialism. To them it was not only against their law but even more so an insult. For those Germans nothing was good enough. Everybody knew that Germany had the most modern and efficient factories. For their joint venture, second-class machinery would do. These Indonesians did not need electronics. In the eyes of the Germans, they were probably not much more than apes. Indonesia had academicians, had universities, a world famous botanical institute, highly skilled craftsmen in many fields, gifted artists. But they were not good enough to run a stupid machine and push some buttons. The argument that a technician had to be flown in at high expense if something went wrong, made the Indonesian customs even more furious. Not only did they have technicians, but Singapore was at their threshold. The whole world knew that Singapore was a leading high-tech country. Even those arrogant German companies had shifted high-tech production facilities from Germany to Singapore. Probably one of the most famous names in cameras was Rollei. And where did the Germans make them? No, not in Germany; they made them in Singapore.

The more the Germans had tried to get their machines through customs in Jakarta, the more they antagonized the Indonesians. As a result they completely lost control over their machinery. It did not clear customs, and they could not ship it back either, because the inspectors were not finished with the inspection process and had not released the machines yet. Two years had passed, and the expensive machines began to rust in the tropical climate.

Lee had found out about the dilemma. He flew with Woo to Germany and offered to buy the whole plant for cents on the Euro. The Germans agreed. They got rid of a headache, and if some more time passed, the machines would turn into scrap metal anyhow. Let Lee deal with the Indonesian customs! It was none of their business anymore, and they were certain that Lee could not do any better than they had done.

Lee had flown back to Jakarta and met with Malik, and Malik set the wheels in motion. Two weeks later all the machines were cleared through customs, and Lee had himself a glue and adhesive tape factory for peanuts. How he had accomplished it remained an enigma to the Germans. For Lee it was business as usual. Malik made all the necessary arrangements. A high-ranking customs official needed a new lawn in his sprawling yard. Lee had sod hauled down all the way from the mountains and then replaced the dead grass with succulent mountain grass. In gratitude the official placed his approval stamp on the shipping papers.

"Where is this damn Malik?" barked Lee.

"I have no idea," replied Woo.

"When I need him the most, he is not here. The machines arrived. How should we get them through customs?"

The Indonesian law was not any different for pencil making machines than for glue and adhesive tape making machines. A joint venture with a foreigner was allowed to bring into the country only the most modern and technologically advanced machinery. Lee and the Ziegler Company knew that this did not make any sense. Unemployment was rampant. A labor-intensive production process would make a lot more sense than an automatic production with a handful of highly paid expatriates running and maintaining the complicated machinery. Whereas in America and Europe the biggest cost factor was labor, here in Indonesia labor cost nothing. A labor-intensive production would be a win-win situation for the people as well as the factory owner. You could get a factory worker for the equivalent of as little as four to five dollars a day. This included even some food allowance and commuting expenses. But it fed the worker and improved his life substantially. A machine that required a lot of labor to operate was much more reliable than those overly sophisticated computer-controlled monsters.

A good, solid machine made of cast iron and steel parts would literally last forever and never break down, for all practical purposes.

Actually Malik did exactly what he was supposed to do. While Lee blamed Ramadan for Malik's disappearance, Malik stepped out of a jewelry store on Orchard Road in Singapore with an old army friend and his wife. While Malik had decided to work for Lee during his retirement, his friend had left the army and joined customs services because it was much more lucrative. It was not as prestigious but made him so much more money. Malik had just bought for his wife an emerald tennis bracelet and matching earrings, and they were ready to head for dinner.

"Where the hell is my driver? I had told him to meet me here by sunset. It is sunset, and he is not here. I have made reservations at the Royal China dining room at the Raffles Hotel."

The driver was well aware that he had to pick up his master by sunset, but he had a different idea about when sunset was, which was not quite unusual. So, he came a half hour late. Malik gave him a thorough lecture about his duties and then had him drive them to the restaurant. The next day the driver took revenge when he bought gas. He overcharged Malik and split the profit with the gas station attendant. Malik would never find out, since he never left the car when they bought gas.

*

The machines whisked through customs with no delay. Customs did not even bother to open the containers. They were satisfied with photos of the machines.

Once the machines arrived at the factory, Eric had to work around the clock to check the machines out, put them up, run them in, train the operators, and so on and so forth.

WOOD-BUYING TRIP

B ut the best machines cannot produce any pencils without wood, and therefore Charlie reminded Eric that it was high time for them to buy timber for their pencil factory.

"Isn't there plenty of wood in Jakarta? In think I saw several lumber-yards. Buying wood should be as easy as buying vegetables," said Eric.

"Not so fast, Eric! Do you have any idea how much profit there is in wood? The success of our factory will depend on how cheap we buy wood."

"Um...?"

"If you are game, we go to the jungle and buy the raw timber—the trees right at the source," suggested Charlie.

"You mean we should go over to Kalimantan, where the big American companies are logging wood. They will laugh at us. Charlie, they cut down areas as big as counties and ship it all to the United States, Japan, and Europe. Now, we two show up and want to buy from them a few cubic feet here and a few cubic feet there. They could as well open up a convenience store for walk-in customers. 'Hey, I need some firewood, don't you have some two-by-fours? Ah, yes, and we make pencils; we need a couple of trees.' Charlie, have you seen their harvesting machines, as big as build-ings? They don't work with axes or chainsaws; they harvest the trees as if they were wheat or rye. Their bulldozers simply drive through the jungle and consume anything in their way. For people like us, you have wholesal-ers and dealers. So, let's look around and visit these dealers right here under our nose."

Charlie grinned. "I know all that what you are trying to tell me, and from time to time we will supplement our requirements from local lum-ber dealers. But we will source the bulk of our need at the source. Not in Kalimantan and not from timber harvesters."

"But I cannot see enough forest here on Java. It is all cultivated."

"Not Java either. We will go to Sumatra. It is much nearer then Kalimantan. Sumatra has plenty of jungle. And logistics are much, much easier. Sumatra and Java are separated only by the narrow Sunda Strait that can even be crossed easily by sailing junks. To get to Kalimantan you need an oceangoing vessel. I never thought of Kalimantan. Our secret treasure chest will be Sumatra. Trust me. Our wood-buying trip will be an adven-ture that you will not want to miss, and it will make us a lot of money."

Eric had not much of a choice, and Charlie had aroused his curiosity. He was a little scared about Charlie's proposal to go to the jungle but decided with Charlie by his side nothing could go wrong.

Charlie felt Eric's insecurity and reassured him. "Look, it is not such a big deal, a short hop by plane from Jakarta to Palembang, over on Sumatra. Palembang is a huge city—I don't know exactly, but maybe with a million people. They have Mc Donald's, KFC, and Burger King. You will feel at home. Then from Palembang we rent a car that takes us to Jambi on the Batanghari River. In Jambi we will hire a speedboat and ride upriver to the logging areas. It is really that simple; you will see. You will love the boat ride. It's like a roller coaster ride on Sentosa Island in Singapore or your Magic Mountain by Los Angeles."

Charlie should not have talked about a roller coaster ride. Eric swallowed; he knew the trip was not that easy if Charlie compared it to a roller coaster ride. Some nerve-racking adventure was waiting for them.

Charlie kept pushing for the trip. "Anyhow, be it as it may, we need to buy the wood as cheap as we can. Wood makes up about eighty percent or even more of our cost," pushed Charlie.

"How come?" countered Eric.

"Look, a factory worker costs us around five American dollars a day. Let's say we have two hundred or three hundred workers. Even that many hands cost nothing. A nice dinner at the Deep Sea Nightclub costs that much. Ah, you might throw in the depreciation of your American machines. We Chinese do not take depreciation into account. If you have the money, you buy the machines for your factory. And when they are used up and worn out, you buy new ones if you have enough money. If not, then not. There you go! As far as power is concerned, you know we have our own generator, and for water we have a well. It all comes back to the cost of wood."

Eric was puzzled. "Fine you can do your internal accounting anyway you want, but I prefer proper American-style accounting, and writing off machines will reduce your taxes, won't it?"

"Not a bit. We do this differently here also. We submit fake statements to the government. And now comes the best part: we pay a negotiated lump sum that includes all—I mean all—taxes: those for the factory, those for the workers, and, best of all, yours and mine. How do you like that? Your salary is totally tax-free!"

Eric liked it but could not see how this would work.

"Easy," said Charlie. "You grease the system a little bit, and then it works like a charm. This is why Lee has Malik. Did I not tell you how imports and how permits work? Well, taxes work the same way."

They decided to spend the week in Jakarta scouting timber yards to get an idea of wood prices. Armed with this knowledge, they would head for Jambi on the east coast of Sumatra.

They learned that wood was a commodity. Its prices fluctuated on a daily basis. But still the spectrum was within a certain bandwidth.

A week later they took off from Jakarta International. As soon as the plane had reached its cruising altitude, they could see beneath them the Sunda Strait. From thirty thousand feet it looked so narrow that you thought you could jump over it. Sprinkled between Java and Sumatra, they could see small volcanic islands floating in the Sunda Strait.

Charlie pointed down. "This is Krakatoa. It erupted, I do not know exactly when, but must have been over a hundred years ago. It caused a big tsunami that swallowed many towns and villages."

Soon the plane left its cruising altitude and began to circle over a web of rivers and creeks. Sprawling in this maze was the city of Palembang, with the majestic Palembang River cutting right through it.

Charlie and Eric did not waste time in Palembang. They rented a car with a driver at the airport and continued their journey to Jambi at the mouth of the Batanghari River. Jambi is about eight hours by car north of Palembang in Central Sumatra. To the west of Jambi are the Barisan Mountains with deep ravines and valleys. And this is where Charlie was going to take Eric. In this mountainous region were some of the last remaining rainforests on Sumatra.

They decided to stay overnight in Jambi to have a full day for their jungle cruise ahead of them. Down by the muddy waters of the Batanghari River, which leisurely rolled through Jambi toward the ocean, they found a small local hotel that was good enough for one night. The Batanghari River reminded Eric very much of the Mississippi back home in America.

To waste no time, they planned on having dinner at their hotel. The dinner menu was about one inch long and contained one item and one item only: nasi goreng, fried rice spiced with sweet soy sauce and shallots and served with a fried egg on top of it. It was good and hearty. They did not mind. Their rooms were clean and airy and had wall unit air-conditioning.

The toilet in the small bathroom was a hole in the floor similar to those you still can find sometimes in Japan or Italy.

The next morning after breakfast, which was the same as dinner—the only difference was they also got very black coffee with their nasi goreng—they walked the short distance down to the riverbank.

"Here we are going to hire a boat and go upstream. This river is some five hundred kilometers long. We will follow it to the mountain region and the forests, where we will buy our wood," explained Charlie.

"Don't tell me you mean we ride in one of those boats." Eric pointed at a cluster of colorful boats, called *keteks*, that the locals use on the river like Dutch people use their bicycles to get around. "As long as you do the rowing, Charlie, I have no objection. What did you say? It's only a few hundred miles," Eric added sarcastically.

Charlie did not bother to answer; he only smiled and took Eric to a different mooring place, where a number of speedboats rocked in the water. They hired a speedboat. You can find these speedboats on all waterways in Southeast Asia. Tourists to Thailand especially enjoy riding these speedboat taxis on the Chao Phraya River, splashing water fountains at the low-riding rice barges that slowly drift down the river with the current. Charlie and Eric's speedboat had a long and slender wooden hull. They had to sit behind each other. At the stern there was a four hundred horsepower Chevy truck engine that some smart entrepreneur had bought with many others at a scrapyard somewhere in America and shipped for great profit to Indonesia.

Charlie and Eric stowed their duffle bags in the boat. Then they went down on their knees, afraid that they might tip the boat over, grabbed the narrow hull on either side with their hands, and carefully crawled aboard. They sat down on the hard wooden planks that spanned the narrow distance from starboard to portside. The same instant the boat owner started the mighty engine. A shudder ran through the body of the boat; the motor growled like a wild animal. Charlie grinned. Eric gripped the sides of the boat with both hands so firmly that his knuckles turned white. The operator let go of the clutch. Pushed by the powerful engine, the bow of the speedboat lifted itself out of the water, the stern dipped deeper, and the boat leaped forward and raced upstream toward the west, the mountains, and the jungle.

Wooden huts on posts at the river's edge flew by. Water buffalo rolled in the mud by the banks. Women washed their laundry, and little brown boys jumped from decks into the water and chased each other. Vendors offering fruit and vegetables from *keteks* flew by so fast that they were only a blur. To both sides of the river were cultivated fields overflowing with the rich produce of the land. The hot, humid tropical climate provided an unlimited abundance of delectable food.

"There, look! Elephants!" shouted Eric at the top of his voice. Charlie did not hear a word. A bow wave splashed in his face. Eric was completely absorbed by the scenery.

In the meantime small trees and mangroves lined the riverbanks populated by screaming monkeys, hornbills, colorful kingfishers, and scary lizards. Charlie did not care about the scenery and the wildlife. He was daydreaming of Brandy.

After several hours the green riverbanks had turned into an emerald wall. They had left behind the cultivated area and were now in the midst of the jungle.

"Watch out!" screamed Charlie, turning around to the boatman. "Wooden crocodiles!" Some logs, called wooden crocodiles, came careening down the river, dashing toward their boat. The boatman, used to random logs in the river, had seen the logs and expertly avoided them. The logs became more and more abundant, a clear indication that they were approaching a logging area. Charlie became excited. They had to be close to their destination.

After a little while, they passed a tributary that was jam-packed with wooden crocodiles pushing and shoving each other out into the Batanghari River, where they dispersed into the wide floods of the main river.

Charlie turned around to the operator so rapidly that he almost lost his balance and fell into the water: "Turn around, turn around. Go into this valley. Yes, this one, from where the timber is floating."

The Indonesian whipped the boat around. It leaned hard into the curve. A huge wave arched from its outside. All three of them were drenched. The boat needed almost the full width of the wide river for its turn.

Charlie yelled at the top of his voice, "From now on, slow down. Slower! Can't you hear me?" He made strong downward movements with his arms. Good, the guy got it. He would have slowed down anyhow without Charlie's instructions.

The boatman maneuvered the boat with dexterity into the narrow ravine. From here on he had to be very careful to avoid a collision with a log, which would have been disastrous. His two passengers had no more nerve to daydream or enjoy the beauty of the jungle. They were fixated on the logs that came heading toward them in clusters. In between there was nothing, then again log, after log, after log. Their boatman had lots of experience and expertly negotiated the random onslaught of timber, but he had to concentrate intently. The Indonesian had no choice; he had to slow down his boat considerably. A conversation became possible again. The GM motor grumbled and growled grumpily that its unlimited power had been reigned in.

"Eric, it looks to me that we have reached a logging area. Look out for a forest aisle that opens up, a trail that leads into the jungle." He was glad that they were near their destination. Had the trip taken much longer, they would have had to moor their boat and stay overnight somewhere along the river.

As Charlie spoke, he saw a mountain trail that dead-ended at the river and wound backward through the thicket, into the mountainous terrain.

"Hey, man. Stop here, right here! We will get off here, and you wait until we return! Listen, we may stay overnight. Just wait for us," Charlie told the skipper, pushing a wad of rupiahs into his outstretched hand. Charlie could not be sure that this was their final destination, but it could well be. If not, they had to continue tomorrow morning.

When the boat ran ashore, Eric jumped off, glad to find solid ground under his feet again, his head still ringing and buzzing. The shaking and bobbing of the boat and constantly being showered with river water had made him nauseated. Eric landed in soft mud and sank into the slime up to his knees. Charlie and the skipper could not help laughing. Eric climbed back into the boat and washed his feet in the river. Then he put on the rubber boots Charlie handed over to him and could now safely step ashore. While the skipper moored his racer to a thick root, Eric and Charlie shouldered their duffle bags and marched off into the jungle, following the muddy trail uphill. Their arrival was greeted by trees full of screaming monkeys flashing threateningly their big yellow teeth at them.

It seemed to them as if the ground was slightly shaking. The two adventurers trotted around the first bend in the trail. The same instant they had to jump aside. A convoy of water buffalo came huffing and puffing down from the mountain. The buffalo dragged behind them roughly hewn timber logs on arm-thick hemp ropes. Sinewy young men with bamboo sticks prodded the oxen forward. The convoy passed the two travelers without paying much attention to them, an occasional glimpse, a smile, a friendly nod. After the convoy had passed them and after having taken deep breaths, Eric and Charlie continued their climb up the trail. They reached a plateau with a clearing in its middle.

When they stepped out of the twilight of the jungle, into the bright tropical light of the clearing, Eric panicked. Charlie, who had walked before him, was bleeding heavily from his back. The bleeding was so bad that his T-shirt was drenched in blood. Blood dripped from Charlie's buttocks to the soft ground, leaving a track of blood behind him.

"Oh my God, Charlie! Help, help! Somebody help!" Eric shrieked. What had happened? Who had done this? He grabbed Charlie in utter despair. Charlie whirled around and looked into Eric's wide open panic-stricken eyes. Eric stuttered unintelligibly.

Charlie grabbed Eric by his shoulders and yelled at him, "What is wrong? What happened?"

Eric pointed at Charlie's back. He pulled himself together, touched Charlie's back, and showed him his hand covered with blood.

Charlie had a hard time calming Eric down. Somehow all this blood did not seem to bother Charlie.

"But Charlie," stuttered Eric.

"No, not 'but Charlie.' I am all right. It's from leeches. You know what leeches are?"

Eric still looked flabbergasted.

"Leeches, man!" Charlie turned Eric around, who was bleeding just as bad, grabbed some of the leeches off Eric's back, and showed them to his friend, who, totally disgusted, backed away.

"Hey, man, you wimp. They are good for you. They are healthy. We use them in Chinese medicine all the time. Do you not do the same?" After a small pause, he said, "Maybe we got too many. They inject blood thinner into your skin. That's why we are bleeding so badly. Let us wipe them off; the bleeding will stop in a few moments. And you will feel actually a lot better. Don't you already?"

Full of disgust, Eric started plucking the slimy monsters off Charlie's skin. Charlie was resolute. He simply wiped them off Eric's back.

"Eric, you are not in a shopping mall in Van Nuys. We are deep inside the Indonesian jungle. I did not think of these leeches. On our way back, we will watch ourselves and wipe them off or pluck them from each other as soon as they drop off the leaves onto us."

"And what if we forget?"

"They let go once they've doubled or tripled in size having feasted on our sweet blood."

Eric needed a while to recover.

Charlie continued, "Look at the Indonesians; they have no problem with those leeches."

When Eric had finally recovered from the shock and had control over himself again, he looked around. In the back of the clearing was a very long, big house. It was built of wood and stood on short stilts. A steep roof covered the house, and the richly carved gables reached toward the sky.

"What is this long house, a church?" wondered Eric.

"You said it. It is a longhouse. These longhouses are quiet common here in the countryside. The whole family or tribe lives in one big house, and since it is so long, it is called a longhouse."

"Isn't that primitive?"

"No way! These longhouses are built of hardwood. They are very expensive, and look at the artful carvings. The stilts elevate the floor; this serves as natural air-conditioning and protects against bugs and flooding."

"Yes, but still, everybody under one roof. They have no privacy."

"Eric, you are wrong again. These longhouses are subdivided inside. Tell me, how is this so different from your apartment buildings? But anyhow, they are becoming too expensive in today's world and are more and more replaced by little houses or huts with corrugated metal roofs. Don't tell me that that is better." And he pointed toward a couple of huts near the longhouse. "See, modern times have arrived here, too."

To the right side of the longhouse, some elephants carrying logs appeared out of the thicket and piled them neatly up in gigantic stacks. The handlers straddled the necks of the docile animals. It seemed as if the elephants did not need their riders at all. The animals knew what was expected from them and carried out their duty swaying from side to side as they stepped back into the forest and reappeared carrying a new load with their powerful trunks.

"Charlie, look, there is more wood than we will need for a long time. Let us walk over to them and ask how much they want for it."

"It is not quite that simple. We cannot use the wood you see over there. It is all hardwood. Very expensive. We need a soft wood. We need jelutong. It is a wood that you can sharpen with a pencil sharpener or a knife, and the wood must have very straight fibers. Jelutong is perfect for our purpose, but jelutong is scattered throughout the jungle. There are no jelutong groves, and it represents only about one and a half percent of the jungle areas where it grows. It is used for tool making, chopsticks, model making, and so on. And jelutong is tapped for latex. Therefore it is very easy to tell if a product is made from jelutong wood. The wood has tiny little pores that were the latex channels. Let us hope these villagers have some jelutong wood."

"OK, let's ask them for—what did you say? Jelutong wood." Eric now remembered. They had given him samples of jelutong slats at the factory in Van Nuys during his training. He had even shown them to Brandy.

"Hold your horses. We cannot walk up to somebody and ask him point blank. We have to be polite and follow procedure. Same as in your country! You would not walk into a factory and start negotiating with whoever you run into. It could be the janitor, a cleaning woman, or an apprentice. We have to talk to the village headman," explained Charlie.

"Good. Do you see the old woman over there by the pond? Let us ask her where we can find this headman."

A few hundred feet from where they had entered the clearing was a pond in which the elephants enjoyed rolling after a strenuous day and in which the women of the village did their laundry.

By the water one old lady squatted with a big pile of clothes dipping them into the water and scrubbing them fanatically with a crude brush. She was very fat and wore a shaggy red coat. After having scrubbed a piece, she would wring out all the water and smash the fabric onto a pile with a thud.

They decided to walk up to her and address her. When they were right behind her and Charlie opened his mouth to say something, this very moment she became aware of them and turned around. Eric's and Charlie's hearts each skipped a beat. Broad teeth the size of Las Vegas dice grinned at them with a wide smile. Her dark eyes were as big as silver dollars. She reached out to greet them with long, slender, sinewy arms ending in boney, hairy fingers as long as pencils.

Eric screamed: "Oh my god, it is not a person. It is an animal, an ape!"

The old lady turned out to be an orangutan.

Later they learned that this orangutan lady had lived in the village for many years; nobody knew exactly anymore for how long. This primate had watched the women of the village do their laundry at the pond and fell in love with this chore. She was very friendly and was considered by all as a part of the village population. Orangutan meant, actually, nothing else but *wood* or *forest person*. For strangers, however, it was advisable to keep a distance from this kind lady, not because she was moody or aggressive. Quite the contrary: she was sweet and caring, always good-tempered and cheerful. Yet she was incredibly powerful. Her rotund body and her thin arms were very deceiving. Although she weighed about four hundred pounds, she could pull herself up on a tree branch with one arm without any effort.

This was almost too much for Eric. They had been only one day in the jungle, and one shock chased the next one. But he had no choice. He had to stay.

The head of the village gave the visitors a very warm welcome. The village was called Bukittinggi, like a city farther north in Sumatra. They were happy to learn that the villagers did have jelutong. There were some trees nearby, and they also had some cut-down logs.

It was getting dark, and so it did not make sense anymore to inspect the wood. The buffalo handlers were coming back from the river, and the village was getting ready for a peaceful evening. Sato, the village head, invited his guests to join him for dinner at the longhouse. Meanwhile the women would prepare a hut for them where they could stay overnight.

For dinner they met with the village elders at the large veranda in front of the longhouse. Behind the veranda lay the formal meeting room. The doors to the meeting room were wide open so that Charlie and Eric could see the inside. Sato offered them nasi goreng with empek-empek, a traditional fishcake that is eaten with a sweet dark sauce made from brown sugar, chili pepper, garlic, and vinegar. After dinner they entered the hall. Young women performed for them a dance in colorful embroidered costumes to the music of a flute-like instrument. Eric lit a kretek and sipped some potent rice wine. When the wine began to take its effect, it transferred Eric back to the night at the Prambanan temple and his encounter with Loro Jonggrang.

Charlie could neither drink rice wine nor smoke kreteks because of his health condition. He was tired but his mind was clear, and he was preparing himself for the negotiations tomorrow.

Outside the longhouse played a different orchestra, an orchestra that no human orchestra could ever match in its multitude of sounds from fortissimo to pianissimo, rattling, peeping, chirping, grunting, mooing, snorting, tapping, sneaking, rustling, hissing, screaming, and squeaking. The orchestra of the forest.

After the exhausting trip from Jakarta, Eric and Charlie retired early. They were guided to one of the huts, where they sank into a deep slumber. The hut had no air-conditioning. It did not need it. The louvered windows and doors without any glass panes provided for a constant, pleasant breeze that kept the hut reasonably cool. The furniture was rattan. You did not sweat on these chairs. And the beds had only a thin linen blanket as cover.

When the sun rose and peeked through the green canopy, the village came to life. Immediately after breakfast a little caravan set in motion to the jelutong trees. At a nearby clearing, Sato showed Eric and Charlie a pile of jelutong logs.

"See, Eric, the typical latex holes: there, there, and there," lectured Charlie. Then he turned to Sato. "The logs have a lot of knots and, what is worse, blue rot. I'd say we could only use forty percent," Charlie said, starting the negotiations. It was vital to talk the quality of the wood down. The profit lay in the discount for poor quality. This had nothing to do with the eventual usability of the wood. It was a way to negotiate price without insulting the other party. Challenging the quoted price would mean suggesting that the seller was unethical and tried to ask too much. Arguing about the quality of a certain quantity of wood was acceptable.

Sato countered, "You do not have to take these logs; we have some beautiful trees a little farther down the trail. Follow me."

They trotted on and on without noticing the abundant variety of orchids. Their minds were on jelutong wood only. Sato must have taken them some two miles, which in this terrain was very arduous, when the forest became lighter.

"Hey, look there." Charlie pointed at a pile of jelutong logs some fifty feet away from them. "This lot is perfect! No blue stain, straight like arrows, no knots."

Charlie wanted to rush over to the wood, but Sato held him back. "Sorry, sir." Sato paused a second as if he did not know what to say. "This lot is sold already."

Somehow it sounded fake to Charlie. "Let me go over and have a closer look. As far as I can tell from here, I have never seen any jelutong of such perfect quality." And he set himself in motion.

Sato stepped in his way. "Please not."

"I do not want to buy it; I only want to show it to my friend here, so that he can learn what jelutong should look like."

"No, please don't go there." Sato became visibly nervous.

"Looking can't harm."

"Yes, it can!" escaped from Sato's mouth.

Charlie frowned, puzzled. What was that supposed to mean?

Sato sighed. "I thought it would not be necessary to tell you, but this pile is haunted. There is something very wrong with it. Please do not even go near it; do not even step into this clearing. Stay with us on the trail." His eyes begged desperately. He whispered, "An evil ghost lives in this pile. He destroys anybody who goes near it. It happened not only once. It happened several times."

Charlie knew he had to respect the superstition of the villagers. He was certain that nothing would happen to him if he inspected the pile. Yet the villagers would be badly insulted, and he could probably forget dealing with them.

Eric saw it differently. "Charlie," he whispered, "we might be able to get this lot very cheap. Keep trying."

"Just forget it."

Charlie's decision was firm and final, and Eric gave in. What other choice did he have? But the day would come when he would return to this pile of jelutong wood, and then Charlie would not stand in his way.

The caravan moved on and came to a stop in front of the first jelutong tree. There it towered in its majestic splendor. Eric was overwhelmed. The tree was some two hundred feet tall and measured in diameter more than six feet. It could well compete with the redwood trees they had in Los Angeles.

Eric thought of the one in Franklin Canyon in the Santa Monica Mountains and the redwood trees in Griffith Park. Well, the ones in Sequoia were even bigger, but this did not take away from the magnificence of this species.

"We have another one back there. Tell me which one you like, and we can cut it down tomorrow." The villagers were masters with the chainsaw and even trees that gigantic would be victims to the teeth of their powerful chainsaws in minutes.

"You've got to give me a minute or two." With knowing eyes Charlie scanned the trees all the way up to the canopy. He stroked his chin. "Well, I am also thinking about the logs you have piled up by the village. Maybe they could do for now, if only they were of better quality. Too much rot, but on the other hand, we could cut it out."

Charlie haggled for the better part of an hour with the village elder. Finally they struck a deal. Charlie bought the logs by the village, all of them. The price they had agreed on left plenty of room for cutting out the bad parts. This would provide them with more wood than they needed for now, and the pile was definitely cheaper than that of a fresh-cut tree. When the pile was used up, they could come back for one of the trees. Neither Charlie nor the village elder mentioned the haunted pile anymore. Part of the deal was that the villagers would drag the logs down the muddy path, the short distance to the river. A handful of young men quickly cut notches into the logs with their chainsaws so that the ropes would not slip off when the buffalo pulled the logs. These notches were a clear indication of illegal logging. Trees cut and moved by licensed companies were moved by forklifts and therefore had no notches.

When the caravan arrived at the river's edge, a rowdy crowd expected them already—raftsmen who vied for their business. In the mountainous terrain around Bukittinggi, there were no roads or railroad tracks, only narrow, zigzagging jungle trails and a maze of rivers and creeks. The only way to get the logs from the logging area to Jakarta was by floating them down the nearest waterway to a point where they could be picked up by trucks. The rafters risked their lives every day for pennies. One wrong move, for one blink of an eye's inattentiveness, and the rafter would lose his balance sliding off the slippery logs and be crushed between the heavy constantly moving wooden crocodiles in the fast-flowing water.

A deal was quickly struck, and the buffalo could dump their heavy load into the river. Rafters with long poles jumped on the logs, embarking on their perilous travel. The rafters deftly pushed the heavy logs away from the banks and into the current of the river. Charlie and Eric had to rush if they did not want to fall behind. As they had expected, the skipper of their speedboat had not left. He had stayed through the night on his boat and was now watching the activities while munching a bowl of rice. Charlie and Eric boarded their speedboat and dashed off, following their newly acquired treasure at a safe distance.

Once the speedboat had left, the village elders scurried back to Bukittinggi and held a summarizing meeting about the visit. They came to the conclusion that they had made a big mistake. They should have sold the jinxed pile of jelutong. What a great opportunity they had missed to get rid of it once and forever! And they would even have been paid top rupiahs for it. They could only hope that the Chinese buyer with his long-nosed friend would return. But too bad, they had revealed their secret to the two visitors.

After half a day of rafting, the river convoy neared a spot where the river met Route 25, the main artery on Sumatra that ran from its northernmost point, all the way down to the south, to the city of Tanjungkarang. A ferry shuttled the short distance from Tanjungkarang across the Sunda Strait to Merak on Java, where Route 25 resumed leading to Jakarta.

Where the rafts reached Highway 25, the picture was the same as at the trailhead. A noisy and waving crowd awaited them at the river-bank. Behind them a number of ramshackle Toyota and GMC trucks were lined up. The truckers knew that they could pick up a log run at this very location. Ten, twenty strong young men jumped in the shallow water, dragged the logs ashore, and began heaving the heavy timber onto the trucks. The price for the run to Jakarta was quickly agreed upon once they noticed that Charlie Wong spoke their language and knew his way around. There was no point in dragging out the negotiations, trying to squeeze some extra rupiahs from somebody who was familiar with the hauling rates.

Charlie paid his speedboat skipper and added a generous tip to the agreed fare.

The boatman thanked him profoundly. "Next time you come back, ask for me. You know where you can find me in Jambi." He bowed and, waving back at them, dashed off with his boat.

Charlie and Eric climbed into the cabin of the first of the five trucks that they had hired. The seats had been patched maybe a hundred times. The speedometer had been pulled out and sold a long time ago. Instead of glass panes, the windows had colorful drapes that could be closed at night so that the cabin served as a bedroom. The heavy scent of kretek and cooked fish lingered in the cabin. The odor would become better once the truck was moving, since it had no side windows and the air draft would blow the smell out through the wide openings.

It was good that they had had only a light breakfast. Even in idle, the truck shook them up pretty bad. Once inside the cabin, a conversation was impossible. They could only throw short bursts of words at the top of their voices at each other. The engine rumble and the clanking of the truck body drowned any conversation.

Rolling down the highway, sitting high up above everything, with a snout in front as big as a minivan was immense fun for Charlie and Eric. They felt like captains of an ocean liner and then again like cowboys driving a stagecoach or simply like truckers on Route 66. They rode through roadside villages, between solid walls of emerald-green foliage and open fields. The trucker had an eight-track music tape in the player blaring Johnny Cash and Elvis Presley. They owned the road; they were the kings of the road!

The trucker swung his baby around a bend in the road when—bam— they hit a road block. State police! An officer who seemed to be the lead officer waved all five trucks to a gravel parking lot that was designed for timber trucks. When they had stopped and killed the engines, they were still dizzy and deaf from the rattle and the noise.

The officer, with broad legs and arms crossed in front of his chest, walked up to their truck and approached them. "Forest Police. Can I see the Blue Paper, sir?" he said to nobody in particular.

Charlie had never heard of a Blue Paper. "What paper, officer?"

This established Charlie as addressee. The officer liked this reply. He had to deal with a rookie. Good. "The shipping manifest. The government license."

The coin dropped; Charlie had no license. The logs he was hauling down the highway were illegally cut. The Blue Paper was a manifest that authorized the transport of logs and proved that the logs had been cut with a permit. To get this license from the government, your woodcutting or harvesting had to be approved by the government. Licenses for "allowable cut" or concessions were issued on a yearly basis by the Forestry Department. The Blue Paper listed the species and quantities that could be harvested and transported.

Charlie Wong had enough experience to realize that this was going to become expensive.

"Sir, step out of your truck." The officer had a stern face and was prepared to squeeze blood out of Charlie Wong.

Wong crept sheepishly out of the cabin, concerned about what would happen next.

"Follow me to the back of the truck…Ah-ha, notches!"

"What notches?"

"These notches in the logs. They are an undeniable indication that these logs have been illegally cut. The notches are cut with axes or chainsaws so that buffalo can pull the logs. The villagers in the mountains go into the jungle with chainsaws and cut down trees to sell them for profit and also to clear terrain to plant grain and vegetables. They do not bother about a license. They just do it. But we cannot allow this. Indonesia has international obligations. The whole world looks at us and blames us for ruthless wood harvesting without environmental concern."

"Uh-oh," thought Charlie Wong. "This guy is taking the time to give me such a lengthy speech. I don't like it. He is raising the ransom." Charlie was smart enough to keep his mouth shut.

"We here in Indonesia have to treat our rainforest with utmost care. You will be going to jail, my friends. Both of you."

Now it was high time that Charlie made his move. "Sir, you said with a license—with what you called the Blue Papers—we would be allowed to transport jelutong."

"Yes, certainly!"

"Is there a way that we could apply and obtain these Blue Papers here in the field? Or is it necessary to go in person to the Forestry Department in Bogor?"

"No, you do not have to go to Bogor in person for such a license. The license can as well be obtained in the field. Let us continue our conversation in the cabin of your truck."

Charlie asked the trucker and Eric to get out of the truck, and he and the officer sat down in the cabin. Charlie Wong was born in Malaysia, had lived in Singapore, and had traveled long enough throughout Southeast Asia to be prepared for such a trap. He knew, like everybody else in the area, how corrupt Indonesia was and that especially the Chinese were the target of the corruption. Not once but several times before, he was escorted by immigration to a separate room when he wanted to fly back to Singapore. They told him that his visa had expired. The immigration officers accused him of having no regard for the hospitality of their country and threatened him with various penalties. The immigration officers as well as Charlie Wong always knew that Charlie's visa was still valid. It was a game, a game for money. And each time, money quickly solved the situation. Charlie Wong could leave and return with no problem. Charlie soon learned that when he traveled to Indonesia without a visa because he had no time to get one or when he left having overstayed the permitted time, all he had to do was put American cash into his passport. Without a word the immigration officer would take the money and stamp the passport.

The situation here on the roadside in Sumatra could not and was not any different, just more expensive. The question was how much. Charlie knew this time it would not be cheap. Once in the cabin, he reached in his hip pocket and pulled out three hundred dollars. The officer looked out the window, bored. Charlie tried five hundred. No reaction.

With a low voice, he said, "Fine, I can do a thousand, but that is all I got."

The officer nodded, took the thousand dollars of US money, and, smiling, handed Charlie Wong the Blue Paper properly signed and stamped by the Forestry Department. Sure it was fake, a good fake, but who cared anyhow?

The convoy was released and continued its journey.

"What happened up there in the cabin?" Eric wanted to know.

"Later. I will tell you when we are out of here."

A few kilometers before Tanjungkarang, they ran again into a roadblock. Charlie's Blue Paper made the road toll a lot cheaper. All participants knew the paper was falsified, but there is honor between thieves.

From Tanjungkarang they took the ferry to Java. The ferry was over-crowded to the hilt. The waterline reached almost to the top of the hull. You would expect the passengers to be still and avoid moving in order not to rock the ship. But quite the opposite was the case. Everybody was milling around. Nobody stayed in his spot. It was a loud and extremely lively crowd with goats and chickens in baskets amid all the passengers. Eric was scared. Had he not read in the papers from time to time that an Indonesian or Philippine ferry had sunk and tens of people drowned? For Charlie, on the other hand, it was nothing unusual. He actually enjoyed the sea breeze.

Back on Java they encountered no more obstacles.

The bottom line of their trip was that they had saved a veritable fortune by traveling north into the jungle, buying the wood at the source, and hauling it down all the way to Jakarta.

🍃

At the factory the two adventurers were greeted with a pandemonium of cheering and dancing workers, barking dogs, bleating goats, and cackling chickens. They were celebrated like royalty entering into town. And then came the big surprise. The factory doors swung wide open, and inside stood a beaming Lee and a joyous Brandy. She rushed out to hug Eric, glad that he had returned unscathed from this odyssey. Eric was unusually cool; maybe he was just tired and worn out.

Lee was beaming with pleasure and pride. "Now that we have wood, machines, and workers, my friends, as soon as the machines are up and running, I am planning a grand opening party at my house!"

Nobody was game for any work this day. Eric and Charlie had to tell their stories. The workers lit an open fire and roasted a goat. It tasted delicious. Later that evening, Lee, Brandy, Eric, and Charlie left. The factory hands continued with their celebration and in the end stayed overnight at the factory.

The next day the normal routine was resumed. The logs were stacked behind the factory to dry from the river-rafting.

The weeks that followed were spent training the machine operators on the pencil making machines and establishing manufacturing-procedures.

Indonesian workers are extremely gifted and skilled with their hands. The training sessions took surprisingly little time, and in no time, the day had arrived on which the factory started operating and churning out thousands and thousands of pencils, which were boxed and whizzed away by Lee's pickup trucks.

Lee upheld his promise and sent out invitations for the grand opening party at his house. The invitations were embossed in golden letters on high-gloss premium stationery.

LEE'S PARTY

Although Lee had his office in Jakarta, he lived in Bogor for its much better climate. Up in the mountains, about a thousand feet above Jakarta, Bogor was cooler, had fresh air, and was not as humid as Jakarta. The British and Dutch knew this as well. Bogor was the capital of Indonesia during the short British occupation and was partly used by the Dutch as the capital. The city houses a presidential palace, with the adjoining world-renowned botanical garden, Kebun Raya Bogor. And as far as Lee was concerned, his home was only forty miles from his office. The commute was a small sacrifice for what he gained by living in the mountains. He did not drive himself anyhow. He rode comfortably in a chauffeur-driven, air-conditioned S-Class Mercedes with tinted windows.

To treat his managers in style for the party, he sent his own Mercedes down to Jakarta to pick them up. Charlie rode in front with the driver, and Eric and Brandy sat in the backseat. Brandy wore a sarong wrapped around her hips. For Eric she had bought an expensive batik shirt, not machine imprinted but one that had been printed by hand with intricate copper batik stamps. For this method, the stamps are dipped in wax and applied to the fabric. Then the fabric is dipped in a bath of dye. The dye sticks to the fabric except on the lines and areas drenched in wax. The process is repeated over and over again until a colorful and intrinsic pattern is achieved. Such a batik shirt is considered formal wear and is on par with a tuxedo, being probably more expensive than a good suit.

As soon as they had left the overcrowded city of Jakarta, the road climbed into the mountains. Extensive tea plantations accompanied the travelers. The little tea bushes stretched like velvety green carpets from the roadside all the way up to the mountain peaks, where high up the tea with the finest quality grew. Rumors had it that monkeys were trained to pick the best of the best tealeaves in perilously high areas that were inaccessible for humans. One pound of such tea leaves could easily cost a thousand US dollars or more.

While passing through the tea plantations, Charlie could not resist telling the two other passengers his tea story. "Mr. Lee and his wife were in Singapore, where they invited Mr. Toepfer—you know, my former boss—his wife, and me for dinner to a Chinese restaurant. After dinner while we had desserts, Lee gave our waiter a small envelope with tea leaves and asked him to brew our tea with these leaves. When the waiter was gone to the kitchen, he told us the monkey story and how exorbitantly expensive his tea was. The waiter returned and poured the tea. It had a rich, dark brown color and smelled to my peasant nose not much different from other teas. Lee's face darkened, his eyes became tiny slits, and he asked the waiter, 'What did you do to my tea?' 'Well, sir,' the waiter responded innocently, 'your tea turned out to be so pale, so we added our tea leaves to give it more color.' Anyhow, Lee could have strangled him. 'My tea was supposed to be pale, you idiot.'"

Along their route they passed through several villages. The houses were mostly small wooden huts, sometimes on stilts, and had covered patios wrapping around the structures, a smart way of keeping the homes cozy without air-conditioning in this part of the world. The stores they passed had no fronts, and they could see the patrons of small country pubs and eateries squatting on narrow, high stools, ladling rice or noodle soup with chopsticks or porcelain spoons into their mouths, sipping tea or very potent rice wine.

Charlie could clandestinely watch in the rearview mirror Brandy and Eric in the backseat. Something had changed. These two used to hug and kiss all the time. But today they sat next to each other looking out the dark windows, absorbing the scenery. This could be curiosity and fascination with the countryside, but if he remembered right, the way he knew them, they would have been closer together holding hands. This would not have stopped them from enjoying the mountain trip. Charlie had the feeling that since their visit to Prambanan, the relationship between Brandy and Eric had changed. He felt so sorry for her; she was such a lovely person, always concerned about her Eric. She was speaking already bits and pieces of Indonesian, contrary to Eric for whom there appeared no need to speak anything else but English. Brandy would come out to the factory frequently to feed stray dogs and cats, and she even introduced recycling to the factory, which apart from her and Charlie Wong, nobody understood. For the workers she went shopping and bought them medical supplies that they could not afford. She did not throw her old clothes in the trash; she handed them out to villagers around the factory who had no jobs. "What a wonderful woman; what an angel. Eric did not deserve her," Charlie mused.

In Bogor they drove past Merdeka Palace, the residence of the president. The building was fenced in and set far back from the road, with a vast succulent lawn in front. Deer grazed on the lawn and followed with big, kind eyes the passing Mercedes.

"The palace is open to the public. If you want to visit it, let Mr. Lee know. You will have to join a group tour. Individuals are not allowed." The driver was proud to show off his knowledge.

Shortly after the president's palace, they turned right into Medan Road. Immediately afterward they turned right again through a wrought iron gate illuminated by torches and into a driveway. The driveway, lined on both sides with little tea lights, led in a sweeping arch up a hill. On top of the hill reigned Lee's house—no, not his house, his mansion: his palace two stories tall with a porte cochere and a flight of stairs leading from the driveway to the main entrance. Lee had put white Christmas lights all around the edge of his mansion and had decorated the porte cochere with icicles of lightbulbs.

When this fairy tale dream unfolded in front of Eric Beck's eyes, he became dizzy. His left hand reached for his forehead. It ached. He felt as if a gigantic hand grabbed for his chest and pressed the air out of his lungs. Eric felt a mixture of admiration and painful jealousy.

"Charlie, this cannot be! This is Mr. Lee's house? This is a king's palace, not a house!"

"Come on, Eric! This is Mr. Lee; you know how rich he is!" Charlie answered, but Eric did not respond; he stared ahead, mesmerized by the mansion.

Brandy, reading Eric's mind, pinched him and teased, "I did not know that you could be so jealous. Eric, we owe him everything."

This loosened him up again, and he looked now at the fairytale castle with interest and curiosity.

With self-confidence and expectation, he stepped out of the elegant Mercedes when the parking attendant opened the door for him. He walked around the car and opened the door for Brandy. "Milady!" Eric reached out his hand; she took it and graciously swung both her legs close together out of the car. She hooked her arm into his, and they strutted up the flight of stairs feeling as if they were royalty themselves.

Charlie trotted behind, glad of Eric's gallantry. Maybe he had been oversensitive or subconsciously hoped for tension between the two because he envied Eric for Brandy.

Lee and his wife expected them on top of the stairs in the nine-foot-high doorway. They stood there to greet all their guests personally.

"Charlie and Eric, today is your day. You made our new factory possible with your dedication and hard work. Brandy, you look stunning. Please walk right through the hallway to the back. We will talk later."

Lee turned to the next group of arriving guests. Eric, Brandy, and Charlie walked into the hallway. In the middle of the hallway stood a Lalique glass table with a stunning bouquet of birds-of-paradise on it.

While they circled the table and headed to the wide open glass doors that led into the backyard, Brandy smiled and nodded more to herself than to anybody else. "I have seen this table on Rodeo Drive. Gorgeous. A dream in glass."

Eric had been with her that afternoon on Rodeo Drive. He recognized the table too. He thought, "If I remember right, it cost over one hundred thousand dollars. If I could only find a way to ever become that rich."

In Lee's backyard, or, rather, in his tropical garden, were already some two to three hundred guests strolling about or chatting happily with each other. Lee had invited all his friends, his customers, bankers, and myriads of government officials and influential army brass. Waiters in traditional Indonesian costume weaved skillfully between the guests, offering wine and champagne, as well as mango juice, papaya juice, and plain water for the Muslims. Other waiters carried on sterling silver trays Indonesian hors d'oeuvres, everything from beef satay sticks served with peanut sauce, soy or hot sauce to quail eggs, krupuks and gadu gadu, a dish of various vegetables sprinkled with a delicious peanut sauce. Those krupuks had been

Charlie's favorite snack until he contracted his jaundice. Other waiters offered Japanese sushi, tofu, crunchy crickets wrapped in citrus leaves or those black, translucent Chinese preserved eggs, which in Western nations are called thousand-year-old eggs or, disrespectfully, rotten eggs.

Some of the dishes were hardly acceptable to the Western palate, such as fried jellyfish and those crickets. Lee's European business friends could pick French quiche, miniature hot dogs with mustard, or mini hamburgers with ketchup. In the middle of the backyard was an octagonal buffet that offered heartier fare, from lobster and salmon, to barbequed chicken and filet mignon cooked right in front of the guests' eyes to their liking. The buffet even featured a Chinese steamboat: thinly sliced beef, tiny eggs, and different vegetables boiled in chicken broth. The chefs would fill little porcelain bowls with this delicacy for those who wanted to indulge in it. In deference to his Islamic friends, Lee did not serve pork although he, as a Chinese, loved pork.

The three friends stepped through the French doors, out onto the patio. It took them several minutes to take in the affluence displayed in front of them.

All around the vast lawn were Malibu lights emphasizing the palm trees that circled the property. It was *A Midsummer Night's Dream* that had become reality. The soft music played by a band in the background was unobtrusive. It did in no way interfere with the animated conversations but mainly served to enhance the magic of the night.

Brandy tried everything from the oriental trays; the more exotic the food, the more Brandy was attracted to it. Eric preferred to stay with hot dogs and hamburgers and a fat lobster tail from the buffet. Charlie celebrated by nibbling on krupuk. Those crunchy chips made out of crabmeat and tapioca flower and fried in hot oil were not good for his liver, but today he did not care. He loved those krupuk chips and because of his hepatitis had refrained from eating them since he had his food poisoning.

When Charlie spotted Woo, Lee's right hand man he had known for years, he headed toward him, wiping his greasy fingers on a wet towel, and got stuck with him in an hour-long shoptalk.

Brandy dived into the party. She was in her element and made many new friends this evening. It was so easy to start a conversation with her. She knew so much about Indonesia, its history, its customs, and its culture. The other guests sensed immediately how much she loved their country, and when she spoke some sentences in Bahasa Indonesia, she won their hearts over instantaneously.

Eric wandered, impressed but bored, back and forth. When Lee noticed that Eric was somehow lost among all these strangers, he approached him and tapped him on the shoulder. "Mr. Beck, may I introduce to you my three daughters? I think you have not met them before. This is Angela, this is Wendy, and this is Anna."

Wendy reached her right hand out politely. Eric took it. It was as if he had touched a red-hot branding iron. A burning, sizzling sensation raced through his arm, past his chest, and settled in his stomach as if it were suddenly filled with glowing embers. Like a robot he shook hands with Lee's other two daughters and exchanged automatic courtesies with them.

This young lady—what was her name? Wendy. She was a live replica of the little statue that had bewitched him at the Prambanan temple. It was as if Loro Jonggrang, the daughter of King Boko, stood in front of him in flesh and blood or as if this young lady had been inside the statue behind the stage during the Ramayana Ballet performance. Her smile— this smile—it was the same the stone figure had radiated at that time, and there, his knees became soft. She blinked, she blinked the same twinkle as Loro had beckoned him with her eyes back then.

Eric had to use all his strength to remain composed.

"Mr. Beck, please forgive me, I have to talk to so many people; I have to move on. We will see each other around. But, please chat with my daughters." Lee moved on to one of the one-legged tables around which a group of Indonesian high-ranking officers had gathered. Angelina and Anna followed in his wake. They sensed that they were superfluous in Eric's company. Eric only had eyes for Wendy. Wendy stayed with Eric. She felt oddly attracted to this American.

There they stood, these two—now just the two of them—silently looking at each other. To break the silence, Wendy suggested, "May I show you our garden?"

She did not dare to address him by his name. Should she call him Mr. Beck or simply Eric? She was introduced as Wendy. She knew Americans always or almost always used first names. She had a strong desire to start a conversation with him and resorted to showing him their garden.

"It is so much bigger than what you can see here. We have the most beautiful tropical flowers and rare trees in our garden."

Eric was only too happy to follow her invitation. It was as if his wife, Brandy, were wiped out from his mind. Eric and Wendy strolled through the noisy crowd, past the music band in the back, and into the unlit section of the vast garden separated from the party area by a colorful hibiscus hedge with dense, dark green leaves and flowers as big as dinner plates. To invite a man to join her into the unlit part of the garden, away from the other party guests, was very unusual for Wendy. Normally she would not dare to leave the crowded area with a man she had met for the first time only minutes ago. But some magic force overruled all her inhibitions and shyness and induced her to do something that minutes before she would not even have dared to think of.

Once the two had stepped into the twilight zone of the yard, lit only by a pale moon, the two became very insecure and shy. And yet they enjoyed each other's company so much and were so strongly attracted to each other. Both did not speak a word. They walked quietly beside each other. His little finger happened to touch her hand, and again he shuddered with a formerly unknown excitement. She responded by looking tenderly up at him and into his eyes. He wanted to move closer, feel the warmth and softness of her body, but he did not dare. She longed for him but was frightened to show it in any way.

After only a few enchanted minutes, the feeling of doing something that was not right and that they could get caught any moment, like a child with his fingers in his father's coat pocket digging for money, took possession of them. It became so strong, so dominating that without speaking a word, both moved back through the hibiscus hedge. Right in the middle of the hedge where the large green leaves and the red and orange flowers covered them, an irresistible urge overcame Eric, and quickly he took and squeezed Wendy's hand. Wendy let it happen. Then they were back out in the open and mingled with the party guests, Wendy and Eric moving in different directions. Nobody had noticed anything but Charlie. A frown formed on Charlie's forehead.

Eric searched for Brandy as if to cover up his infidelity. He found Brandy with a group of English bankers from Singapore who were impressed by her knowledge of Indonesia as much as by her beauty and charm.

"The Dutch used to call Bogor 'Buitenzorg,' which means 'beyond worry'…"

Brandy had not the vaguest notion that Buitenzorg was the place where a disastrous future would take its course. Had she known, she would have been worried to death.

"Ah, Eric, there you are. Where have you been?'

This was only a courtesy question. She was too absorbed by her conversation and new acquaintances to notice anything. Eric's answer was as hollow, but he stayed with her for the rest of the party.

Wendy left the party and went upstairs, straight back to her room. Without undressing, she lay down on her bed staring open-eyed at the ceiling, with nothing else on her mind but the fleeting encounter with Eric.

On their ride back home to Jakarta, the monotonous whirr of the powerful engine and the lulling sway of the heavy Mercedes body had the effect of a sweet narcotic on the three, and soon Eric, Brandy, and Charlie were asleep.

A GHOST AT THE FACTORY

Down in Jakarta the enchanted night was replaced by daily routine. The brand new factory ran as smooth as a Swiss watch, churning out an endless stream of pencils. Pickup trucks kept lining up at the main gate, hauling hundreds of boxes full of pencils to Lee's warehouse from where they were distributed to Lee's wholesalers and dealers throughout Indonesia.

It did not take long, and Wendy announced her visit. She wanted to see how all these little pencils were made. She was especially curious to find out how they managed to get the lead slips into the wood casing. Did they drill holes into the wood or what?

As soon as Eric learned about Wendy's plan, he became extremely excited and talked all day long about the forthcoming visit. Charlie could not help it; an uneasy feeling was creeping into his mind. Wendy's curiosity seemed to be about Eric and not the pencil-making process.

When the day of Wendy's visit arrived, Charlie went about his business as usual. Eric scurried excitedly back and forth between his office and the factory, with one or two workers in his wake. He arranged a little dining table with chairs and a flower arrangement in his office that was suspended in the mezzanine ten feet above the factory floor like the other two offices, the one for Charlie Wong and the other one for the office girls. Then Eric dashed off to Jalan Thamrin, the main business and shopping street of Jakarta. He came back with all kinds of goodies, which he arranged on the sideboard in his office for what he called a business luncheon. He chased a girl with a broom around the mezzanine to make sure everything was spotless; not a speck of sawdust from the pencil-making process was allowed to be found in and around his office. He had just enough time to change into a new shirt, when Wendy's arrival was announced.

Charlie told himself he owed it to Brandy not to leave Wendy and Eric alone. Grudgingly the two had no choice but to play along. They had both envisioned the visit differently. After the obligatory factory tour, Charlie, ignoring Eric's angry looks, joined Eric and Wendy for lunch in Eric's office. On purpose Charlie had schlepped a box full of samples from the pencil-making process into Eric's office and explained in all detail how pencils were made. Wouldn't Wendy want to know how the lead slips got into the wood casing? Well, he would show her.

Wendy actually could not care less. She thought, "Why can't this impertinent man not leave us alone?"

While Charlie gave his lecture and Eric arranged various snacks and treats for Wendy on a white porcelain plate, the machines down below were clanking along busily. The pencil-making process produced a certain medley of noises that Charlie and Eric, already after a few weeks at the new factory, did not notice at all anymore. The noise of the factory was to them not any different than the air around them with its typical wood scent of a carpenter shop. To Wendy the noise and the scent were new, and she was aware of them all the time, even in Eric's office and during lunch: clack, clack, clack, clack, clack, clack, clack...

Suddenly, it was as if the sharp blade of a guillotine had dropped and cut off the noise: Complete, utter silence. No shuffling of feet, no chatting of human voices, no metallic clanking of machines, no banging of wood, no humming engines, no grinding of cutting knives through wood planks, no slamming of doors. Nothing, absolutely nothing. The stillness was so acute that it hurt the ears, the ears that were used to the constant background noise level. The depravation of noise was as painful as if the air that they breathed were suddenly cut off.

Bam! Blackout—complete noise blackout!

The three in Eric's office were stunned; they sat there motionless and looked at each other, bewildered, confused, and insecure, as if transferred in one instant from their world into another universe.

Charlie recovered first. "A ghost...We have a ghost!" he whispered.

Wendy grabbed Eric's arm, her face as pale as a shroud. Even Eric, the self-confident American, felt an ice-cold hand reach down his back.

Charlie got up from his chair first, grabbed a handful of pencils, and left Eric's office without any further explanation. Wendy and Eric followed him, Wendy still hanging on to Eric's arm. When they reached the head of the stairs and looked down to the factory floor, they noticed that not one living soul was in the factory. The entire workforce had disappeared. All the machines stood still.

Charlie marched down the wooden stairs with purpose and determination, ready to confront the ghost.

"I will not go down there. Not even ten horses can make me go down there," pleaded Wendy with Eric, looking up at him in despair. Eric would have loved to agree with Wendy and retreat with her to the safe haven of his office. But he knew with acute clarity that this would be detrimental if not disastrous to the high esteem that Wendy had for him. He had to show strength now.

"Wendy, I am with you. Remember, I beat the ghost before. He tried to bury me under a wall, but I escaped his attack." And he added, lying, "I am not afraid; I will protect you. Come, let's follow Charlie."

Charlie was by now already crossing the factory floor. If they did not want to be too far behind him, they had to move right now. Wendy dug her fingers into Eric's arm and, hiding behind his big body, followed Eric down the stairs, across the deserted factory hall, toward the main entrance. Charlie had left already the factory.

When Wendy and Eric stepped outside, they were at first blinded by the intense sunlight. As soon as their eyes had adapted, they saw Charlie disappear into a huge crowd that had gathered in the front yard.

Everybody was there: their complete workforce and many locals from the street. They formed a big circle three or four deep. No cheering, no rooting, no clapping of hands—complete silence! They were all staring into the circle, concerned of what would happen.

Charlie forced his way through the motionless crowd to the center of the circle. Eric and Wendy decided to stay behind at a safe distance.

Inside the circle was a young machine operator. She was not more than eighteen years old. The young woman swayed broad legged like a swash-buckling seaman, back and forth in the circle, throwing her body around as if she had epileptic convulsions. The spectators murmured and sheepishly moved backward whenever she headed in their direction; her body was bent over, and her fingers contracted like claws. Her eyes were bloodshot and piercing, and she stammered brutish sounds as foam dripped from the corners of her mouth. Charlie knew her as a sweet young girl, friendly, almost submissive, and very dedicated and hardworking.

Wendy was behind the last row, cuddled up against Eric, shivering. He put his arm around her and pulled her closer.

Now Charlie was in the circle. He and the girl were like Roman glad-iators circling each other. Every time she approached Charlie, hunching down, ready to pounce on him, Charlie could not help it, and involuntarily he moved back. Suddenly he realized this was bad, real bad. He displayed weakness. It was high time that he turned the table and took the initiative.

"Charlie, Charlie, don't make a mistake now!" he warned himself. "Let me see what she and her ghost are made of." To test her resolve, Charlie made a quick lunge right at her. She backed away.

"Ah, look at that. You are not as tough as you want us to believe."

Charlie repeated his lunge several times, and each time she retreated and a rumble went through the crowd. In the last row some of the specta-tors began to flash rupiah bills. They were betting on the two combatants in the circle as if it were a cockfight—a very common pastime in Indonesia.

"She is insecure, yes. She is afraid, afraid of me. If I manage to calm her down, I may be able to approach her." Charlie began to talk to the young woman quietly and with a soothing voice. As hard as the spectators strained their ears, they were unable to catch what he said. But it had an effect on the girl; she stood motionless watching Charlie as a cornered tigress. He approached her ever so slowly, constantly talking to her.

When he stood right in front of her, he pulled a few of the pencils from his hip pocket. She did not notice; she stared him in the eyes.

Charlie placed the pencils between her fingers. The crowd expected her to jump on Charlie and rip him to pieces, but she did not move; she did not even register his action, just stared at Charley with fiery hateful eyes. Once Charlie had placed the pencils between her fingers, he immediately squeezed her hand as hard as he could. She screamed in pain like a stabbed pig. Charlie, who lived and had traveled extensively in Southeast Asia, had experience with ghosts. The excruciating pain he inflicted on the girl made, through her as a conduit, the ghost receptive.

Charlie had the ghost's attention now. He was ready to address the ghost. "Tell me, spirit. What is all this about? What do you want? Why did you take possession of this poor girl?"

The girl's eyes became even wider. She moved a step back. Hunched over and watching Charlie warily, she began to speak, swaying from side to side. "You thief, you criminal! This land is my land; it is my home! You stole it from me," shouted a deep guttural voice from out of the girl's mouth. "I want my land back; give it back to me!"

"You know I am your master. You tried to kill me once—no, twice. You tried to poison me, and you tried to crush me. And both times I survived. You can see I have more power than you do." On purpose Charlie spoke loud enough so that the crowd could hear him. The crowd murmured in agreement and full of respect for Charlie's courage.

"He is right. I saw the wall come down."

"I remember they had to take him to the hospital when the ghost struck against him."

The ghost responded to Charlie's statement. "I will try a third time, and this time I will succeed. Everything is ready for my assault. You will bitterly regret your intrusion into my realm." And the girl grinned knowingly.

"This smirk is serious," thought Charlie. "Something is hidden behind it; some real danger is lurking in her eyes. I must reconcile with her or the ghost or whatever this is." He said to the girl, "Yes, you are right; we should have never taken your land without your permission. I am so sorry. I had no idea; I simply did not know. If only I had known, I would have approached you. Maybe we could have come to an agreement. But now, the factory is there! So many people depend on it. Do you really want to destroy all this?"

The girl listened intently. It almost seemed to Charlie that the ghost did not know what to do anymore.

"Look," Charlie continued, "weren't you lonely before, all by yourself, no company? Nobody dared to come near your land. And now, look at all these people and the chickens and the dogs and cats and goats. Does this not make you happy?"

Instead of arguing with Charlie, the girl hunched down and uttered with the deep voice of the ghost, "I am hungry. I want a chicken. Give me a chicken."

Charlie knew he had made progress, yet he could not give in too easily. He had to stay in control. He was the master of the spirit. He had won twice, and he had to dominate again.

He argued, "It is only a short time since we started production. We are a poor company. We cannot afford to give you a chicken."

Foam came out of the girl's mouth and ran down her chin and her chest. She raised her arms high above her head; her fingers contracted like talons. Her eyes became bloodshot and exuded animosity.

"You greedy bastard!" bellowed the girl. "I will destroy you and your factory. You will see."

Charlie knew if he gave in now, he was lost. Everybody in the crowd would consider him the loser of the altercation with the spirit. He had hoped the girl would accept his reasoning. But she did not. He had no choice; he had to try a different approach. One thing was clear to him: he could not give the girl a chicken. This would mean capitulation. Therefore he tried a different, albeit similar, approach.

"Our company is a young and fragile company. We have not established ourselves yet. If we go around and squander our money, this could mean our end. Do you really want this? Look around, look at all these people; they need their jobs here at the factory. A chicken is way too expensive. Just because we cannot afford a chicken, you want to destroy all these lives?"

For Charlie a chicken was nothing, but for the girl it was the ultimate in luxury. For her it was what white truffles would have been for Charlie and Eric.

Charlie also knew he had to give the girl a way out of this deadlock. He continued, "I give you my word that you will get a chicken once we are stronger, once the factory makes money and we can afford it."

Charlie noticed that the girl became insecure.

He made her an offer. "Tell me, is there anything else we can give you for now?"

After a short hesitation, she demanded, "Then give me bananas. Now! I need to eat." And still with a very deep voice but much kinder, she added: "If you promise me that you will keep your word and give me a chicken later on, I will tell you a secret that only I know."

"I give you my solemn oath that you will get a chicken as soon as our profits allow this."

Charlie gave the audience a sign. Some of the workers rushed outside to get a bunch of bananas.

When they came back, Charlie offered the bunch of maybe thirty to forty bananas to the girl. She greedily grabbed it. With shaking fingers she ripped the skin off the first banana and stuffed the whole fruit right into her mouth. Munching and gobbling, she peeled the second banana and stuffed it into her mouth in the same way as the other. Charlie could not help thinking she reminded him of a goose being force-fed. The girl continued in this manner through a dozen bananas before she slowed down and ate the next dozen or so in thumb-length bites and finally the rest in smaller and smaller bites. But she would not stop until all of the thirty some bananas were gone.

The workers had never seen anybody consume that many bananas in one sitting. It was near impossible, but the tender girl did it. The spectators knew this was not the girl it was the spirit.

Done with the bananas, the girl, sweating profoundly, belched and belched and belched and spit out some of the undigested bananas. Then she went down on her knees and threw up a yellowish-white banana pudding with chunks of bananas and some whole bananas in it. Almost at the end of her strength, crawling around on all fours, she resumed the negotiations with Charlie Wong, her cheeks glowing with satisfaction. "Maybe you are right. Maybe I should let you stay, Mister, but then you must give me a new home, a place where I can live. You must build me a shrine and feed me every day."

Charlie knew it was vital to agree with this demand. If he rejected it, he would have the whole workforce against himself. He had already achieved so much; the ghost was prepared to compromise.

"Yes, we will build you a nice shrine. We will do it today! And we will offer you food at your shrine from now on every day." After a short pause, he continued, "Where do you want your shrine? You must tell me."

"I want my shrine behind the factory, there where the generator is," demanded the ghost.

Anybody would have picked a better place, but if that was where the ghost wanted his shrine, then so be it, Charlie thought.

"I will do as you say, but before I build your shrine we have one more business to complete. You promised to tell me a secret. What is it?"

She grabbed Charlie's pants and tried to pull herself up. Charlie reached down and helped her. She was sick and bloated and a splitting headache haunted her, but the ghost gave her strength one last time. Cupping Charlie's head with both hands, she pressed her mouth against his ear and whispered, "Soon, very, very soon, there will be a big fire. It will consume everything. If you had not accepted my terms, I would have let it destroy you and the factory. But since we belong together now, I warn you of the firestorm. You must protect my house, my shrine, and my people. You must protect yourself and your factory."

With this she collapsed and fell in a deep, dreamless slumber. Four strong workers brought a blanket and rolled her onto it. They carried her into their lunchroom. Charlie sloughed behind. He felt as drained as she was. The four men laid her down on a sofa; Charlie took a chair from one of the tables and dragged it over to the sofa. He sat down and took her lifeless hand to comfort her. She slept through the rest of the day, the night, and half of the next day.

While Charlie sat by her side, he pondered what the ghost had meant and how he could protect himself against an imminent disaster. At this moment Charlie had not the slightest doubt that a spirit had possessed the young lady and that the spirit had talked to him. He took the spirit's advice very, very seriously.

As pressing as preparing for a firestorm might have been, something was more urgent. He had to deliver on his promise. He had a handful of his workers build on the very same day for their ghost a beautiful new home between the back of the factory and the generator. They formed three walls out of wood and filled the form with concrete. In an hour it had dried, and they could remove the wood form. The front of the shrine stayed open.

A sheet of plywood covered with corrugated metal served as a roof. The shrine was only two and a half feet tall and wide and deep, but this was plenty for the ghost according to the opinion of Charlie's workers. Then they painted the little house in a bright yellow color. As soon as they were done, other workers brought a little red-and-golden altar and put up candles and incense sticks that they lit, and then they sacrificed a selection of tropical fruits. From this day on, there would always be somebody back there by the shrine praying or sacrificing. The ghost had become part of the Ziegler Indonesia family.

FIRE IN INDONESIA

During the following weeks, Charlie built an eight-foot wall all around the factory. Such a wall would not only protect against a fire, but it was common sense to protect the values inside the property from the overcrowded and incredibly poor slums that surrounded it.

He built a corrugated metal roof over the lumberyard similar to a carport. It kept the wood dry from the daily rain showers but was also good protection against flying embers in case of a fire. These few measures might make a big difference, just in case.

And he did what he should have done in the first place anyhow. He had ABC fire extinguishers installed throughout the building and, for good measure, a water tank outside.

*

Not long after Charlie had completed these projects, his phone rang in the middle of the night. His hand came out from underneath the warm blanket and reached for the phone.

"Yeah?" snorted Charlie.

The voice from the other end came screaming through the phone with such shrill anxiety that it took Charlie a minute to understand.

For an instant he froze, but then the adrenaline made him act like a robot. It had always been his strength under extreme stress to turn into a high-tech machine functioning ice-cold without emotion and without a sign of nervousness. His alarm button had been pushed.

He leaped out of his bed, slipped out of his pajamas, and pulled on a pair of jeans, hopping on one leg while he did so.

"The whole neighborhood is ablaze! The flames are several hundred feet high. It is an inferno," the caller had screamed into the phone.

Once dressed, Charlie ran to the safe and dialed the combination. His hands shook, he missed the right number, and he had to dial it again. At least a trace of nervousness. He flung the heavy metal door open and stuffed all the cash he could find in his pockets. Then he grabbed his wallet, tore it open, searching for more money. He found some.

The old harbor area where their factory was had to be an inferno according to the caller. He would probably not even be able to get close to the plant, so what he could do he did not know. He would have to see once he was there. He tore open the little cashbox he kept under his bed, grabbed all the money, was of out the door, and revved the engine of his Toyota four-wheel drive. No time to look for his driver. The wheels spun in the dirt road, the Land Cruiser fishtailed and raced off.

While steering with one hand, he reached for the glove compartment, took the cell phone out, and dialed Eric's number and then Lee's.

While Eric pulled his Toyota out of the driveway, Lee woke up his driver and was ready to leave, when Wendy tore the car door open.

"I will come with you, Dad." She was barefoot and wore nothing but a skimpy nightgown. In one hand she held a pair of sneakers, and under her arms she had tucked jeans, thong panties, and a blouse.

"No way; you stay home. Go back to bed."

She did not listen and hopped into the backseat. There was no time to argue. If it was so important for her to come along, so be it. Lee instructed the driver to get going and floor the gas pedal. The big Mercedes lurched forward and left the driveway with screeching tires. It glided almost soundless through the sleeping Bogor and flew like a big, dark bird through the moonless night, down the mountains toward Jakarta, with Wendy in the backseat.

Without a thought about the driver, Wendy took off her nightgown, slipped the blouse over her head, and put on her thong panties. Lee in the passenger seat sighed disapprovingly yet was somehow amused. The driver pretended to be oblivious of the activity in the backseat. But now came the difficult part of Wendy's endeavor. She had stuck her feet into her jeans and, while lifting her fanny off the seat, was pulling hard on her jeans to get them over her hips and her buttocks. She wiggled and pulled but did not manage.

Lee could not help laughing. "How about buying your jeans one or two sizes bigger? If you don't get them on, you will have to stay in the car. I will instruct the driver that he does not let you out."

Wendy sulked. "This is not funny. They do fit; it's just so narrow in here." Then she had an idea. She lay down flat on the backseat and lifted her legs with the pants stuck on them up in the air. This was better. Wiggling like an earthworm, she finally managed to get her jeans on with a hard yank above her hips. Breathing all the air out from her lungs and pulling her tummy in as hard as she could, she managed to close the button and pull up the zipper.

Lee could not resist; he had to comment again. "You know, in America the girls soak their jeans in water before they put them on and then let them dry on their body." Actually he was proud that he had such an attractive and sexy daughter.

She replied, "This is not funny."

The driver remained stone-faced although his manhood began to stir. If they would notice, he could kiss his job good-bye.

❦

Down in Jakarta, even from far away, Charlie could smell the smoke and the fire. He drove right toward the blaze in the distance.

"Why do I even try to get there? It is hopeless. God Almighty, if that had happened during the day with hundreds of people working at the factory…" At night they had only a couple of night guards patrolling the factory. They had called him when the fire broke out.

He turned with screaming tires onto a main street and joined a group of fire engines thundering toward the inferno. When they came near the fire, his hope rose that he might have a slim chance to rescue the factory. Closer up he realized that the fire had not started at the factory, which he had been afraid of.

The fire was burning in pockets, huge big pockets, with the flames licking up to the sky. But between these pockets the streets still seemed accessible. The intense heat made him sweat profoundly, and his T-shirt clung to his tanned skin. Firemen and soldiers were running around, evacuating city squatters from their wooden shacks that might burst into flames any moment. An ambulance passed him. Police officers were blocking off streets. He would never have been able to get close to the factory had he not been driving in a group of fire engines, and probably everybody thought he belonged to the fire department. His dark red Toyota Land Cruiser certainly helped his disguise. So he slipped with ease through all the barricades. Once inside the blockade, he stepped on the accelerator and pushed it right to the floor. His car careened out from the convoy. He overtook the fire engines in front, his spinning tires showering pebbles and sand from the rough road onto them. Once he had passed the leading truck, he hit his brakes and pulled over. His car slid on the mud and ashes that were everywhere and finally came to a halt. The fire truck behind him had also braked but a split second later than Charlie. Before it came to a standstill, it hit Charlie's car and pushed it forward. Behind them five more fire trucks came to a screeching halt. In no time the captain was out of his truck and at Charlie Wong's side yelling frantically at him and prepared to hit Charlie Wong with his ax. Just before he could do so, Charlie reached into his pocket and pushed a big roll of rupiah bills into the firefighter's free hand. This stopped the man dead in his tracks. He opened his hand and looked at the money. The corners of his lips twitched in a hint of a smile, and he looked with expectation at Charlie Wong.

In the meantime several other firefighters had come to the support of their captain, ready to kill Charlie on the spot. Who would care? When they realized that their boss had relaxed and was talking to that asshole in the SUV, they stepped back and waited respectfully at some distance.

Charlie was shouting at the top of his voice to compete against the roar of the fire.

"You want more money? Lots more? We have this factory at the old harbor. It is all lacquer and wood. If the fire gets closer, the factory will go up in flames like tinder. If the factory goes up in flames, everything—the whole neighborhood—will be destroyed..."

The chief did not quite understand Charlie.

Charlie grabbed him by his arm and looked him into his eyes. "You want ten times of what I gave you and money for all your people?" Charlie screamed, "Come on, I give you a hundred times more! All cash!" Charlie reached in his pocket and stuffed another handful of money into the greedy fire captain's hand.

The fireman, still not understanding what Charlie wanted from him, reached both his hands out, expecting more.

"Look, I have a whole stash full of this stuff. You can have it all. It is in my factory. If you don't take it, the fire will. For me it's gone. But if you guys rescue my factory, you can have it all. I don't give a damn fucking shit."

"How much is it?"

"Lots, even more. I think thirty thousand or so US dollars. No rupiahs, all dollars." They had the money prepared for their next wood buying trip.

When the captain heard the number, this was all the incentive he needed: "Man, hurry, it might already be too late. Damn it, can't you get in your car and show us the way?" With this, he shoved Charlie into his jeep and ran back to his fire truck, flinging his arms and shouting commands.

With his forearm, Charlie wiped his forehead gleaming with sweat and wet ashes, turned the ignition key, and started the engine.

"Boy, oh boy! What luck!" Thankfully his experience had told him to take the cash. He had not known what for, but he knew Indonesia was corrupt and if he wanted anything done he would need money.

While the fire engine convoy was dashing down the main street, the fire captain kept talking over his CB unit, mustering every fire truck within reach. Firemen abandoned their jobs, letting fires they had already almost put out rekindle again to follow the call that came over the walkie-talkie. The magical word that did the trick was *money*. Once they heard that they could get some share of the squeeze, they were on their toes.

"What did he say? Somebody was giving away US dollars if we put out his fire."

The captain would never tell them how much he really expected. He considered it absolutely legitimate to keep two-thirds for himself and split the rest between a hundred firefighters or even more. This was still an enormous amount for everybody. And the captain had no choice anyhow. He had to protect himself. He had to keep the lion's share. His superiors would squeeze blood from him. They could sentence him to lifelong imprisonment and deportation to an isolated island for abandoning his duty. But they would not do so, because they knew he must have made a fortune for doing what he did, and they would go like vultures after their share. The system worked, everybody knew the mechanics, everybody followed the rules, and everybody was kept happy.

Whereas factory workers were content to make a living on a handful of dollars a day, a fireman, like any other government employee, was not prepared to live on the dismal pay he got. He had to find a second source of income. The government expected their agents to find a way to make a living on their own. The fire department would not mind setting a neighborhood on fire from time to time so that they could get bribed for putting it out again. Mostly the squeeze did not even come close to what this tall, thin Chinese guy was offering, because the people simply did not have so much money.

At about the same time when Charlie arrived with his escort at the factory site, fire trucks were zeroing in from all over as if it were a star rally of firefighters. The factory guards could not believe their eyes. They cried in joy and skipped around like little children. When Charlie jumped out of his jeep, the night guards forgot their respect and gave Charlie a huge, big hug.

"I knew it. I knew it. I knew you would do it. I could not tell how, but I knew you would manage."

"I am so glad you are alive—and, let me see." He turned one of the guards around. "Good, you are unharmed. Tell me, nothing happened to the factory yet?"

"No, nothing. We are pouring water over the wood like crazy, and we shoveled tons of sand onto the lacquer shack. But there is only so much we can do. You came just in time. We were at the end of our wits. But how did you manage to get half of the firefighters of Jakarta to come with you?"

Charlie only smiled. The inferno was not over yet. If one spark hit the wrong spot, everything would go up in flames.

Around them the fire was hungrily licking over the eight-foot tall walls. The wooden shacks outside around the factory site were already all ablaze.

In the meantime Eric had arrived and stood around helplessly. An hour and a half later, Lee's Mercedes drove through the factory gate. Mr. Lee rushed toward Charlie Wong, completely ignoring Eric as if he did not exist. Charlie briefed Lee in a few short words about what had happened to this point and how he had managed for the firefighters to follow him.

Lee did not need any details; he caught on immediately. "Forget about your wood money, Charlie. I will take care of the firefighters from here on."

He walked over to the fire captain and talked intently to him. Both went to Lee's car. Lee invited the fire fighter into the backseat. Wendy had disappeared. In all the commotion, Lee had not noticed.

Wendy rushed to Eric, hugged, and kissed him. "Let me see. Did anything happen to you?"

"No, nothing. I am fine." He did not tell her that he had played no part in the battle against the flames.

"You are my hero," and the word "darling" escaped her.

"Boy is she hot. She is making me so damn horny," thought Eric, but he said with a cool and professional voice, hiding his thoughts, "We should check the offices to see whether there is any damage." Eric said with a wolfish smile, "Our timber money and all our files are there." He had a strong urge to be alone with her.

Wendy caught on right away. She followed him through the dark factory hall.

"Ladies first. It may be slippery from all the embers. It is better if I walk behind you, just in case you should slip." Eric pointed to the steep staircase leading up to the mezzanine, which was about ten or eleven feet above the factory floor.

Wendy raised her right leg and set it on the first step. Her right buttock muscle strained, stretching the tight-fitting denim. At the same time, she straightened her left leg. A crisp crease appeared between her left butt cheek and her hamstring, sucking in and squeezing the denim. Then with hips swaying from side to side, she raised her left leg and straightened her right leg. The crease changed sides and moved over to her right side while her left butt cheek became round and firm. Eric was mesmerized by the view, his eyes fixated on her derriere. Wendy, without turning around, was acutely aware of her backside and the game it played with Eric's psyche. She practically felt his eyes burning holes into her buns.

Once they reached the landing, Eric took her by the hand; she closed her hand firmly around his. They turned right into the hallway and right again into his office. He closed the door. There, in the twilight of the office, he could not resist; he had to touch her cheeks. They were sizzling hot. She stood motionless, let it happen, and looked with big black eyes into his eyes. He took her in his arms. She pressed her body onto his as if she wanted to be absorbed by him and become part of him. At this instant all their inhibitions went by the wayside. With shaking fingers he opened up her blouse. She let it happen. Tenderly he touched her porcelain-white skin. God, it was so soft. As in a trance, she began to unbutton his shirt, and her fingers went farther down to open up his pants. He did the same with her, and when he opened her zipper, the back of his hand running down her smooth, flat stomach, desire overran him like a thundering tornado. He pulled her gently down to the floor, and the moment they hit the floor, he penetrated her, his penis as hard as a steel rod. She screamed in pain and in lust.

"Oh my God. She is a virgin," flashed through Eric's mind.

At the same instant, both froze in panic, her hands digging into his skin in sheer terror, squeezing droplets of blood from it. They heard heavy steps coming up the stairs. An eager firefighter had decided to check the mezzanine and, carrying a fire extinguisher in one hand, was hauling his heavy body up the wooden stairs. He reached the landing. They were lying completely motionless. The firefighter turned right into the hallway. They did not dare to breathe.

"Seems to be OK," she heard him say in Indonesian. He turned around, and his heavy steps faded down the stairs and into the factory hall. There could not have been any better aphrodisiac.

Enhanced by the raging disaster around them and by almost being caught in the act, they had wild sex rolling on the floor. She scratched and bit him over and over again. He penetrated her so deep and so hard that she felt certain his cock would come out by her belly button. He ejaculated inside her and on her stomach. They did not care. Finally they calmed down and lay next to each other quietly for a while. Then they got up, and he cleaned her carefully with a stack of paper towels and half a dozen wipes from his desk. When they returned and joined the others, nobody noticed their soiled clothes in all this helter-skelter. Had anybody noticed, one would have thought it came from the fire and from whatever rescue effort.

Without the need for any further instructions, the firefighters got the picture why they were called to this place and had gone to work immediately. They pumped water frantically into the flames and hacked away at smoldering beams and wooden structures. They tried to push the fire away from the property line of the factory with everything they had.

By now there must have been some thirty-fire engines forming a protective wall around the factory, with close to two hundred firefighters struggling for the survival of Ziegler Indonesia. A few dozen of them were running around the factory grounds, pouring and hosing water over everything flammable, putting out the beginnings of fires kindled by falling embers and sparks from the outside.

By late morning it was all over. The whole neighborhood was nothing but smoldering charcoal, here and there a thin ribbon of smoke meandering to the gray clouds above. A few forlorn chickens and goats were roaming about the rubble. The locals who had been surprised by the roar of the midnight inferno were barely clothed at all and searched the debris in the futile hope to find a piece of their belongings.

Like Mont-Saint-Michel, the monolithic monastery off the coast of France, at low tide, the Ziegler factory reigned unharmed over the wiped out shanty town. Its walls had been blackened. The roof of the main factory building had caved in in one place. This had happened when the fire managed to get its first bridgehead across the outside walls. Without the firefighters and their powerful water guns, nothing would have stopped the fire in its advance from this starting point on the roof. It had been that close. But the Ziegler factory was the only structure that survived the fire, and this only because of Charlie Wong's assertive and resolute action. And last but not least because Charlie Wong had been forewarned by the ghost, the ghost he sort of did not believe in but whose advice he had heeded anyhow and prepared for such an onslaught.

All the firemen gathered in the yard. Lee stood in front of them and handed a brown paper bag to the captain. What nobody knew was that already, when the struggle was in full force, Lee had given the captain another package as soon as it had become obvious that they were winning the battle against the fire.

After having completed his part of the rescue effort, Lee and Wendy, equally satisfied, rode back home to Bogor: Lee because his factory had been rescued; Wendy because of her fiery romance with Eric.

"See, I told you, you should have stayed at home," commented Lee on their way back. "Look how dirty you got from all the soot and ashes."

"That's OK," answered Wendy, "I will shower and change my clothes as soon as we are home."

*

When Eric came home to Brandy, she felt so sorry for him, yet was very, very proud of him. In her opinion he had battled the fire till almost total exhaustion. His clothes were dirty and torn, and he himself had bruises and scratches and cuts on his face, on his neck, and his upper body. She was convinced that he had given everything to rescue the factory. She prepared a hot bath for him and mixed in lots of soothing bath salt. He drank half a glass of wine in the tub. Then she rubbed him down with a fluffy towel and tucked him away. He fell asleep the same instant with a smile on his face. She kissed him tenderly on his forehead.

Later a rumor circulated that the fire had been started on purpose by the government. This neighborhood had always been a shanty town. In recent times it had deteriorated to such a degree that it became a serious health hazard. Deadly diseases might spread from it. When even cholera bacteria had been identified by the health department, it had become necessary to clean up this neighborhood, to tear the old contaminated shacks down and erect new ones. The local people, however, would fight such a measure tooth and nail. The simple solution was to burn the whole area down. There was no better disinfectant. After such an action, the government could show its generosity and hand out small grants to the people to enable them to put up new huts and resume their lives. And then there was another very secret reason behind that fire. The government needed to build a monsoon drain through this area that required the confiscation of a vast number of homes—a complicated, expensive, and time-consuming procedure. It was much cheaper and more effective to burn the whole mess down. Landownership was no problem anyhow. The land had always been owned by the government. Poor people all over Jakarta used to build their huts on public ground (where else?) and the government tolerated it to a degree (what else could they do?).

The only structure of real value in this slum area had been the Ziegler factory. In the end everything had gone well. The factory survived, the neighborhood was soon rebuilt, leaving open space for the storm drains, and the germs were extinct, leaving room for new germ generations to establish themselves. Only a few rats, chickens, cats, and dogs had bitten the dust, and a few dozen people, most of them elderly and sick anyhow, who were not able to run away in time. Ziegler Indonesia helped and supported the locals in every possible respect to get their lives back on track.

Charlie was seen between the factory building and the generator house by the little shrine murmuring, "Maybe you exist after all. Maybe! We had some disagreements. This time you were on our side. Thank you, thank you so much." And with that he placed a plump barbequed chicken, which he had denied the ghost before, in front of the altar.

DIVORCE

From the very day of the fire. Brandy observed that Eric had changed. It was as if he had become a totally different person. Brandy at first blamed his reserve and silence when he came home from the fire on total exhaustion. But this restraint and reserve toward her did not change. This took Brandy completely by surprise, and she did not understand what had happened. Before he was happy to come home from work and tell her over dinner what had happened all day long at the factory. Afterward he would enjoy going with her to a local market to buy fresh produce or stroll arm in arm with her along the banks of the Ciliwung River. But now, she hardly saw him anymore. He always had to attend some meeting or work long hours at the factory, or Lee wanted to meet with him in Bogor, or he even had to go on business trips to Singapore or Sumatra to scout out new wood-buying sources. This was at least what he kept telling Brandy. The two started arguing and fighting, which was so much against Brandy's nature. When he screamed at her, she could not help but scream back or rush to their bedroom, throw herself on the bed, and cry bitterly.

In her despair she sought help from Charlie. "Charlie I am at my wits' end. Whatever I am doing is wrong. It is as if Eric avoids me. Charlie, please..." Her eyes were pleading with Charlie for help.

Charlie had no concrete knowledge of how close Eric and Wendy were, but he had an uneasy hunch. He could not tell Brandy his suspicion. How could he? What should he say? What should he do? How on earth could he help her? He blamed himself for being a coward, but he dodged the issue and comforted Brandy with empty words while desperately searching his brain for a solution.

Oh God, if he only knew himself what was going on. He was afraid that Eric and Wendy were a lot closer than what he had noticed so far. And what could he do to help Brandy in her misery? He could only hope that the situation would change for the better and Eric would return to his sweetheart, Brandy.

*

While Brandy pleaded with Charlie for help, or at least for an answer to what was going on with her husband, Eric in the meantime spent the afternoon with Wendy at Ancol Dreamland, by the waterfront not far from the factory. Ancol Dreamland was Asia's largest tourist resort and Jakarta's favorite amusement park. Ancol Dreamland offered many different attractions: a Fantasy World, Water Adventures, Jaya Bowling, and even a golf course. Eric and Wendy enjoyed this afternoon riding the Gondola, a sky lift cable car high above the other attractions, with fabulous views of the shoreline as well as the city. At other times they had dared to stay overnight at one of the three hotels within the vast compound, Eric pretending to be in Jambi or Singapore.

Their cable car was like a love nest on wings. Eric caressed Wendy's hair. "Wendy, you are my princess." Looking deep into her dark eyes, he added, "You are a real princess!"

She teased him, "You are only calling me a princess because I am the daughter of Lee, the king of Bogor. Tell me, do you love me? Do you really, really love me?" Her eyes were gleaming mischievously, expecting Eric to engage in a playful banter with her.

But Eric was serious. "Wendy, you are a true princess, as real as any royal princess."

The seriousness in his voice surprised her.

"Do you believe in reincarnation, in life after death, Wendy?"

"I don't know." She shrugged her shoulders. "What are you up to, Eric?"

"Well, many hundred years ago, you walked this planet already, here on Java. And at this time, you were a real princess of flesh and blood."

"And you, Eric, were the king of Sheba." She still believed Eric was playing a love game with her and the princess story was nothing but part of his courting.

"I was not, but you were. Listen to me; don't interrupt!"

"Oh my God, he is serious. An American, of all people, is talking about reincarnation," flashed through Wendy's mind.

Eric continued, "Soon after I came here to Indonesia, Brandy took me and Charlie to this dance thing at the Prambanan Temple near Yogyakarta. While we watched the performance, I noticed a little statue carved from stone at the back of the stage. Brandy explained to me after the presentation that this statue was Loro Jonggrang, the daughter of King Boko; hence she was a princess. This Princess Loro Jonggrang looks exactly like you. When I saw this little statue, I was attracted to it as much as I was attracted to you when I saw you the first time in your dad's backyard."

"Are you trying to tell me that you love a stone figure as much as me?" she scolded him.

"No, no, please stay with me. The eerie part is this statue was as much alive as you are. It smiled at me. I did see the corners of her mouth move up. And she winked at me. I did see her eyelids move, not once but several times. And you know we humans have a facial expression that is alive, that keeps changing. There is movement in a person's face. The same was true for Loro's face. It was not a frozen stone mask; it was a human face." With this his fists hammered the handrail of the cable car to emphasize that his story was true.

Wendy was now still, perplexed, bewildered.

"And, Wendy, I kept telling myself, 'It is the moonlight playing tricks with me.' But no, it was not the moonlight. It was the statue; it was her. I felt this attraction to her; I felt her desire, her longing for me. How can a stone long? I once was in a room with a person who died, and although I

107

was looking out the window the moment the person passed away, I knew instantaneously that life had left his body. I turned around and he had expired. We sense life! And life exuded from Loro's statue. There was a communication going on between her and me. She flirted with me. I blushed; I got aroused. At the very same time my feelings for Brandy cooled off, right then and there."

He looked at her; she looked back, not daring to breathe a single word. Eric's story was gripping; it was as realistic as it was hard to believe.

"It becomes still more unbelievable. When I saw you at Lee's party, you were the spitting image of this princess, and at the same instant my blood started to boil in desire for you. Not only do you look like her, your facial expression, your smile, your saucy eyes, the way you carry yourself—everything is the same. Loro is you, just smaller. Now you know why I am convinced that you lived before, long before, and that you were a princess at this time."

Overwhelmed with a whirlwind of emotions, Wendy fell on her knees. "Will you marry me, Eric? I love you with all my heart. Please, marry me!"

Eric laughed. "I should be on my knees and proposing. Yes, darling, I want you as badly. I wanted you the moment I saw you. I do want to marry you, as fast as possible." Then his face darkened, and he became serious. "But I am still married. I completely forgot about it. Let's elope to Guam or Las Vegas!"

"No, Eric, I will talk to my dad. He will get us a divorce, and then we can marry in Bogor. Dad gets anything he wants."

"But a divorce? What could we blame on Brandy?" He rubbed his nose with his forefinger.

"Daddy got your machines through customs in no time, he bribed the firefighters into saving the factory from the big fire, and he will get you a divorce."

After this eventful gondola ride, Eric dropped Wendy off at her father's office on Jalan Thamrin. Lee was so busy with all his projects that he had not noticed Wendy's absence. As on most of the days, she joined him on his ride home. At first both sat next to each other in the backseat quietly. When the car eased out of the last outskirts of Jakarta, Wendy grabbed the bull by its horns. She had to spill her heart before they reached home. At home with her two sisters, her mom, the servants around, and dinner being prepared, the television blaring in the background, she would never be able to talk about such an important matter with her dad. She pushed the button to raise the glass panel that separated them from the driver.

Once the barrier was up, she took a deep breath and tucked at her dad's arm to gain his attention. He turned toward her. At first her words trickled haltingly. The more she talked, the more she gained courage. Eventually she talked like a waterfall rushing over the edge of a cliff. She told her dad about her love for Eric, that he compared her to Princess Loro Jonggrang. She confessed her secret meetings with Eric and that she was dying to marry him and that Eric was still married, and if her dad could help her get Eric divorced and, and, and…

Lee gave his little angel a big hug. "What a wonderful story, the story about Princess Loro Jonggrang and you. I always knew that you are a little princess." He kissed her. "Maybe Eric's story is true. But be that as it may, for me you are my princess, my princess full of mystery and beauty! And don't worry! I will take care of Eric's divorce."

For the rest of their ride home, she leaned her head against his shoulder, surrounded by an aura of happiness, warmth, and protection. She had known that her dad would grant her this wish, but she honestly had not expected that her wish would be accepted so surprisingly fast. She had been prepared to argue with him, plead with him, cry, even act up. None of this was necessary. The touching story of Loro Jonggrang must have convinced him. She had no other explanation.

*

Not even a week had passed, when Brandy's doorbell rang. A man dressed in some official garb stood outside. He had a big envelope for her and asked her for her signature. Somehow she felt uneasy. What could that be? But she signed and took the package inside. Once she had closed the front door, she opened the envelope. It contained the divorce papers.

Brandy collapsed. When she recovered, she was not her cheerful, confident, enterprising self anymore. Her world had been shattered. Everything she had lived for had been taken away from her. With an ashen face, slumped over, she crept around the house.

From then on she did not have the energy anymore to do anything purposeful, not even the household chores. Her brain seemed as if it had been replaced by a ball of cotton. She could not think clearly. She kept sobbing all the time. She was horrified. After the papers had been served, Eric did not come back to their house anymore. She had no idea where he stayed, what he did. And worst of all, she had no idea why Eric wanted to divorce her. What had she done? What was wrong with her? Why? She blamed herself but did not know why.

Her only hold and support was Charlie Wong. She had called him the same evening. When he answered the phone, he could only hear her sobbing. She was not able to utter a single word.

"Oh, my God, what has happened? Brandy, talk to me!" he shrieked into the receiver.

She could not.

"I am on my way, Brandy." And with that, he had run to his car, not bothering to look for his driver, and raced over to Brandy and Eric's house.

The door had been open. He marched in. Brandy sat at the kitchen table and held some papers in her hands. Without a word she handed the papers to him. Still standing, Charlie read.

"This swine, this dirty pig," had shot through his head. "I suspected they might be having an affair, but a divorce!" He knew instantly that Wendy was behind this, that she was the reason for the divorce. And he knew that Brandy still had no idea what was behind the divorce papers.

From then on he spent every minute that he could spare, with her, sitting at the kitchen table. He told Brandy about his hunch. But would this be of any comfort to her? If only he could know. But when Brandy began to blame herself, Charlie decided it was necessary to tell her everything that he had observed. Brandy and Eric had been such a wonderful couple full of tenderness and sweetness toward each other. She had sacrificed her career for him; she had embraced her new home, Indonesia, with all her heart. And now this disaster! He had noticed Eric slowly slipping away from Brandy. If he remembered right, it all had started at that ballet in Yogyakarta. From that time on, Eric was no longer that close to him as well. Eric was like a different person. It definitely had nothing to do with Brandy, but Wendy could very possibly be behind the change in Eric's personality. Charlie's presence may have prevented Brandy from ending her life.

Then came the court hearing. Brandy had no chance. She was paralyzed with fear and confusion. She did not know how to answer to the ungrounded accusations from Eric's attorney. She just stood in front of the judge, looking at him with red, swollen eyes, shivering, her arms crossed in front of her chest. Charlie sat in the back. He could have murdered Eric and Lee as well. He knew very well that without Lee's connections this divorce would never go through. They had no case.

When the judgment of divorce was handed down from the bench, it hit Brandy like a sledgehammer. She swayed and staggered back to her seat. Charlie jumped over the barrier, grabbed Brandy just in time, and led her out of the courtroom. Eric passed them on their way out gleefully and completely unaware of Brandy's misery. Nothing could stop him anymore.

CHAPTER III

BACK IN LOS ANGELES

After Brandy had recovered from the initial shock, she realized that she was stranded in Jakarta with absolutely nothing to call her own, not even enough money to pay for her flight home to America.

"Charlie, should I go to the American embassy for help? I cannot stay here; I need to go back home."

"No, you do not need the embassy. Brandy, I will take care of everything. The Ziegler Company owes you so much, and I am the president. We will pay for your return ticket."

"And what about all the furniture?" Brandy asked timidly.

"I will ship it to you in a container. Eric does not care anyhow!"

This was all Charlie could do for Brandy at this point. Brandy wanted to get away from it all as fast as possible, in the hopes that back in the States the deep, gushing wound would heal. Charlie understood. He convinced her to stay with him until her departure to America because he did not want her to be alone in her house. Who knew what she might do to herself?

When the day of the departure had arrived, Charlie drove Brandy to the airport, where he handed her a one-way business class ticket to Los Angeles. At the check-in counter, they heaved together two heavy suitcases full of necessities onto the scale to make sure she would not arrive barehanded in the States. The digital numbers on the scale raced past the free weight limit. Charlie did not care how much he had to pay for excess luggage. Brandy did not notice it. She turned away from the counter; she did not want Charlie to see that thick tears rolled down her cheeks. Indonesia had become so much a part of herself that she was afraid of flying back to America. Charlie had always been at her side in the most difficult times of her life. And now all this would be over. But she saw no alternative. Quietly they walked slowly together to the security checkpoint.

Charlie took her by her shoulders and kissed her good-bye on her wet cheeks. He wanted to kiss her mouth, but he was too shy. His heart was screaming, "Please do not leave me! Brandy, I love you, I love you so much!" But his mouth did not say a word.

She turned around and walked through security. One last glance over her shoulder, and then she disappeared in the dark tunnel that led to the boarding area. Charlie stood frozen and looked after her. Even when she had been gone for quite some time, he was still looking into the tunnel, a furtive tear running down his cheek.

◢

This time the flight across the Pacific stretched out forever. Brandy slept on and off fitfully. She kept sipping on a bottle of mineral water even after it had been empty for a long time. She did not eat anything, and she was neither interested in a magazine nor any of the many movies that were offered. Her mind was stuck in a rut, thinking the same thoughts over and over again. Why did Eric leave her? Why for Wendy? What was so special about Wendy that she could not offer? Where had she failed? What had she done wrong? All this was so unreal. What was going to happen to her now?

Where would she go? What would she do? Would she be able to support herself having sacrificed her career for Eric's education?

Finally the plane landed at Los Angeles International Airport. Still numb and lost in thought, she walked down the ramp and into the Tom Bradley International Terminal. The moment she set her feet on American ground, she felt already better, securer, and more confident. God, did it feel good to be on American soil again! It was as if she had been away for an eternity although she was only gone for less than two years. Immigration and customs were nice and friendly.

"Hey, madam, you have been away for quite a while. Welcome back home, and God bless you," greeted the black lady in the immigration booth. She radiated warmth and typical American optimism.

This rubbed off on Brandy, and she replied confidently, "Yes, you are right; it is good to be back home." And to herself she murmured, "I will get over Eric. I will start out new. I have to be strong now, but I can do it. I will start all over again. I can do it."

Nobody checked her heavy luggage that she pushed on a cart through customs and up the rather steep incline to the welcoming area. Nobody was waiting for her. She pushed her cart through the throngs of people on the lookout for family members, friends, and business partners arriving from overseas. Once through the automatic sliding doors, she took a cab to Hollywood Boulevard and checked into one of those cheap but pretty decent hotels that could be found all over Hollywood. At the check-in counter, she made a monthly arrangement with the clerk. This was probably the best. She had no apartment, and her furniture was floating somewhere on the ocean. Her room was OK, old and small but clean, and it had a TV set, a telephone, and a bathroom with shower. This was all she needed at the moment.

Her highest priority was to find a job to make a living. The very next morning she went down to the corner of Hollywood Boulevard and Cahuenga Boulevard and bought the *LA Times* at the newsstand, then she walked across the street to a little corner diner, where she bought a cup of coffee and a muffin. She could not afford to dwell on Eric and the divorce anymore. She had to get her life together. She leafed through the huge newspaper and stopped at the classified section, her eyes scanning column after column.

"This might be something," she muttered, pointing with her index finger at one of the many, many ads. "Haven't I worked as a secretary before and paid for Eric's education?" She circled the ad with her lipstick.

The Pestalozzi School off Los Feliz Boulevard was looking for a secretary to the principal. Since the school was not too far away, Brandy decided to go there in person right away. After having finished her breakfast, Brandy took a bus going eastward down Hollywood Boulevard. On Western Avenue the bus turned left. Western Avenue became Los Feliz Boulevard. Brandy got off at the Vermont Avenue intersection and, after backtracking some fifty feet on Los Feliz Boulevard, walked through the gate of Pestalozzi School. It had not occurred to her that it might have been prudent to call in first and try to get an appointment. The school was nestled against the slope of Griffith Park, a complex of old Spanish buildings overgrown by ficus and ivy plants. Two mighty palm trees stood to the left and the right of the gate to the property like sentries guarding the entry. The bright morning Californian sun painted the school in friendly and inviting colors.

"I like it." With confidence and expectation, Brandy marched up the graveled driveway toward the main building.

She caught up with an elderly man. She greeted him politely and cheerfully. He greeted back. They began to chat, and for whatever reason, Brandy told him that she had arrived from Indonesia only yesterday, where her ex-husband had started a factory.

"Fascinating. Why don't you join me in the cafeteria for breakfast? By the way, I am Peter Stadler," he said, inviting her.

Although she had already had breakfast, she accepted. The gentleman was a good and patient listener. Brandy felt comfortable and secure with him. She spilled her life story to him. That she could talk to somebody about all that had happened helped her overcome some of her lingering sadness and recover some of her self-assuredness. The breakfast took well over an hour, and at the end the nice gentleman introduced himself as the principal of the school.

"What an incredible story. I have to admire you. I am looking for a secretary, and I would be delighted if you took the job and worked for me. I think I've found a real gem in you. What do you say?"

Brandy accepted wholeheartedly and had a job on her very first day back home in America. And not just some job, but something she had done before and was good at. Best of all, she liked this man, her new boss.

*

As time passed her wounds began to heal. Step by step the nightmare of her divorce was replaced by fonder memories. Memories of the wondrous world of an archipelago far, far away in the tropics, a world filled with history, mystery, culture, craftsmanship, colors, a unique fauna and flora, and, last but not least, with ghosts and spirits, some good, some evil. Memories of a world where she had encountered the worst deceit and unfaithfulness one could imagine but, at the same time, true friendship and support.

CHAPTER IV

THE WEDDING

It did not take long for Eric to erase completely from his mind Brandy, who had been his high school sweetheart, who had sacrificed her career to pay for his engineering school, who had supported them both before he found employment with The Ziegler Pencil Company—Brandy, who not so long ago had been the love of his life.

The wedding preparations for Eric and Wendy were in full swing. If one of Lee's daughters got married, this was going to be a major social event, and the expectations of the guests would not be disappointed.

Then there was something else. Lee held a top, top, top secret meeting with his trusted right hand, Woo, in his back office, where all of Lee's important decisions were made. This time only he and Woo sat at the filigree rosewood table. Each had a little cup of steaming tea in his hand, their heads close together. Lee whispered intently; Woo kept nodding. Not even the maid was allowed to come in and fill the teacups. Lee himself kept pouring tea once in a while from the porcelain tea pot into the tiny cups that had no handles.

The very next morning, Woo was on his way to Yogyakarta, where Indonesia's finest and most skilled craftsmen had their shops.

They hammered intricate *wayang kuit*, leather puppets, with endless patience from ordinary pieces of leather. They carved wooden puppets, *wayang golek*, and painted them in all the colors of the rainbow. They dyed batik shirts, batik scarves, and sarongs and even designed batik paintings depicting vividly the stories from the *Ramayana* epic. Silversmiths squatted on the ground with not much more than an awl and a hammer, turning sheets of silver into water carriers, pill boxes, jewelry cases, or horse carriages, with attention to the very smallest detail.

From wood, artists carved detailed and colorful Garudas. Every craftsman tried to outdo his competition by making his Garuda even more colorful and more intricately carved. With incredible patience and skill, they cut every feather of the bird from a block of wood and even showed the texture of the feathers not only in color but with their carving knifes, their chisels, and their rasps.

And stonemasons were breathing life into stone with the same artistry and skill as their ancestors who had created Borobudur and Prambanan many centuries ago.

Woo wasted no time; once in Yogyakarta, he headed straight for the shop of a master craftsman.

When he left the shop after little more than an hour, he stopped and turned around. "Once again, I need it in not more than three months."

"It will not be easy, sir, but I think I can do it."

"And it has to be perfect."

"It will. I have never done any job that was not perfect."

Satisfied, Woo flew back home to Jakarta.

While the craftsman drove to the mountains looking for a suitable rock, Lee's home and office were humming like a beehive in preparation of the wedding reception, the *resepsi pernikahan*.

The actual wedding ceremony would be in the presence of family members only. It would be strictly a private affair. The reception would be a very different affair. The Lee family planned on inviting literally everybody they knew to the *resepsi* and then some more. All the members of Wendy's family were invited. Nobody cared about Eric's family. He himself did not seem to care either. Did he even have family? Further invitations had to be extended to all employees, all vendors, all customers, all bankers, many, many government officials, representatives of the city, travel agents, and even fitness trainers and beauticians. There was no end to the list. The reception had to be fit for royalty. Lee's reputation was at stake. Endless lists were drafted and revised and rejected and redrafted. Everybody had a different opinion. Some people were not invited on purpose. This was meant as an insult and to teach them a lesson. Others had to be on the list although nobody in Lee's family knew them in person. If you forgot the wrong person, it could have far-reaching consequences. Finally the list was hammered out. Well over a thousand people were on the list. The most conservative estimates were that at least nine hundred, more likely over a thousand people, would attend. Everybody knew that as much as it was an insult to forget somebody for the invitation, it was as much an insult not to attend without a very strong reason.

Lee's home in Bogor, despite its big backyard, was out of the question. The family decided on the Grand Ballroom of the Prambanan Hotel and its poolside, with the Olympic-size swimming pool for welcome drinks. Despite the fact that the hotel was in the center of Jakarta, and thus was convenient for all the guests, it had twenty-three acres of tropical gardens.

It was going to be a sit-down dinner, a sit-down dinner for an army. To answer the questions of who was allowed to sit at a reserved table and who to the right side of whom was more excruciating than solving a Rubik's cube. How much easier it was to decide on the food selection, the music band, and room decoration. And then the proceedings: they had to be rehearsed, fine-tuned, rehearsed again, and fine-tuned again, and rehearsed again. For three months Wendy and her wedding were the center of the universe.

❦

The first hurdle was cleared when the invitations were mailed. Charlie Wong sat at his desk in his office and held his invitation in his hands: embossed golden letters on heavy stock, handmade paper with its typical tell-tale jagged edges.

"You would do our family great honor by attending and extending your blessings on the bride and the groom," ended the invitation.

"They will need a lot of blessings if this wedding is going to work. Eric used Brandy, cheated on her, and dropped her like a hot potato as soon as something better—nah, richer came along," hissed Charlie between his teeth.

Three months passed and Woo returned to Yogyakarta with a cordless reciprocating saw in his duffle bag. He checked into a small hotel at the outskirts of the city and then drove to the stonemason. After a short while, Woo left the shop again with a heavy object wrapped in an old blanket under his arm.

He was extremely satisfied with the work of the stonemason. The craftsman could not have done a better job.

With a mischievous smile on his face and murmuring to himself over and over again, "Perfect, wonderful, great, a masterpiece...," Woo drove back to his hotel. He went straight to bed after setting the alarm on his wristwatch to 3:00 a.m., because the hours of the night before the sun rises are the darkest and people sleep the deepest.

At three o'clock his watch chirped. He pushed the button to quiet it, quickly got up, and stealthily, without a noise, snuck out of his room. He loaded his heavy object into the trunk of the little rented Toyota Corolla and pushed the car out of the parking lot. Once on the road, he started the engine and, without making hardly any noise, drove off. It was a moonless night, shrouds of clouds chasing each other on the tropical sky. Woo drove a short distance through the jungle. When eerie stalagmites reached out of the dark foliage by the side of the road, he pulled his car over, went to the back of it, and opened the trunk. He lifted the mysterious object in its blanket out of the trunk, squeezed the saw under his arm, and with his heavy load disappeared like a shadow between the dark structures. He moved from temple to temple until he reached the center of Prambanan. It took him several minutes to find what he was looking for in the darkness of the night. He breathed a sigh of relief when he spotted her, Loro Jonggrang, on her pedestal. He lifted the saw to sever her from her stand. To his surprise he did not need the saw. He could lift her up. She was heavy but not attached to the pedestal; only gravity had kept her in place all these hundreds of years. With a moan he lowered her down, stood her next to his package, and unwrapped an exact copy of Loro Jonggrang. He switched on a powerful flashlight and intensely compared both figures. Nobody would be able to tell the difference between the original and the copy. How this craftsman did it, Woo did not know and did not care. Probably the craftsman had spent a lot of time out here at the temple.

"Nobody will ever find out!" With this he lifted the copy up unto Loro's pedestal, wrapped Loro in his blanket, and toiled back to his car. Once the lid of the trunk had closed with a thump, he took a deep breath of relief. Back at the hotel—by now it was six in the morning—he enjoyed a hearty and well-deserved breakfast, checked out, and headed back to Jakarta, where he unwrapped his loot in Lee's back office.

❧

Finally the great day arrived. From the *akad nika*, the actual wedding, at which Eric and Wendy exchanged their vows, they were whisked in a rented Rolls Royce to the Prambanan Hotel. They entered through a back door and disappeared unnoticed by anybody into the Wedding Suite.

In the meantime an endless convoy of limousines and cars lined up at the main entrance to the hotel, and elegantly dressed couples in traditional Indonesian costumes or Western black tie and evening gowns stepped out and strutted with pompous bearing into the main lobby. Hotel guests and tourists stood all around gawking. It was much like on Hollywood Boulevard in front of the Dolby Theater when the movie stars have their great entrance to the Academy Awards. Many men wore long-sleeved batik shirts, all uniquely handcrafted and hand painted works of art. They cost easily as much as an Italian custom-tailored suit. The Chinese ladies sported skintight batik skirts with golden embroideries, showing the movement of their legs and derriere through the expensive fabrics with every step they took. The bustiers were as tight as the skirts, lifting up and enhancing their breasts. Muslim ladies covered their hair with the traditional scarf. European ladies preferred long evening gowns, and Indians wore saris of the finest silk, endless long scarves wrapped around their heads, then down their busts and around their waists. It was a lavish feast of colors and styles for the eyes, as colorful and multiethnic as the people of Indonesia.

In the main lobby, the guests signed the guest books, received their thank-you token for attending and honoring the bride and groom. Lee had decided on a dozen pencils from his factory. The pencils were imprinted with Wendy's and Eric's names and the date of the wedding, and they were presented in a filigree sterling silver box. After depositing their presents on sheer endless tables, the guests entered, heads high up, in measured strides through the welcoming lane formed to the left and to the right by Lee, his wife, his two unmarried daughters, and some other family members. Some guests shook hands with the family members, and others bowed, their hands on their thighs or folded in front of their chests. The guests exchanged a few words with the hosts and disappeared from the rubbernecking crowd of onlookers into the reception hall, where the lane was extended by young men and women holding flowers, the fence of beauty, *pagar ayu.*

Soon after all guests had arrived, the bride and groom, Wendy and Eric, held their million times practiced grand entry preceded by traditional dancers in their inimitable grace. The bride wore a white wedding dress with an eight-foot long train, a diamond diadem adorning her hair. From head to toe Wendy exuded royalty. Self-confident, Eric wore a black tuxedo and a winner's expression on his face. They had exchanged their marriage vows in the morning. She was all his.

Eric and Wendy were followed in procession by her parents and other important family members. Once they were seated, all other guests followed from the reception hall and took their allocated seats. Now followed the less pleasant part of the wedding. Speeches, speeches, and more speeches—some short, some lengthy, some witty, most boring. And then there was again a receiving line. The guests came to the stage, climbed up the three steps, and shook hands with Wendy and Eric and Lee and his wife.

A beautician was always at Wendy's side to dab her cheeks with powder, to apply a new layer of lipstick, or to tuck a loose hair back where it belonged.

Unnoticed by anybody, Wendy and Eric disappeared after a while, hands hurting from all this shaking. They had to take a break and get ready for the dinner. In the meantime the guests could step outside to the pool area for some refreshments or stroll around in the garden.

At sunset the guests had gathered again in the Grand Ballroom. Ushers led them again to their tables and helped them sit down. Before dinner was served, bride and groom reappeared from their retreat. They had changed from Western attire into traditional Indonesian costumes. Her costume was similar to those worn by the guests: bustier and tight-fitting ankle-length skirt with hand-painted batik motifs from the *Ramayana*, threads of real gold woven into the fabric. As the bride Wendy was the only one who again wore a head gear. This time it was made of pure gold and radiated like the rising sun. Eric wore a slim-fitting frock, running from his shoulders to his knees, of the same fabric and with the same batik motifs as Wendy's skirt. Under the frock he wore a sarong. But his was wide and loose fitting and by far not as ornate as Wendy's. His head was covered by a black, round hat with no brim, similar to the pillboxes that had been in fashion in Europe and the United States during the time of Doris Day. This hat was a favorite head gear of many Muslim Indonesians but was also worn as part of a traditional Indonesian outfit.

Before they sat down, Wendy and Eric exchanged hair. Indonesians believe that the life force of a human being is in his or her head. The head is the vessel of one's soul, or *semangat*. Eric noticed that the dancers performing at their wedding had human hair attached to their dance costumes.

Wendy explained, "Darling, this promotes *semangat*, life force—like we just exchanged our hair and thus our life force."

Then they were allowed to sit down at the head table, and dinner was served.

𝄢

As the party began to wind down and the first guests were leaving, Lee felt it was time to present to the couple the very special wedding gift he had for them. It could not be done in front of the guests. This present had to be kept a secret for all times. Lee asked the newlyweds into his suite on the top floor of the hotel.

As they rode the elevator up, Wendy almost burst with curiosity and expectation. "Tell me, what is it? Why is it such a secret? Should not all the guests enjoy and see your wedding present?"

"No, no! Wait and see. We are almost there."

They walked down the long hallway, and at the end Lee opened the door to his suite. There she was in her full splendor. Loro Jonggrang. Lee had replaced the flower bouquet on the round table at the entrance to the suite with Loro. At first Wendy and Eric did not get the magnitude of this present. Lee explained it to them. He told them how touched he was by Eric's heart-warming story. He had decided to give them as a symbol of their eternal love the most precious gift he could come up with: the little statue of Loro. Not a copy—no way—it had to be the real one, as real as their love for each other. His trusted friend and advisor, Woo, had the assignment to procure the ancient princess, and, as always, Woo had come through.

The two were overwhelmed. Both had tears in their eyes. They touched and caressed the statue with shaking hands. They looked at each other and then again at Loro Jonggrang.

"Wendy, look, she is you! Look at her features. She even has your personality, your charisma!" stuttered Eric in amazement. He had remembered right.

Lee had been as overwhelmed by the similarity as Eric. It was almost creepy. In all the jubilant joy, there was a hint of evil in Loro's aura. Lee seemed to sense it, if ever so slightly.

Wendy unwittingly brushed Lee's premonition aside when she asked, "But, Daddy, will they not find out. What then?"

"No, nobody ever will." Lee was his usual businesslike self again. "Woo exchanged Loro for an exact copy so perfect that nobody can ever tell unless they use this radiological or carbon thing... You know what I mean. And who is going to do this? Nobody, because nobody will ever suspect anything."

"Eric, I want you to have Loro in your office," cooed Wendy over a late breakfast, "so that even when we cannot be together, I am always with you."

He reached across the table, took her slender hand, raised it to his lips, and kissed it.

ERIC PROMOTED—WONG LEAVES

After spending an enchanted honeymoon in Hawaii, Eric returned to his daily routine at the factory.

Somehow the chemistry between Charlie Wong and Eric had evaporated. Eric looked after the machines. Charlie Wong ran the company, taking care of personnel matters, sales, purchases, government relations, and all the other many tasks that are required from management. Charlie did not involve Eric in any of these jobs anymore as he had done before.

From the beginning Charlie had been of the opinion that both should know as much as possible of each other's responsibility. After all, they were only two, and it was for the sake of the company and their own protection to be able to substitute for each other if need be. This had changed. Charlie did not feel like doing it anymore. He did his job and Eric his. They were still friendly with each other but preferred to stay out of each other's way.

Eric suffered under the fact that Charlie seemed to avoid him and did not involve him anymore in his daily activities. He had not done anything wrong; he had always been cooperative, nice, and friendly; yes, he had almost been submissive and accepted Charlie as his superior, guide, and mentor. Was it that he had divorced Brandy and married Wendy? But what was wrong with that? He had been truthful and faithful to himself. How could he have stayed married with Brandy when he loved Wendy with all his heart? It was better to accept one's feelings and draw a line. Brandy would find a new love. It did not occur to him that the divorce had been merciless and left Brandy stranded with nothing in a foreign country and that without Charlie stepping in she might have ended up in the slums of Jakarta begging for a piece of bread.

For now Eric had more important business to conduct than to linger over his relationship with Charlie. He commissioned a carpenter to put up a sturdy pedestal in his office. This done, he hauled Loro Jonggrang from Bogor to the factory and placed the little statue on the wooden pedestal. Then he walked back to his office chair behind his desk, sat down, and looked at her, stroking his chin. She gave him comfort and company! Not like Charlie, who was shunning him. After a while he stood up, walked over to Loro, and caressed her. She smiled at him; it was as if she liked his touch. She felt warm and full of blood. Could this be? She was stone! Maybe he was just tired, daydreaming, his thoughts wandering. But it was as if she was trying to tell him something.

"Loro, oh Loro, what do you want to tell me?"

Eric nodded almost absentmindedly, almost as if in a trance.

"So, Loro, you mean it is not right that Charlie is president and I am nothing but a glorified machine operator, a subordinate to this Chinese guy from Singapore? Why did I leave my homeland, come all the way down here, to become a nobody?"

He shook his head as if to shake off the dreariness from his mind, walked back to the chair behind his desk, and shuffled some papers. After a while he had to support his head; it became heavy, and his eyelids wanted to shut. He took a deep breath and looked weary-eyed at Loro.

"Are you talking to me again? What do you want? Yes, I am Wendy's husband. I am married to Lee's daughter; Charlie Wong is not married to her. It is a disgrace for Wendy that her husband works under a hired hand."

"Eric." Loro became loud and outspoken. She came down from her pedestal and walked over to Eric's desk. She planted herself on the desk, right in front of him. "You must talk to Mr. Lee! Do it! Do it for Wendy; do it for me! I want to be the wife of a president, not of a lowly machinist. What do my friends think of me? How can I have a party, go to charity events, when I am married to a nobody? I am Lee's daughter, and you as my husband should be the president." Loro's eyes had become piercing and demanding.

Eric fell off his chair, his head hitting the floor with a thud. This woke him up. He looked around drowsily. Loro was on her stand, immobile, smiling at him, mute.

"This damn heat and this monotonous singsong of the machines; I must have fallen asleep," he thought. He stood up, supporting himself at the edge of the desk, left his office, walked down the stairs, and tinkered with one of the machines to distract his mind.

At home over dinner, he told Wendy about his eerie experience at the factory. Wendy wholeheartedly agreed with Loro. She should have come up with this idea herself. Nothing would have to change in the daily routine at the factory. The only difference would be that her husband would be president, and Charlie would get some other title, like manager or director or whatever her dad came up with.

It was easy enough for Wendy to convince her dad. She had him wrapped around her little finger anyhow. She wiped her dad's weak objection—how Charlie Wong would take it—away with her big eyes and pouting lips. Nothing would be taken away from Charlie Wong. His job responsibilities would be unchanged, only his title adjusted a teeny weenie little bit.

The next morning Lee called Charlie at the factory and asked him to come over to his office. When Charlie arrived at Lee's office, they had a cup of tea together. Lee asked Charlie how things were at the factory and if they needed any help.

Charlie thought, "This is odd; Mr. Lee did not call me over for such small talk. What does he want?"

It was clear to Charlie that Lee was dragging his feet. Something was in the bush. Lee was not his usual self-assured and composed self. Face to face with Charlie, it was not that easy for Lee to tell Charlie about his decision. It had been much, much easier to agree with his daughter and promise her that he would do it.

Lee fidgeted in his chair. He knew it was not right what he was about to do. But he did not dare to go home to his family without the desired result either.

"Come on; what is bothering you? What do you want to tell me! Spit it out!" Charlie thought.

Well, he would soon find out what was bothering Lee. Taking a deep breath, Lee bit the bullet and let the cat out of the bag, trying to play down his decision as much as possible.

Lee resorted to the standard phrase used in such a situation: "You have to understand...," which, in effect, meant the opposite.

No matter how Lee tried to justify his decision, the fact remained the same: Charlie was demoted and was not prepared to understand.

Charlie sat there, stone-faced, showing no emotion. Maybe his chest was heaving a little more, yet he kept his face blank and did not allow Lee to look into him. When the meeting was over, Charlie Wong got up, saying, "I guess there is not much that I can do to change your mind since you decided already. Thank you for the meeting and your frankness, Mr. Lee."

With that, Charlie Wong left Lee's office. Lee was unable to fathom how Charlie Wong took it. He would have preferred it if Charlie had started an argument with him, which would have enabled him to explain his decision, maybe even apologize for it. He could have told Charlie that for him Charlie was still and would always be the boss at the factory. But Charlie did not do Lee the favor of letting him explain and apologize.

*

At Bogor Wendy had been eagerly waiting for her dad to come home. "How did it go? Tell me, how did it go?"

Lee shrugged his shoulders. "I have no idea. I told him our decision, but Charlie showed no emotion."

"He will get over it," replied Wendy, carefree, and she scampered away to the kitchen to help her mom with dinner preparations.

*

The next day Charlie did not show up for work, and he did not the day after and the day after that. On the fourth day after his meeting with Charlie, Lee received a letter in the mail. In this letter Charlie told Lee that he had resigned and that he would, by the time that Lee was reading these lines, be already back home in Singapore. He thanked Lee for the good times they had had together and the trust Lee had had in him in the beginning. He was disappointed but did understand Lee's predicament and decision. He could not get himself to wish Lee good luck for the future and ended the letter instead with a rather formal "yours sincerely."

*

Lee had some remorse and doubts about his decision, which Eric managed to dispel convincingly. Until Eric divorced Brandy and married Wendy, Charlie had involved Eric in everything he did. He, Eric, knew the ropes by now. And then there were Lee's team and Lee's connections. Nobody would miss Charlie Wong.

THE HAUNTED TREE

With Charlie gone, Eric had become the kingpin at the factory, king of all kings. Loro had given him good advice. He in turn took his new responsibilities very seriously. The Lee family had been so good to him. He wanted to give something back to them, and he also wanted to prove to himself and to the Lees that he could run Ziegler Indonesia without Charlie Wong. And Eric did a surprisingly good job. Ziegler Indonesia ran as smooth as a freshly oiled sewing machine. Lee was very satisfied with the performance of his son-in-law and glad that despite some scruples he had made the right decision.

Weeks passed and then months, and nothing extraordinary happened. What had been a big challenge in the beginning and demanded Eric's full attention and dedication became routine and, after a while, drudgery. As a matter of fact, Eric had a lot of idle time at the factory sitting around, doing nothing. All kind of ideas, imperceptible to him at first, crept into his idle mind and slowly began to affect his thinking, as if being poisoned by arsenic, the victim not aware of what was happening to him. He developed a habit of talking to Loro.

The day after his promotion to president, he had bought from a street vendor at a traffic signal a whole bunch of flowers and placed them at Loro's pedestal.

"I don't know whether my scheme was just a dream or whether you really advised me. It does not matter; it worked. And as far as I am concerned, dear Loro, you gave me this tip, whether it was while dreaming or awake. Thank you, thank you so much, my darling."

Mornings when he entered his office, he would greet her, "Hey, there. Hope you had a good night."

When he left in the evening, he would say, "See you tomorrow, and stay good."

He talked to her like many people talk to their dogs or cats or plants, making her part of his thoughts, his desires, his hopes, his fears, and his victories and happiness.

Many months had passed. One of these days, Eric, as he did so often, lounged in his swivel leather chair, rocking back and forth. From down below the machines murmured their lullaby. Eric was totally relaxed, his eyelids becoming heavy as he looked at Loro. She looked back at him. She smiled. He smiled. She blinked. He did the same. He looked at her, mesmerized. For him she was so real. Comfortable warmth embraced him. He let his thoughts drift, and there again—bam—Loro started talking. He kept looking at her and let it happen.

"Eric, Eric, my dear. They are so rich, so wealthy, and have you work for pennies. Why did Lee not make you a partner? You married his daughter. You run one of his companies. And he feeds you table scraps. You are a member of the family. They should acknowledge it; they should make you part of everything. What if your marriage turns sour? What if Wendy drops dead? So much can happen. You will be down and out in the streets, a pauper. Eric, I am your true and only love. You must protect yourself."

This was not possible. He had been wide awake. He was positive he had not fallen asleep, and yet he clearly had heard her talk. He had been in a trance-like state, maybe drowsy but not—no, no, no—not asleep. Admittedly, he had been very relaxed, but he had been alert; he had been focused. He had followed every word of her. And now he mulled over her words in his mind.

Bewildered by what had happened in his office, he left work early and drove straight to the library. He was unable to read most of the books since they were in Malay, Bahasa Indonesia, or whatever other oriental language. But there were more than enough books in English. He disregarded books on spirits and ghosts; they were nonsense, old wives' tales, oriental hocus-pocus. Self-hypnosis! That may have been it. He had been relaxed. He had been in a trance. He had been conscious and focused. All these were signs of self-hypnosis. This would mean that Loro's words were his own thoughts, which his trance brought from the subconscious to the surface. Yet again, her speech was so real. These could not have been his thoughts. And what about her smiling and winking? His American background did not want to believe in ghosts or spirits. On the other hand, he had experienced so much during his time in Indonesia that he was not sure anymore. He had a real human relationship—a relationship like between a man and a woman—with this stone statue. Her magic had bewitched him. He was unable to escape her spell. Yes, she exercised immense influence on him. Ever since he had attended this ballet performance at Prambanan, Loro Jonggrang determined the direction his life took. It could not be denied; her advice had been good so far. When he left the library, he was not any wiser than before. Maybe he should not have disregarded the books on the supernatural.

The next day he marched into his office and challenged Loro Jonggrang right away. "Fine, Loro, and how do I do this? I cannot walk up to Lee and ask him for a cut of his business. He'd be mad. He would blame me that I am never satisfied, that I am greedy, that I have no patience, that I do not trust him. Everything is running so smoothly. A demand as you propose won't work. So, tell me what I should do!"

Loro showed no reaction, not even her enchanting smile. She was just a piece of rock on a wooden stand in his office.

"Loro, come on! Wake up. Come to life. Smile. Talk to me!"

Nothing, nothing at all!

"Don't try to tell me you are just a piece of rock. You are more than that."

He remembered every time that Loro talked to him, he had been in a sort of a trance, relaxed, slightly tired.

"So, I am going to relax!"

He tried hard, very hard, but he remained tense, focused, and expectant and was disappointed all around.

"Yeah, I know. You always talk to me when I expect it the least. And now that I need you, you are hiding inside this stupid rock, you bitch."

Maybe he should have never insulted her. Immediately after he called Loro a bitch, an idea flashed through his brain.

"See, I don't need you. I know what to do."

He was kingpin at the pencil company. Lee did not seem to care; he let Eric do whatever he pleased. Had not Charlie taught him that the profit lay in the wood purchasing process? After Charlie Wong had left, Eric had bought his timber at local lumberyards. The timber cost down in Jakarta was so much more than in the jungle, but it was for Eric so much more convenient, and the company still made lots of money. If he started to buy again from the villagers on Sumatra, the prices he had paid in Jakarta so far would serve as a yard stick. Anything less would look good. The purchasing was all done without any paperwork; the transactions were all cash as long as he bought from illegal logging activities. And not to forget, his vendors were hidden somewhere in the mountains, not around the corner. Perfect! It could not be any better. What had Charlie taught him: Nobody can tell what a tree trunk costs with all these knots, latex channels, blue stain, cracks, rot, bark thickness, and insect infestation. The buying price depended on your negotiation skills. If he went back to Sumatra again and bought his wood there, he could charge Ziegler Indonesia anything he wanted as long as it was below the market prices in Jakarta, and the difference to the real deal would go into his pocket. Ingenious. Yes, he was a genius. He would become a partner of Lee, and Lee would not even know it.

"There, smarty-pants. Loro, I can do it without you whispering in my ear, you capricious woman. Fuck you!"

And he turned to leave his office. On his way to the door, it was as if he saw out of the corner of his eyes Loro's features harden, her mouth become thinner, her eyes turn irate. She appeared to clench her little fists, turning the gray rock white for an instant. Even her breasts seemed to heave. Bewildered, Eric swung around. Loro stood immobile, just like a statue—what she actually was, not more and not less. He shrugged it off, left the office, and went about his daily business.

For a little while, a thought nagged him. Had Loro hissed a warning or a threat at him on his way out?

"If you think you can do without me, without my advice, be careful you might get badly burnt!"

"Ah, nonsense," he mumbled to himself. "All these ideas were mine, stupid rock." And with this, he did not waste a thought on Loro anymore and went about his business.

*

"The sooner I start, the sooner my cash register will begin to ring." Eric was so excited about his clever scheme that he could hardly wait to go back to the mountain region on Sumatra where he had been with Charlie Wong.

This time the trip was by far not as much fun as with Charlie. On top of everything else, he had difficulties communicating with the Indonesians although he spoke some broken Bahasa Indonesia, which Wendy had taught him or which he had picked up around the family table. Some of the Indonesian loggers and rafters knew a little English. Communication was complicated but possible, and greed drove Eric on. He could not take an assistant from Lee's company along. This would jeopardize the whole idea. This trip he had to do alone.

*

Toiling up the muddy mountain trail, fighting off leeches, dodging buffalo caravans, stepping into buffalo manure, he remembered the pile of premium logs hidden in the jungle behind the village. What nonsense did the villagers tell them about this pile? It was haunted or some such thing? For these Indonesians everything had to be supernatural, mystic, or something. Bullshit! If he could convince these hillbillies to give him the pile cheap, just to get rid of it, he could charge Ziegler Indonesia a premium price, justified by the extraordinary quality. Little did he know that the villagers had had similar thoughts since the Singaporean with the long-nosed white devil had left them. They regretted that they had let the opportunity pass to free themselves from the curse.

◢

Eric had no choice but to sit around, bored in the mountain village for three days to wait for two young villagers who had worked for American logging companies on Kalimantan. These two young men spoke enough English to act as interpreters during the negotiations.

The negotiations were like a poker game. The villagers would have given Eric the stack of haunted wood for free as long as he took it. On the other hand, they wanted to squeeze as much money out of this foreigner as possible. Eric held an ace that helped him win the deal at his terms in the end. During his last visit, the villagers had made the mistake of telling him and Charlie that they were deadly afraid of this pile of logs. In the end Eric got it for a pittance. Yet, he needed much more wood, so that the villagers also made some nice profit, and both parties were highly satisfied.

◢

The trip back to Java and Jakarta was almost identical to the odyssey with Charlie, with one exception. Something happened at the very beginning of the trip, which, for the people of Bukittinggi, was a clear indication that their decision to get rid of the cursed tree was right. For Eric it was a minor event of no significance. While floating the timber down the river, the head of one of the floaters hit an overhanging tree limb. The floater lost his balance on the slippery surface, fell into the river, and was crushed to death between the constantly moving and turning heavy logs, the wooden crocodiles.

On Highway 25 Eric bribed his passage through roadblocks as he had learned from Charlie Wong and got home safely. This one trip alone had made Eric a ton of money. With the money he had made, he could easily buy a house here in Jakarta. And with every trip up north, Eric became richer and richer. He did not need to ask for a partnership in Lee's company anymore; de facto he was already a silent partner anyhow.

At the factory Eric stored the haunted stack separate from the rest. He planned on keeping this wood for the back-to-school business in the United States. With Ziegler Van Nuys as a partner of Lee in Ziegler Indonesia, Eric could be certain that he would receive a lot of business from America. To protect and develop this business, he wanted to ship pencils of the highest quality at a premium price.

And, chuckling under his breath, he would add stealthily to himself only, "Well, I will squeeze as much as possible out of the Americans. What is very profitable for us is still very cheap for them. I guess if I go twenty-five percent below the production cost of Van Nuys, the Americans should be pretty happy and we'll make a lot of hay. And I will tell Lee I will have no choice but to offer dumping prices to be competitive in America and develop this gigantic market. What does he know? And all the difference will end up in my piggy bank." With this scheme on his mind, Eric prepared the offer for Ziegler Van Nuys's back-to-school business.

"I am a genius. I will make money on both ends, buying raw material and selling finished products. Watch out, Lee, one day I will be as filthy rich as you!"

SUSPICION

J oe Manner sat in his dingy office at the factory in Van Nuys. With his left hand he scratched himself behind the ear, and with the index finger of his right hand he dialed 01162, the country code for Indonesia, then 21, the city code for Jakarta, and then the number of Lee's office.

"*Selamat datang*," came out of his receiver.

"Ah, yes, good morning." It must have been around nine or ten in the morning down there. His watch showed 7:00 p.m. "Could I please talk to Mr. Lee or Mr. Woo?"

The female voice at the other end said something that did not mean anything to Joe Manner, but he caught something that sounded like *Mistel Woo*, and then he heard her put the receiver down and scurry away.

"Good, she understood; she is getting him." While she looked for Woo, Joe Manner studied the offer from Indonesia that lay in front of him on his desk.

"Mr. Manner? Hello, Mr. Manner, are you there?" came out of the receiver.

"Hey, Harvey, yeah, it's me."

Woo addressed Joe Manner by his last name. As an Asian he did not feel comfortable with first names. Joe Manner, on the other hand, used Woo's first name, Harvey, which nobody else, not even Lee, did.

After they had exchanged the usual courtesies, how they were doing, how the weather was and so on, Joe came to the point. "We are about to place a rather big order for back to school with you guys. Today I received the offer from your factory, from Eric Beck. You guys must be kidding. The whole idea of our joint venture was to beat the hell out of our competition here in the States. Pencils from Indonesia were supposed to be damn cheaper than we can make them here."

Woo listened without saying a word.

Manner went on. "We need to be especially competitive in the school business. These are big orders, not these fucking orders from stationery stores: a box of this and a box of that. The prices your Eric is quoting us make no sense. He is just a smidgeon cheaper than our cost here. What's wrong with you guys?"

And he went on ranting, "Don't tell me we went through all this trouble for nothing. Your prices should not be more than half of our cost. What did I say? A third or a fourth, but not a lousy twenty-five percent lower. Are you trying to cheat me?"

This was tough. This was not a subtle insinuation; Joe Manner's last remark was an insult. Woo swallowed it. "Mr. Manner, there is not much that I can say right now. I will have to talk to Mr. Lee about this. Could you please fax me a copy of the offer, and then I will get back to you tomorrow at the same time."

"You got it, and don't try to play tricks on me. The offer is already running through my fax machine. You should have it any moment."

Harvey Woo reported to Lee every detail of his phone conversation with Joe Manner.

Lee was fuming; Joe Manner had uttered a massive accusation.

"Me, Lee, to be unethical, a cheat!"

Lee could have strangled Eric, but to preserve face he did not show his emotion. Harvey Woo knew his master from many years of loyal service and knew that Lee was irate.

"Mr. Woo, what did Eric think? We never cheated on anybody. All my life I kept my word. My word is stronger than any written contract. We had agreed to treat our American partners honestly and fairly. How can Eric ask so much more from the Americans than from us and our distributors? They will look at us as thieves and criminals. How can I ever look Mr. Manner in the eye?"

Then he stopped abruptly. Woo did not say a word and sat quietly across from Lee.

After a while Lee continued as if talking to himself. "Maybe Eric is overzealous. Maybe he wants to prove himself and make as much money for us, for his little company, as possible. Maybe he is even right. He knows America. Maybe they can pay that much and Mr. Manner is playing poker with us."

Lee did not even believe his own words. He was trying to vindicate his son-in-law. He brooded again.

"You know, Woo, since Charlie Wong left us our wood-costs went up drastically. Maybe Eric is trying to recover the higher cost?"

He pulled the fax from Manner out of the fax machine and looked it over. Suddenly his eyes got bigger. At the bottom of the offer to Ziegler Van Nuys were instructions to remit the payment to a bank account in Singapore.

"I do not know this account. Do you?"

Harvey Woo shook his head. "No, never heard of it."

Something here was fishy. Lee sensed it with painful clarity. He prayed he was wrong.

"This is nagging me. Mr. Woo, I want you to go to the factory—yes, tonight. Look around and see if you can find anything. Check the file for the school business from America. Maybe we'll find an explanation in there. And also look at the timber purchases. Why do we have to pay so much more? You know what? Take a copy machine with you. Do not use the one at the office and copy anything that strikes you."

"Why not the one at the office? These copy machines are so heavy."

Lee explained, "The copy machine at the office might record everything and I do not want Eric to find out that we are investigating him."

*

Woo left for the factory around midnight together with a locksmith. The uniformed guard at the gate snapped to attention, clicked, his heels and hurried to open the big steel gate for Woo. It did not occur to the guard to ask himself what Woo wanted at this time of night at the factory. Woo was so high up above him, like a god on mount Olympus. Woo and the locksmith walked quietly through the dark factory, up the stairs to the offices.

First Woo looked around the general office. He quickly found the timber file and made copies of all the documents. Purchases from Jakarta had proper invoices; purchases in the logging region were all cash, and therefore all documents were drafted and signed by Eric himself. Never mind. Woo copied all of them.

Eric's office was locked. The lock was a cheap entry lock. It took the locksmith not more than a minute to open it with a simple lockpick. There on Eric's desk sat a manila folder marked "Pestalozzi School Los Angeles." Woo copied everything that was in this folder.

Hidden in the pitch-black background, Loro Jonggrang watched him with piercing, knowing eyes as if wanting to say, "Hey, Eric, this is what you get for your betrayal. I would have never allowed you to send false quotes to Lee's partner. How dumb can you be? Or better: how greedy can you be?"

Every time the green light from the copy machine cast an eerie light flash at her, she seemed to come to life. A shiver ran down Woo's spine, and he was glad when he was done and could leave the office. The locksmith locked the office, and soon the night swallowed the two intruders.

*

Woo's loot confirmed Lee's worst fears. Oh, how much he had hoped that his suspicion was unjustified and that Woo would find a plausible explanation. But this was not the case.

Lee and Woo studied the copy of the Pestalozzi File that Woo had made in Eric's office. Two things were different from the offer Joe Manner had faxed them, devastatingly different. On the copy of the Pestalozzi File from Eric's office, the quoted price for the pencils was much lower, and the instructions to pay to a bank account in Singapore were missing all together.

"This does not look good. Eric seems to be working with two prices and plans on pocketing the difference." It was not easy for Woo to say this, but his loyalty to Lee left him no choice. "And there, look, Mr. Lee, the timber purchases from lumberyards here in the city cost more; we know this. What I do not understand is why Eric paid in this village near Jambi so much more for wood than Charlie Wong used to pay."

Lee still tried to defend Eric. "Well, Mr. Woo, we both know that it is very difficult to determine the price of wood, and so much depends on your negotiation skills. Maybe Eric is not yet as experienced as Charlie. I need absolute certainty. After all, Eric is my son-in-law. I need ironclad proof. If I do not know, I will eat my heart out. I might be feeding a snake on my breast. Let's do this." And Lee laid out his plan to Woo.

🖋

This time in his broken English Lee talked to Joe Manner in person asking Woo to help him with his English several times. It was not easy for him. He swallowed the bitter pill and let Joe Manner in on his suspicion.

"Mr. Manner, please understand. We do not know for sure. It would be disastrous if anybody knew about our plan. I need you to go through with the order as submitted by Eric, all the way through to the bitter end. I even want you to remit the payment to this account in Singapore. This is the only way I can gain certainty. Afterward we will straighten things out between us, and I will reimburse you for any loss or overpayment."

Joe Manner had caught on immediately and was only too happy to play along. It was in their mutual interest.

Yet Lee was not satisfied with this trap; he wanted to find out whether there was more. The prices Eric paid for the wood seemed to be awfully high. Where did Eric buy his logs from? All they knew was that the lumber was from some village in the jungle near Palembang or Jambi. To find a needle in a haystack was easy compared to finding this village. And in addition, would the villagers trust him? There existed only one solution to this challenge. Charlie Wong! It was not going to be easy making amends for his wrongdoing. Lee knew that he had treated Charlie Wong very badly, that he had done him a great injustice, and still he had done so for the sake of his daughter and his son-in-law. To go back to Charlie Wong and atone, ask for his forgiveness, went against his grain, his upbringing, the whole culture he lived in.

"Mr. Woo, I cannot do this. But then, is it not enough if we follow through with Eric's invoicing fraud? You have to help me. What should I do? You go—you see Wong!"

"Mr. Lee, you know as much as I do: only you can go this stony road."

"Um."

"It will haunt you if you do not know for sure, Mr. Lee."

"Then it will haunt me!"

"And who is going to run the pencil company if you have to fire Eric?"

One thing was ironclad: if Eric was caught embezzling, Lee would fire him. Nothing on earth could stop him from doing so, not even the love for his daughter Wendy. Lee would not tolerate a criminal in his business or in his family.

"Are you going to tell me that if I fire Eric, I will have to rehire Charlie Wong?" Lee knew he had no choice.

Lee was faced with two strong reasons to kowtow to Charlie Wong.

Finally Lee jumped over the hurdle. "But I will not go alone! You must come with me."

"Certainly, sir."

Woo, the faithful friend and confidant, accompanied the penitent Lee on his trip to Singapore. Charlie had not found suitable employment yet after leaving Ziegler Indonesia. He lived in a one-bedroom apartment on the twelfth floor of one of those new high-rise buildings subsidized by the government that burgeoned in Singapore.

Woo rang the doorbell. Almost instantaneously Charlie opened the door. When he saw the two visitors, he did not say a word, only looked perplexed at them, a frown on his forehead. Lee was fidgeting with his fingers, looking at the concrete floor.

Woo broke the silence. "Mr. Wong, may we please come in?"

Charlie shrugged, opened the door a bit wider, and showed with a gesture that they could enter his lair. Lee crawled like a beaten dog into Charlie's apartment. Woo followed sheepishly. Charlie's apartment was pretty barren: a bed, a bookshelf (Charlie was an avid reader), a stove, and a kitchen table with two chairs. Charlie offered Lee one of the chairs and sat down across from him. There they were, sitting now. Charlie looked stone-faced across the table at Lee, elbows on the table with both hands supporting his chin. Woo had no choice; he had to stand, leaning against the whitewashed wall. It was obvious that Charlie was still sulking. It was just as obvious that Charlie was not too well off. His stint in Indonesia had been too short to build some wealth.

Lee knew painfully well that he could not buy Charlie with money no matter how dearly Charlie Wong needed some income. Charlie had left Ziegler Indonesia because of hurt pride. He would return to work for Lee only if he was appeased. To discuss any money issues with Charlie today would have shut the door right away.

Lee decided not to play any games with Charlie but to be totally candid with him. He planned on hiring Charlie back if his horrible suspicion about his son-in-law should turn out to be true. But it was too early to talk about it. He explained the situation to Charlie and for now only asked him to accompany Woo to the mountains. Charlie kept looking at Lee. For Lee he would not do it, no. The wound was too deep. First they cut his throat, and then they came kowtowing and telling him how sorry they were! They deserved what they had coming.

"Eric is taking revenge for me. How sweet," crossed Charlie's mind. "May they fry."

On the other hand, getting back at Eric would give him great satisfaction after what Eric had done to Brandy. This would be sweet revenge. Over and over he had regretted that he had sent Brandy home to America. He missed her. Only after she was gone had he realized that he actually had fallen in love with her.

"Yes."

This yes came out loud and forcefully, so strongly that Lee and Woo jumped. They had not expected it after enduring Charlie's stone-faced silence for that long. They had no idea what motivated Charlie Wong to this sudden decision, and he would not tell them either.

Satisfied with the result, Lee flew back to Jakarta. Woo stayed with Charlie and left the next day with him for Palembang. They took a flight out of Singapore.

Charlie enjoyed the trip back into the mountains and the jungle; for Woo it was pure horror: leeches, snakes, beetles, mud, eerie sounds, and the terrible moisture. Was he glad that this was going to be a onetime trip and other people took care of wood procurement! On his own he would have never found this place. Well, he would have turned around halfway there anyhow.

When they approached the village, Charlie pointed out to Harvey Woo the orangutan who was sitting in her usual spot by the pond.

"I will certainly not go near this monster lest it bites me or abducts me onto a tree," said Harvey Woo, shuddering. Next to the orangutan sat a white man in camouflage carpenter pants. He was talking to the animal, making big signs with his arms. The beast mimicked each of his moves. When the man spotted them, he waved and wore a friendly smile on his face. The orangutan waved in exactly the same way, a broad smile from ear to ear exposing her big yellow teeth.

"*Grüezi, miteinand*," the friendly stranger greeted them.

Charlie and Woo looked bewildered.

The stranger corrected himself: "Ah, *selamat datang*. You speak English, you guys?"

"Yes, we do," said Woo.

"What the hell are you doing here in the jungle?" inquired Charlie curiously.

"As you can see, I am training this cute forest lady," answered the white guy jokingly. A little more serious, he continued, "Please go over to these tents. I will catch up with you as soon as I have finished my session with my girlfriend here. In the meantime my colleagues will tell you everything you want to know."

The village had grown by a number of tents interspersed between the wooden huts. At one of the tents sat a young, blonde woman looking into a microscope.

They learned from her that she belonged to a group of Swiss scientists from Bärli Pharmaceuticals, a Zürich-based drug manufacturer. They had set up camp in this part of the rainforest to search for plants that could be beneficial in medical treatments.

"How long are you guys planning to stay?" wondered Charlie.

"No idea; we just arrived a short while ago. Maybe we stay two or three months. But we might stay as long as a year. Depends on our findings. The rainforest is a treasure trove for pharmaceutical plants."

The Swiss scientists invited Charlie and Woo for dinner. Charlie told them that they were buying their timber in this village for a pencil factory they had in Jakarta. The Swiss showed Charlie and Woo samples of plants and told them about their medical benefits. Roland Weber, the head of the Swiss scientists, steered the conversation toward the importance of the rainforest for our future and how disastrous the clear-cutting by international companies was.

"In the end we will all regret it. It is all about greed. Even the clear-cutting that some of the villagers do should be stopped. With no concern about their own and our future, they even burn down the forest to gain arable land."

Charlie defended their wood buying.

"Yes," agreed Roland Weber, "this is different. You need such a minuscule quantity. It does not affect anything." He said this more as a courtesy than out of his own belief. In his opinion all these little needs added up to a gargantuan crime regarding our ecosystem. It was a pencil here, a picture frame there, an entry door, a chopstick, a few beams. Forests the size of countries disappeared with no replanting and with no responsible forest management. The region's dense rainforests were normally damp environments, but once they had been thinned by timber poachers, they dried out and became prone to catch fire. England once had dense forests, and they were all gone, gone forever, sacrificed to the British shipbuilding industry. The Adriatic coast of today's Croatia had eroded over the centuries. The Venetians needed the trees for their ships. Today was so much worse, burning and cutting down everything that was left of our green lungs in Southeast Asia and South America.

The villagers of Bukittinggi were happy to see Charlie return. Ziegler Indonesia had developed into their biggest customer and their main source of income. Charlie and his sidekick (this is how they looked at Woo) spoke their language, which made it a lot easier to converse and negotiate with them.

Charlie had instructed Woo that they were going to buy a shipment to make their visit seem inconspicuous. They could store the wood for an interim time at one of Lee's warehouses.

As always Charlie stayed overnight. Woo had no choice but to stay with him. The next day Charlie checked cut lumber and scoured the vicinity for suitable trees, talking incessantly with the village people. The villagers did not realize that Charlie was sounding them out. And in the end, Charlie had collected all the information that Lee was after.

"Mr. Woo, your buddy Eric is cheating you blind; he is squeezing blood from your pencil company." Charlie could not help it. He had to show his sarcasm. It was written all over his face. Nothing tastes sweeter than a good measure of revenge. They had asked for it. They got what they deserved. In the presence of Lee, Charlie would not have gloated that openly; he still had too much respect for him. "Hey, Woo, I hope Lee rips Eric's liver out and throws it to the Sumatra tigers for lunch."

Woo winced but had to admire Charlie's effectiveness.

Woo had heard enough; he had completed his mission and returned back to the village and to the group of Swiss scientists. He had enough of wandering around in the forest, where any moment a snake could drop on you out of a tree or a giant centipede might crawl over your feet. Charlie Wong, however, continued his foray into the forest with the village head and the elders. When the small company came to the clearing where the haunted pile of logs had been, Charlie's eyes widened. It had disappeared. Bang, all gone.

"Did your genie pack up and leave with all his belongings?" Charlie Wong was in a good mood. He nudged the village head in his side while he asked him.

"You don't know?" The village head was surprised. "The long-nosed devil took it all."

"Don't tell me." Charlie shivered. Eric had bought the whole stack. "Yeah, but why did you give it to him? You warned us we should not even go near."

"He wanted it. He even laughed at us and our concern. I don't understand these foreigners anyhow. And we were glad, to tell you the truth, to get rid of this wood. We made him a super low price. Maybe these long-nosed devils have a stronger magic; he was not afraid at all."

Inadvertently Charlie was about to step out into the clearing. As if bitten by a tarantula, the village head jumped, grabbed Charlie by the arm, and held him back. "Don't. This part of the forest is cursed."

Charlie stopped dead in his tracks, but could not resist saying, "Why? The wood is gone. And did you not say the long-nosed devils may have a stronger magic?"

The village elder raised a hand, expressing doubtfulness, "Well, maybe, maybe not. When they began to float the logs from this cursed pile down the river, one of the floaters was careless. Maybe a tree branch hit him; maybe the ghost reached out of the water and pulled him down where the logs crushed him to death. This logger had a lot of experience. To a man like him, this accident should never have happened. And who can say that the area where the pile had been is not still haunted? We do not go there, whether there is a pile of wood or not."

Charlie turned around and continued with the villagers on their way back to the village. He kept telling himself that he did not believe in ghosts, that he had an English education. But in the end, he could not escape the effect the report by the village elder had on him. Maybe this ghost was real after all. He could not deny that the village head's story was scary, no question.

On another level Charlie knew now that Eric had acquired this premium quality wood for a pittance.

Back in the village, he told Woo that they had completed their mission and achieved their goal. "Now, let us go back and see what Eric charged Ziegler Indonesia for the wood" Charlie saw no reason why he should let Woo in on the ghost story he had just learned.

When Charlie Wong was done with all his business in Bukittinggi and ready to pack up, Woo breathed a deep sigh of relief. He had done his duty; he would go home to beautiful Jakarta and never ever come back. Woo even convinced Charlie to leave all the wood they had just bought behind and to pick it up at some later date.

Charlie's response was, "No problem. What do I care. I don't work for Lee anymore; you do. It's your decision."

They took a speedboat and, with the speed of lightning, shot down the Batanghari River. In no time they were in Jambi and back into civilization. When Woo stepped off the boat, his legs were shaking, and he was drenched from the bow wave, but he was happy as a clam that he had survived this suicide mission.

ERIC'S ARREST

Eric's fate was taking its course.

Lee had patience, the patience of a cat waiting in front of a mouse hole. Joe Manner placed his order with Ziegler Indonesia exactly as per Eric Beck's order confirmation. Eric was jubilant. America was going to be his goose that would lay golden eggs for him. For the back-to-school order from Pestalozzi School, Eric decided to manufacture their pencils from the premium quality wood stack from Bukittinggi, the stack with the old wives' tale. There was no better wood. The school would love his pencils, he would get repeat orders, and he could continue filling his coffers.

In export business it is customary to pay an invoice after ninety days to allow for shipping and customs clearance. If you paid earlier, you could take a cash discount. Joe Manner deducted a cash discount of two percent and paid as soon as he received the shipping papers. From this point on, he had control over the merchandise although it was still swimming somewhere on the ocean. The payment went to the ominous bank account in Singapore. Eric skimmed off his profit and transferred the remainder to Ziegler Indonesia's bank account at a local bank in Jakarta. The trap snapped shut.

"Mr. Lee, we have a perfect paper trail. There is no escaping for Eric Beck anymore. We have his signatures on every incriminating document, and, best of all, the money trail leads right into Eric's pocket." Woo wanted to continue bragging, when he noticed that Lee was very stern and serious. Woo stopped immediately.

"Mr. Woo, we knew early on that this would be the outcome of our probe. It still hurts, hurts me in my heart. Woo, my heart is bleeding. Don't forget his wife is my daughter. Woo, I don't know what to do."

Woo stayed quiet. He did not know what to say; the issue was too delicate.

"I could talk to Eric, give him a stern warning and forgive him…No, the leopard does not change its spots. Eric will do it again. I have no doubt about this. He went too far."

"I am afraid you are right," agreed Woo. "How about you fire him and divorce him—uh, I mean, Wendy divorces him."

Lee sat in his chair rubbing his forehead with his left hand, tapping the table with his right. All his life he had been honest and straightforward. He had not become successful because he was tricky or ruthless. He had never cheated, had never taken advantage of other people. He had become so successful because he was always kind, helpful, and understanding of other peoples' needs. He was always prepared to compromise—yes, to give in. His word was as good as gold. And now he had this poisonous viper soiling his nest, destroying his reputation, cheating him out of his money, abusing his daughter. The more he thought about the situation, the more enraged he became.

"I have given him everything, and this is not enough for him, Woo," began Lee. "He did not only take my money, he took my partner's money, he took my daughter, my trust, my honor. If I let him walk, he will shake us off, like a dog shakes off water. We will become the laughing stock of the trade, of our friends, our family. I cannot let him walk. And, Woo, don't even try to tell me it won't come out. Maybe people whisper already about our naivety, our stupidity."

Lee's chest was heaving; he was breathing heavily.

"They call me Sura Baya: *sura* the shark, *baya* the crocodile. I will show Eric what it means to mess with Sura Baya. This is the only way to reestablish my honor and my reputation."

Woo understood what Lee meant.

After a pause, Lee concluded his meeting with Woo. "Let us do what we have to do."

When Eric came to the factory the next morning, as every morning, in a good mood and proud of himself and his smarts, he had for a moment this odd feeling that everybody was watching him. Yet he did not pay much attention to it. He climbed the stairs to the mezzanine, taking two steps at a time, unlocked the door to his office, and opened it. To his complete surprise, he encountered two burly police officers in uniform.

"Officers, how did you get in? What happened? Can I—"

He stopped in the middle of the sentence because the two officers did not waste any time. They grabbed him, threw him against the wall, searched him expertly, and before he knew it, his hands were cuffed behind his back.

"Sir, you are under arrest. Please follow us." With that they led him out into the short hallway.

Eric was completely confused. He had not the slightest inkling why they placed him under arrest. This had to be a horrendous mistake. He tried to talk to the two officers, asking for an explanation. Either they did not understand him or they did not want to. Anyway, they led him away through the factory, with everybody ogling, and outside to their patrol car that was hidden around a corner.

On his way out, Eric yelled to everybody in sight, "Call Mr. Lee, please! You hear me: Mr. Lee."

None of the factory workers dared to move. Frozen with fear, they watched Eric being hauled away to an uncertain destiny.

The officers drove Eric straight to a jail somewhere in Jakarta. There, in a small cubicle, somebody read to him something from a stack of papers. Eric did not understand a word. He had to hand over his personal belongings and sign an inventory for later proof. Then two prison guards grabbed him and led him down several hallways and through a number of barred doors. They stopped at one of the many cell doors, unlocked it, and threw him in. The jail cell was more a hellhole than living quarters. Six inmates squatted already in the room; Eric was the seventh. In one corner of the jail cell was a toilet with a waterspout above the toilet tank. The lid of the tank had the shape of a bowl with a hole in the middle. Eric knew these odd toilets. They were typical for Indonesia. You could wash your hand with the water that came out of the spout to refill the empty toilet tank. To his utter dismay, he would soon learn that here in this jail the same water was the only water supplied for drinking purposes. Eric looked around the confined space: no bed, only some rice mats on the floor, no chairs, no table, no shelves, no nothing. In shock and desperation, he whipped around, banged the door with his fists until they were bleeding, and screamed like a stabbed pig.

It did not do him any good. His inmates watched him, motionless. It was not the first time that they had observed such behavior. In the end Eric slumped down and squatted next to the six Indonesians.

At eleven a guard came by with some slices of bread, a few bananas, a papaya, and a small bowl of boiled vegetables and some bean curd for each prisoner. Eric tried to hold him back by his jacket. The guard kicked him in the groin and left. It turned out that this was all the food each prisoner got per day.

In the afternoon the prisoners were allowed into a small, crowded courtyard. Many of the other prisoners were smoking kreteks, drinking canned coffee or tea. Some enjoyed a bar of chocolate.

"How is this possible? They give us nothing. And these guys get everything: coffee, chocolate, cigarettes...everything," wondered Eric, longing for some coffee and American cigarettes.

He would quickly find out that the guards were not much better off than the inmates; to make a decent living, they depended on what they called donations from the prisoners. As a Westerner, by definition he had to be rich and an excellent source for extra income. Only minutes after Eric had entered the courtyard thinking his jealous thoughts, he was approached by a guard, very politely and, to his surprise, submissively. The guard asked him in broken English if there was anything he wanted: toiletries, clothes, food, coffee, or tea. Or did he need some medication?

Eric's eyes widened and he gained some hope again. It turned out he could buy almost any favor for very little money. What he had in his wallet when he had been checked in would hold him over for a long time.

The night was terrible. He had to sleep on the ground, touching the inmates on both sides. He was sweating like a pig, and the air was unbearable. For the hundreds of large, black and brown cockroaches, his body was like a roadblock. Most of the roaches decided to circumvent him, and some more daring roaches climbed right over him.

The next day an attorney came by, comforting Eric, telling him that it would not be so bad. From this attorney Eric learned that Lee had filed embezzlement charges against him, but he as an American would most likely be treated mildly by the court. The attorney, although a public defender, wanted his attorney fee up front. Eric had not enough on himself, but he had a bank account in Jakarta. He wrote a check for the attorney and one for himself.

When the attorney returned the next day with the money from Eric's bank account, Eric could pay for an upgrade to his own cell. He had a little more space now, and it did not stink that badly. He could even buy a fan and a TV set for his cell. He also ordered bottled water from now on. As far as his case was concerned, the attorney proved rather useless. It was disgusting how little he knew about the accusations. Yet, the attorney was of extreme importance to Eric: he was his only access to his money. The attorney knew this, and whenever Eric needed to replenish his funds, the attorney took a cut.

As the waiting for the trial dragged out, Eric bought himself a bed and even some hard liquor to help him through his misery.

Eric became the favorite of all prison guards since he was the wealthiest of all inmates and also the one who suffered the most. Together with the public defender, they milked him as good as they could.

❦

Week after week went by, and Eric sat incarcerated waiting for his trial day. Lee had managed to win Charlie Wong back as president of Ziegler Indonesia. It took some convincing from Lee, but in the end Charlie Wong gave in and accepted. Eric had no knowledge about this. Lee had his daughter Wendy divorced from Eric. He did it against her will. She was still in love with Eric.

Charlie moved back into his old office that Eric together with Loro Jonggrang had occupied during his absence. Every time Charlie entered his office, it was as if Loro stared at him reproachfully and full of hatred, as if blaming him for Eric's arrest.

"You will not stay here, my dear! You know what I would like to do with you? I would love to throw you in the trash, and you would end up in a garbage dump. But I will be kind and Mr. Lee can have you, and then he can do with you whatever he wants. He gave you to his daughter and Eric as a wedding present; I give you back to him. He may keep you or give you to his daughter or throw you in the Ciliwung River. I do not care."

He did not even want to touch her, although he had no idea that she was the real one. He still thought she was a copy. He called his driver and told him to take this statue to Lee's office on Jalan Thamrin. When the driver arrived with Loro, Lee did not know what to do with her either. He told the driver to put her into his back office where the hand-carved filigree table was. Actually it might make a nice addition. After all, it was a valuable artifact. Who knew better than Lee that it was the real thing? And to his back office, only his closest friends had access. No need to parade Loro Jonggrang in front of everybody.

There she stood now in her new home, watching with piercing eyes Lee and his friends, her features hard and bitter as if she was pondering revenge for the injustice that had been done to her, robbing her of her great and only love, Eric.

CHAPTER V

PESTALOZZI SCHOOL

Eric's shipment of pencils from the haunted stack of logs near Bukittinggi was riding in a twenty-foot container across the Pacific Ocean, heading toward the Port of Long Beach. At Long Beach the shipment cleared through US customs unopened, and a trucker picked up the container and hauled it on the 5 Freeway to its destination, the Pestalozzi School off Los Feliz Boulevard in Los Angeles. Near Glendale the driver took the Atwater Freeway Exit and carefully drove down the crowded Los Feliz Boulevard with his gigantic box on the trailer. He crossed Vermont Avenue that led to the Greek Theater, and right afterward he made a sharp right turn into the driveway of Pestalozzi School. He drove past the main school building that faced Los Feliz Boulevard and up the graveled driveway to the storage shack in the back. Joe Manner had arranged for a so-called drop shipment. No need to channel the shipment through Ziegler's Van Nuys warehouse. It could head straightaway to the customer's warehouse.

At Pestalozzi School the principal's secretary, Brandy, was responsible for receiving merchandise and signing the papers. When she noticed that the shipment in the twenty-foot container was from Indonesia, she could not help it but had to open one of the crates and take out a box of pencils. The beguiling scent of kretek and tropical wood rose from the pencils and found its way into her nostrils and from there to her brain, on which it had the effect of some exotic narcotic, lulling Brandy into a deep sleep, raising a medley of pleasant and terrible pictures from the depth of her memory. Sam the janitor found Brandy, and he called the school nurse. At her advice, he carried Brandy to the infirmary and laid her down on the gurney. Brandy stirred and moved from side to side, sometimes smiling, sometimes appearing to be horrified and desperate.

BRANDY WAKES UP

It took quite a while before Brandy slowly opened her eyes, still drowsy. She was at the infirmary of Pestalozzi School; the school nurse, Sarah, was bent over her.

"Brandy, are you OK?"

Brandy looked at her, wide-eyed. "Where am I? Where is Charlie? I must see him. Please get him." She was still confused.

"Brandy, there is no Charlie. You are here, right here at the Pestalozzi School, in my nurse's room."

"At what school? This is odd. I am in Jakarta. Am I not?" Brandy slowly pushed herself up on her elbows and swung her legs from the stretcher.

This effort revitalized her blood circulation, and she looked around. Her memory came back. She rubbed her forehead.

"Ah, yes…the Pestalozzi School." She was still a little confused. "I remember now. I work here, don't I?"

"Yes, Brandy, you are the principal's secretary. You fainted, out there by the supply shack."

"The principal's secretary, hmm? What shack?"

"Brandy, you have been the principal's secretary for almost two years! Don't you remember?"

"Ah yes, I remember now. A shipment came in from Indonesia. Yes, that's it. I fainted." Brandy remembered now, and to hide the true reason why she had fainted, she quickly added, "I had no breakfast today. I need to go to the cafeteria and eat a bite." With that, she stood up forcefully and headed for the door.

Sarah held her back. "Brandy, not so fast. You may faint again. Let me take your vitals first."

The nurse took Brandy's blood pressure. It was not quite normal; it was about twenty points above Bandy's statistics. Brandy's pulse was also faster than normal. The nurse agreed that Brandy should have something to eat but afterward she should go home for the day and lie down. Brandy was only too happy to comply.

Nothing was wrong with her, but she needed some time by herself. It was the sudden confrontation with her past. After she had left Indonesia, Charlie had called her two or three times. He had told her that Eric had married Wendy. Lee had promoted Eric to president of Ziegler Indonesia and demoted Charlie. Charlie's honor had been badly hurt; he had left Ziegler Indonesia and had moved back to Singapore to look for a new job. But it was tough to find something suitable. Brandy told Charlie that thanks to the lucky meeting with the principal of Pestalozzi School out there on the driveway, she had found a new job immediately and was trying to move on with her life.

The shipment from Jakarta brought so many memories of her time in Indonesia back and tore old wounds open. Brandy was determined to get over it a second time.

And she did. The stress to get prepared for the new school year and the many duties of her daily routine helped Brandy to erase her gloomy thoughts. By the time the students arrived, Brandy was her old self.

The school year took its usual course. It was not any different from all the other years before, until this ominous day late in September.

EERIE EVENTS

It was a few minutes before two in the afternoon. The signal turned red, and Angie the friendly, overweight bus driver stopped her school bus at the red signal. Her mind was on the little incident that had happened on the bus today in the morning. One of the boys had pulled a girl by her long hair, and she had given him a bloody nose in return. Regulations required Angie to file a report about the incident. Writing reports was certainly not one of Angie's strengths. While she was waiting the some ninety seconds at the traffic light, she chewed on the yellow pencil, which one of the children must have dropped on the floor, mulling in her head how to word her report so that it would have no consequences for the two children. The light turned green, and she drove on.

The school bell rang. School was over for today. As if on command, the boys and girls of the eighth grade jumped out of their chairs and ran out of the classroom and down the stairs to the front door. Every day they played the same game—who would be first in the school bus?—and almost every time it was Johnny. He was the fastest runner in his class, and his coach foresaw for him a career as an athlete. But today Gregory was at his heels, determined to beat his classmate, if only once. They dashed through the huge main entrance, down the flight of stairs, and across the lawn in front of the school. The bus was not yet here. They saw it rumble down Los Feliz Boulevard. Probably they would reach the curb at the same time as the bus. Johnny and Gregory crossed the walkway and raced on to the little strip of grass between the walkway and the road.

Angie saw them coming. "Oh, these wild boys! I only hope they never break a leg."

She stepped on the breaks, ready to pull the bus over. That very instant, Johnny's right foot hit a sprinkler head, and Johnny was catapulted directly in front of the bus. Angie threw all her weight into the breaks. Johnny came down on the asphalt an inch in front of the right front wheel. The heavy bus had too much momentum. The right front wheel climbed up Johnny's skull and cracked it with a thundering sound. Gregory was hit by brain and blood. Angie collapsed behind the steering wheel. Gregory reeled to the "no parking" sign, held on to it, and threw up convulsively

155

over and over again until only green bile came up from his stomach. When he recovered a little bit, he staggered across Los Feliz Boulevard and continued homeward. Nobody noticed him leave in the complete confusion that followed the accident.

Gregory schlepped himself all the way home as if he were a zombie. His mind was completely shut off. It felt as if his brain had been replaced by dense, impenetrable fog. At home he stumbled through the front door.

His mom called from the kitchen, "Gregory, you are late today. I cooked steak pie. Hurry up; wash your hands."

He continued up the stairs to his room. She did not notice that he did not answer. By the time Gregory reached his room, his mom was wondering if Gregory had said something when he came in. She was not sure and shrugged it off.

She set the table and, when she was done, called, "Gregory, dinner is ready. Come on down."

No response. She called again. Again no response. This was odd. She went upstairs to Gregory's room. When she opened the door, she screamed out in utmost despair. She raced to Gregory's desk, grabbed his survival knife, and desperately started cutting on the rope from which Gregory dangled from the beam in his attic room. Finally, it seemed an eternity, the rope snapped, and Gregory's lifeless body thumped down on the floor. She opened the noose, tore his shirt open, and tried CPR. Frantically she pumped his chest, then forced his mouth open and breathed into it with all her strength. She did it over and over again. She did not know much about CPR, just what she had learned from TV shows. It made no difference anyhow. Gregory was already dead. Why, why, why had he done this? Gregory was such a happy-go-lucky child, always cheerful, always upbeat. Why, why…why?

Meanwhile, at the scene of the accident there was total pandemonium. The police tried to make heads and tails of what had happened, but all the students tried to talk at the same time.

"Listen, the critical witness here is the bus driver. She seems to be still in shock. Robert, get a paramedic in here; I need to talk to her," snapped the lead officer, standing in front of the bus, at one of his police officers.

Robert climbed with a paramedic into the bus, where Angie was still slumped over the steering wheel, the pencil she had been chewing on still in her mouth.

"Exodus," said the paramedic, wrapping his findings into one cold, unemotional word. He was right. Angie had suffered a massive heart attack and had died behind the wheel, probably only seconds after Johnny.

The media had a feast. A gory accident, a suicide, and a heart attack! All three somehow connected. The local TV stations interviewed each and every student they could get a hand on and paraded them on the news, hugging each other and crying bitterly. By sunset flowers began to pile up at the site of the horrendous accident, and when the next day broke, the sidewalk was buried under flowers, candles, teddy bears, and letters of sympathy.

Attorneys condemned the school administration, and the city and threatened with gigantic lawsuits. How could the school be so irresponsible and allow their students to race each other to the bus? Were the brakes of the bus good enough or worn out? What about the sprinkler head? Was it not buried deep enough in the sod, thus being a stumble trap? Oh yes, the attorneys would sue, and they would sue big, for millions and millions of dollars. Not because of the money, but they had to send a strong message to the school district. Politicians were strutting on TV, debating the pros and cons of busing. Parents were demanding a fence between the sidewalk and the road and the installation of road bumps. The horrible tragedies became a circus in the local media; the national networks picked up the "story" too and gave it quite some exposure. Their viewers liked blood and horror stories as much as the Angelinos. The media hand-picked classmates and fellow students who were best at crying, hyperventilating, and mourning as expertly as the old mourning women in the Middle East. The calm, introverted, and composed mourners, who may have suffered the most, were of no interest to the media.

CNN International picked the story up and aired it around the world. After a hard day at the factory, Charlie Wong sat in his living room eating baked beans. He had opened a can and emptied the can into a skillet, which he heated on his gas stove. He did not care that some of the beans got burnt at the bottom of the skillet. He scratched the burned beans out with his spoon and ate them too. While he spooned the goop into his mouth, he watched CNN. The events at this school in Los Angeles drifted by him like most other news. The news was so packed with gory stories that a few horrible deaths in America did not affect anybody. They only served as filler. Charlie had to go to the bathroom. He stuck his spoon in the remaining beans, got up, left the living room, and headed for the bathroom. Right at the moment when he had left the living room, the newscaster dropped the name, Pestalozzi School. Charlie missed it. He returned to his dining table, finished his beans, turned the TV off, and slouched to his bedroom. He was tired and needed a good night's sleep. On his way to his bed, he thought of Brandy. He should call her and inform her of what had happened in the meantime in Indonesia. She would be surprised. And he definitely wanted to hear her voice again.

"I wonder how she will react when she learns that Eric is rotting in an Indonesian jail awaiting his trial. She does not know yet. The last thing I had told her was that Eric had been promoted and I had left Ziegler. I think she will like this latest change of events." He uttered a dirty chuckle, crashed into his bed, and fell immediately asleep, still fully clothed. He dreamt of Brandy.

CHAPTER VI

JUDGMENT AND PUNISHMENT

The wait for the court date seemed to Eric like an eternity. All by himself in his private cell, Eric had ample time to think about his situation and how to defend himself in court. He came to the conclusion that his situation was not that bad after all. He would claim that he had not done anything wrong. Yes, he had charged a very high price for the back-to-school order. But was he not supposed to work in the best interest of Ziegler Indonesia. He had picked the very best wood for the order. Ziegler Van Nuys got the pencils from him for 25 percent cheaper than for what they could produce them. But what if they found out that Ziegler Indonesia got only part of the money? No problem there either. He would argue that he had opened the account in Singapore to build a slush fund for the company. Singapore was so much safer than Indonesia. He only helped Lee to get money out of the country. And for the Americans, he would argue, their share would be tax-free and well hidden from the IRS. In his mind the whole hoopla was only caused because Lee was hurt in his honor as businessman because of overcharging a business partner. The court hearing would clear him of the embezzlement charges. And then what about Bukittinggi? No documentation existed. Nothing! Nobody could prove anything. They would not even know where on Sumatra he had bought the wood. He was confident that his wood-buying scheme would not even come up in court. His case did not look too bad. Maybe a slap on his wrist and then, good-bye, fucking Indonesia.

Finally the court day arrived. Eric did not understand most of the court proceedings. His public defender was an incompetent asshole. Eric remained even rather relaxed when the district attorney handed to the presiding judge bank statements and remittance slips that unveiled Eric's Singapore transactions. So, they had found out about his Singapore account! This was not good, but he had taken this scenario into consideration and prepared a plausible explanation. He could only hope they would buy it. But suddenly the picture changed to the worst. Naked fear gripped Eric when Harvey Woo was called to the witness stand, and several times Eric picked up the word "Bukittinggi" in Woo's statement. How on earth did they find out about Bukittinggi? It was as if an ice-cold hand reached for Eric's throat and began to squeeze it. Eric's defense, including his lukewarm explanation of the Singapore account, crushed under the weight of Woo's words. Eric did not understand much, but what he picked up was devastating.

Eric's public defender did not offer much of a defense other than empty platitudes. When it was Eric's turn to take the stand, he radically changed his defense strategy on the spur of the moment. In his fear, desperation, and confusion, he blamed everything on Loro Jonggrang, the little statue in his office. Didn't those Indonesians believe in ghosts? Well, then it was a ghost who was responsible for all that had happened. He was only a tool in the hands of this ghost.

Wendy sat in the last row of the audience, crying silently into her silken scarf. She looked pale and vulnerable like never before.

Already on the second day, the judges were ready with their judgment. In Indonesia there were no jurors; a panel of professional judges heard the evidence and would hand down the verdict as well as the sentencing. The Indonesian criminal law was still based on Dutch law, which played to Lee's hand. He had bought all the judges.

The bailiff ordered, "All rise," and everybody in the courtroom stood up.

The presiding judge began to read the judgment. The public defender translated the judge's words as well as he could into Eric's ears. Each guilty count pierced Eric's chest like a white-hot dagger: guilty of embezzlement, guilty of breach of trust, guilty of theft, guilty of fraud, guilty, guilty, guilty!

Immediately after the guilty judgment, the presiding judge handed down the sentencing: eight years in jail. The sentence hit Eric like the blow of a sledgehammer; his knees became soft, they gave, and he sank onto the defendant's bench. His attorney caught him in the last instance; otherwise Eric might have landed on the floor. Wendy could not take it any longer. She slipped quietly out of the courtroom. The corners of Lee's mouth twitched fleetingly, displaying a satisfied smile. As fast as it had appeared, it was gone again. He had had a hand and a wad of money in this court hearing anyhow. The sentence was no surprise to him. It had been prearranged with the judges.

In his subsequent opinion, the judge explained that the punishment had to be harsher than usual. Not only did Mr. Beck cheat on his employer, but he broke the trust of his father-in-law and his wife. He could hardly imagine a more despicable case of embezzlement and fraud. It was not enough to display such abominable behavior, but Mr. Beck's defense, that a stone statue hexed him, could only be interpreted as contempt of court and ridiculing the culture of Indonesia.

*

Back in his jail cell, Eric sat motionless on his bed and stared bleary-eyed while he leaned against the bare wall. His life had ended. It was all over. He would never survive these eight years.

To comfort him, the guards told him that Lee probably bought this sentence. "Lee bought the prosecutor, the judges, and, most likely, your attorney."

"This sure makes me feel better. Now I know it was not justice; it was revenge. Eight years are still eight years."

"Who knows?" continued one of the guards. "You can buy anything in the justice system. We know about an Australian who brought his sentence down from twelve years—this is longer than yours—to five and then in the appeal hearing to a mere year and a half. And guess how he managed to do it!"

"Why did you not tell me this before the court hearing?" wailed Eric.

"Because you are no match for Mr. Lee! You had no chance against him. No matter what you tried, he would have crushed you like a cockroach."

"Why did the guards have to tell me this? Do they enjoy to make my misery hurt even more?" Eric asked himself.

At first Eric did not see the point the guard tried to make. He was fixated on the fact that Lee had so much power and could buy anything he wanted. After a few days, it dawned on him: "Now I understand what the guards wanted to tell me. Everything and everyone is for sale in this justice system. This means I should be able to buy my way out of this rat hole. That is what the guard tried to tell me."

The guards knew exactly what they did. On purpose they had waited for the sentence. A harsh sentence like this played in their favor. During detention, awaiting his trial, this long-nosed white devil would have been much harder to negotiate with. As long as he harbored hopes for a lenient judgment or even a not guilty verdict, they could not expect much from him. Their patience was, for them, a ticket to unheard-of wealth.

Eric and the prison guards cautiously moved inch by inch toward their mutual goal. Finally the guards showed their cards. Eric would have to pay four guards ten thousand US dollars each. In this case they could arrange his escape. They would have to flee together with him and could never return to their duties as prison guards, which they did not mind. They would submerge in the ocean of people in Jakarta and start new lives with new identities. Ten thousand dollars was more than they could save as prison guards all their lives, even with all the donations they could squeeze from prisoners. They warned Eric that they had to act fast before Lee got his fingers on Eric's bank account in Indonesia. Eric agreed. And one night all five of them had disappeared. The next day Eric cleaned out his bank account and paid off his liberators.

When Lee learned about the prison escape, he was furious. As soon as his rage had subsided a little bit, he hired two bodyguards and installed an alarm system in his house that was hooked up to the nearest police station. He sent his car to Singapore, where it was armored with bulletproof windows and Kevlar lining in the doors. He did not really expect an act of revenge from Eric. Probably Eric had left the country immediately and was on his way back to the States. If Eric would resurface and get caught, he was facing a very long jail sentence, much longer than the eight years. But then you could never be one hundred percent sure of what went on in Eric's head. Who would have thought that Eric would jeopardize everything Lee gave him for some measly rupiahs he had embezzled.

"It is better to play it safe, than to be sorry. The money spent on the security of my family and myself is money well spent." Lee convinced himself.

CHAPTER VII

INVESTIGATIONS AT PESTALOZZI SCHOOL

Far, far away in Los Angeles, Pestalozzi School had after this disastrous day no choice but to hire a renowned psychologist as counselor. Dr. Arthur Journal got up from his chair and escorted the mother and her daughter to the door. This had been the last counseling for the day. For over a week, from morning to night, Arthur had counseled distressed students as well as parents, teachers, and even administrative staff members. The horrible three accidents had left deep scars on anybody who had to do with the school. The sheer endless counseling had left its mark on Arthur. His job was not easy. He actually had to be the strongest of them all, and he had to change his approach when talking to a child or an adult.

Before he closed the door after his last two visitors, he poked his head through the crack and said to the nurse who had her office just outside his, "I need a few more minutes, Sarah. I want to jot down some notes on the last meeting. How about, if afterward, I invite you to a cup of café latte in this new mall on Hollywood Boulevard? "

"Hollywood and Highland. Wonderful. I will wait."

Arthur closed the door and slouched back to his chair. He slipped and almost fell but caught himself at the desk.

"Stupid cleaning crew! Why do they always wax the floor? I am glad nobody fell today."

With that, he sat down behind his desk, took a notepad out from the drawer, and started to pencil some notes on it. His ear itched. He dug the eraser on his pencil into his ear and turned and twisted it. Ah, it felt so good. After he pulled it out, he looked at it. It had yellow stains from earwax.

"Um."

His ear itched still. Arthur turned his pencil around and carefully eased the pointed end into the ear channel, pulling bits and pieces from his ear. It was addicting. He dug a little deeper and, in the course of it, scratched his ear canal. A drop of blood soaked into the soft wood. When Arthur pulled the pencil out and saw the blood stain, he knew he had gone far enough and stopped his stupid behavior. He concentrated again on his notes. He had misspelled a word.

He turned the pencil around and began to erase the wrong word. While he did this, he leaned forward on his chair. The chair tilted and was now on two legs only. The very same instant, the two legs slipped on the glossy floor, and Arthur fell forward. He screamed out in agonizing pain. His right eye had hit the nicely sharpened pencil. The nurse raced into the office, startled by the terrifying scream, and saw blood gush out from Arthur's right eye. In a reflex he had pulled the pencil from his eye. Some gel-like substance dripped from the tip of the pencil. Sarah raced outside, got an eye patch, and put it over his damaged eye. She wrapped gauze all around his head to hold the patch in place and then called the paramedics. Arthur was slumped over in his chair, whimpering. She managed to give him three Vicodin to take the edge from his pain. Down at the Kaiser Permanente Hospital on Sunset Boulevard, the doctors had no choice but to break the devastating news to Arthur, that his right eye was gone. What had promised to become a pleasant and relaxing evening had turned into a nightmare.

This new incident led to total hysteria at Pestalozzi School. How was it possible that so many gory accidents happened in such a short span of time, and all of them at the same school?

At the emergency PTA meeting, principal Peter Stadler tried desperately to calm down the enraged parents.

"This is just a string of unfortunate incidents. They have nothing to do with each other. Let's hope that our unlucky streak is over and nothing will happen again."

A young teacher in the back shyly raised a hand.

"Yes, Sandy, what can I do for you?" asked Peter Stadler politely.

"Well, sir...I don't know how to put it. It appears to me that in all the accidents somebody was careless or made a mistake. You know Johnny ran too fast and tripped; Arthur played with his chair."

"This is nonsense. What about the bus driver? And what about Gregory's suicide?" interrupted her Peter Stadler.

One parent stood up. "Please let her finish."

"Well, sir, could it be that all these victims had some sort of poisoning that affected their mind? You mentioned Gregory. He was a bright and athletic young man. You should know, always cheerful and upbeat, and then, out of the blue, this. Yes, and you mentioned the bus driver. Who told you that nothing was wrong with her? You know how overly careful these bus drivers are. Anyway, you may think what you want; as far as I am concerned, I cannot help it. I still wonder whether there is some sort of mind-changing poison behind all this. I keep asking myself if maybe this came from some sort of mold."

The instant she said the word "mold," the meeting got out of control and turned into a shouting match. The teacher had hit a nerve with the parents. Peter Stadler could have strangled her.

On the next day, half of the students did not show up for classes. Peter Stadler had no other choice but to report the stupid thought of the young teacher to the school district. The school district did not take any chances but immediately ordered a thorough and comprehensive mold inspection. In the meantime, Pestalozzi School was shut down. Nobody was allowed in all the school buildings anymore, not even teachers or Peter Stadler. Hordes of attorneys began to drool and sharpen their knives.

A certified mold inspection company went with the literal microscope over all the school buildings, making sure that not the smallest nook or cranny was overlooked. They even went so far as to open the wall in various places where they suspected mold nests. The EPA ordered supervisors on the site. No chances whatsoever were taken. They found some mildew, some wet and dark spots in hidden corners and inside the walls of the bathroom area, and some wood infected by dry rot. Samples were taken and sent to a laboratory. Later the results came back. It was harmless mildew and harmless dry rot. Not one single spore of mold was found.

The school opened its doors again. All parents received a letter with the result of the inspection. Peter Stadler let the young teacher know in private that her thought had not been such a good one and that she would be well advised to keep her mouth shut or talk to him in private.

Case closed. The students trickled back to the school—first a few daredevils, then a few more—and in the end, all of them. Teaching was resumed. Only the attorneys were disappointed. Their pot of gold had turned into a mirage.

CHAPTER VIII

LORD'S REVENGE

After escaping from prison, Eric decided to stay for now with his four liberators. He had unfinished business to take care off before going his own way. The four prison guards took him to an abandoned warehouse of the Dutch East-India Company down by Pasar Ikan, the fish market where they decided to hide out.

Eric had been to the fish market before. Brandy loved to go with him there to buy fish. He hated the area. If they did not manage to go there early in the morning, the market would smell awful, and the area was overcrowded, dilapidated, and probably polluted. The market was at the mouth of the Ciliwung River. When the tide came in, the water would spill over the banks, onto the streets. And even at low tide there were puddles everywhere. The streets were always wet and slippery. Why couldn't they have their fish in one of the elegant restaurants or buy it at a gleaming new supermarket and then fry it at home? Brandy would explain to him that the restaurants and the markets also bought their fish here and pointed out the many delivery trucks, the two-wheeled oxen carts, and motorcycles with wooden crates full of fish.

"This is the place where the fish are brought in from the Java Sea. You will not get any fresher fish than here. And look, nowhere will you find such an endless variety," she had said.

He had to admit that Brandy's fish was the best and the freshest. However, in his opinion, the area was still grubby and seedy, and Brandy could not even change his negative opinion by pointing out that the fish market was the nucleus of Jakarta and therefore a sightseeing spot. He drudged along because she had insisted.

Yet after his prison break, he saw the fish market in a very different light. This slum-like, bustling, vibrant, and overpopulated area was the perfect hideout. Nobody on earth would guess that this was his refuge.

Due to his time in jail, Eric's clothes were raggedy. His skin became darker every day because of the intense sunlight at the market. His hair was greasy and matted and had grown much longer since he had been arrested, and he had not shaved since the court hearing. It was almost impossible to recognize him anymore. Eric felt safe here.

As a matter of fact, neither Lee nor the penitentiary system cared much about Eric's whereabouts. Lee was glad that he was gone, and with the Damocles's sword of a very long jail sentence hovering over Eric's head, he probably would never see him again. This was good enough for him. The government did not care either. Who at the government should have any interest in persecuting the five fugitives? What would they get out of it? The satisfaction to have them apprehended? You could not buy anything from this satisfaction. Who would pay them anything for apprehending the five? Nobody! Therefore nobody did anything. From Eric's perspective, the situation was quite different. For him the game was not over yet.

The botanical garden of Bogor, Kebun Raya Bogor, is world famous. Some visitors to Indonesia do not bother to spend time in Jakarta but immediately upon their arrival in Jakarta continue on to Bogor for no other reason than to visit the botanical garden. It is situated right in the center of the city and covers a vast area of 215 acres. The garden is proud to house fifteen thousand species of trees and plants. Sweeping lawns stretch over gentle hillsides, with streams and ponds and groups of trees and flowers and ferns. Fifty different kinds of birds chirp and peep and sing and crow and croak. The Ciliwung River cuts through the park on its way to Jakarta and the Jakarta Bay. The park is so gigantic that visitors are allowed to drive with their car on some of the roads in the park.

Lee's mansion was not far from the botanical garden, and one of the joys of Lee's life was to get up early and run for the better part of an hour in this park. Sweaty and invigorated, he would then be driven home by his chauffer. At home he would shower until his skin turned pink and tingled, and then he would head downstairs to have breakfast with his family. After that daily ritual, he felt refreshed and energetic and ready to tackle the challenges that the day would have in store for him at his office in Jakarta.

As every day, Lee's driver, who also served as his bodyguard, stopped at the pay booth by the entrance to the park to pay the little extra fee that was required to admit cars to the park. And as every day, the man in the little pay booth stepped out of his booth, bowed to look inside the car, and saluted Lee politely. After the driver handed the guard the fee plus a little tip, the heavy Mercedes eased quietly away from the booth into the park. They drove on, passing trees as tall as church spires in Europe and gliding forward under tree canopies as cavernous as the naves of cathedrals and abounding with life and the penetrating noise of thousands of bats that early in the morning. Lee had no idea what all these plants and animals in the park were called, but every day they filled him with awe and admiration for the wonders of creation.

"Take me to the Lady Raffles Memorial," Lee requested of the driver.

The memorial was a small rotunda with columns supporting a domed stone roof. The memorial had been built in honor of the wife of Sir Stamford Raffles, who established the botanical garden and founded the city of Singapore. Most tourists, however, were more familiar with the Raffles Hotel in Singapore, which was named after the great British statesman.

"Stop right here!" Lee ordered his driver. "I'll start from here."

Lee's driver stopped, got out of the car, walked around to Lee's side, and opened the car door for his boss. Lee shuddered. It was chilly. He quickly reached to the backseat, grabbed a sweatshirt, and pulled it over his head.

"Ah, this is better."

Then he swung his legs out of the car, bent over, and tightened his shoelaces.

"I am ready, Wait here by the rotunda; I will be back in about three quarters of an hour."

While the driver made himself comfortable in the luxury car, Lee flapped his arms and jogged a narrow path that led away from the paved road, up the hill, through a bed of fiery red and yellow flowers. The flowers were taller than he. He disappeared from his driver's view, who tried to follow him with his eyes as good as he could since he was not only Lee's chauffeur but also his valet and his bodyguard. Farther up the hill, Lee reappeared. His pace had picked up, and he was heading toward a grove of a variety of palm trees, many cut in such a way that they looked like huge fans that a giant had stuck into the rich soil.

The eyes of the driver were not the only pair of eyes that followed Lee's course as well as they could. From a dense thicket of foliage, four pairs of dark eyes and one pair of light brown eyes also followed Lee. As Lee moved farther away from his car, the five pairs of eyes moved with him from a safe distance. Lee reached the crest of the hill, and, crossing it, he disappeared from the driver's view. The driver leaned back into the plush car seat, crossed his hands behind his head, and was ready for a little morning nap.

Lee had reached his target heart rate and was now racing down a long, stretched-out slope. Out of nowhere a sharp whistling noise cut through the air by his right ear. Bewildered, he stopped and looked around. "Was that a gun shot?" At this instant, a second bullet from a Kalashnikov hit him in his right shoulder and shattered his shoulder joint. The pain was excruciating. As the agonizing pain raced through Lee's shoulder, he realized what had happened. He was hit by a bullet. Instinctively he flung himself to the ground. He had survived the shot—two shots. The first one had missed him; the second one had hit only his shoulder. The assailants had to be far away somewhere up the hill in the dark green leafage behind him. They must have waited until he was far enough away and out of sight from his bodyguard. He must have passed them. The bodyguard must have heard the shots and would be on his way to come to his aid. All this raced simultaneously through his mind. If he only managed to survive the seconds that it would take his bodyguard to show up! Nearby, where he had fallen, was a plant the shape of a bowl as wide as a man could stretch his arms, and from its middle a yellow phallus pointed toward the sky. This was the only protection in his immediate vicinity. The plant was big enough to hide him and maybe strong enough to stop a gunshot from a great distance if he could only reach it.

His driver had also heard the shots. As if a cobra had bitten him, he was torn from his sweet slumber and sprang into action like a robot. With shaking fingers, he turned the ignition of the car on, smashed the stick shift into drive, and gunned the big Mercedes up the hill, right across the lawn, leaving two deep furrows behind in the wet ground.

There another shot and another one...

The Mercedes fishtailed on the wet grass. The driver eased off the gas, and the car steadied itself. Within seconds the heavy car reached the top of the hill. The driver fumbled with his right hand in the glove compartment for the 9mm Heckler & Koch, while he steered with his left hand.

There, about five hundred feet ahead of him, in the valley by this tall plant, something was moving. It was Lee. He was on the ground! The driver could only see Lee's legs. His body was hidden by the plant.

"Oh my God! I hope he lives!"

He reached the plant. He hit the brakes, and the car broke out and came to a standstill inches before Lee's legs. The driver jumped out of the car, looked feverishly around to protect himself against further attacks, and sprinted around the plant—it smelled awful—to help Lee. Blood was on the ground. Lee lay on his face. Blood came out of his shoulder and—oh no—his back and his neck. There was nothing the bodyguard could do for his master anymore. The last two shots had both been deadly. They had caught Lee before he could hide behind the plant. The driver knew Lee was dead, but he did not want to comprehend it. He turned him over. Lee's eyes were wide open and glassy.

172

"I must give him CPR." The guard pumped Lee's chest frantically. Blood came out of Lee's mouth. The guard stopped. No use; it was all over.

Lee had died at the trunk of an *Amorphophallus titanum*, the symbol of the botanic garden. The Indonesians call this plant *bunga bangkai*, which means *corpse* because of its pungent odor.

Desperately the driver jumped back into the Mercedes to hunt the murderers down, to run them over, to shoot them with his handgun, to kill them dead! While he thrashed the car all over the wide lawn, plowing through the wet grass, up the hill, down the hill, toward the thicket— everywhere—he kept dialing the emergency number with shaking fingers. The killers had disappeared from the surface of the earth.

MANHUNT

When the news about the tragic death of Lee reached his family, it was as if a black shroud were pulled over the family, placing them into a twilight zone of grief and mourning. For hours Mrs. Lee sloughed around the house, unable to cry—the pain was too much. In an instant the woman in her best years had turned into an old widow, hopeless, listless, and paralyzed. Wendy locked herself in her room and cried bitterly. Only a little stone statue in Lee's back office seemed to have changed its expression from bitterness to great satisfaction. Nobody noticed. Nobody had any reason to go there.

Within hours, Lee's mansion was bustling with police officers trying to look busy but, in actual fact, doing nothing.

The chief of police of Bogor himself was present. "Mrs. Lee, may I offer you my deepest condolences. I am heartbroken. Is there anything I can do for you?"

She did not register what he said.

Early in the afternoon, Mrs. Lee suddenly pulled herself together, her eyes still red with silent crying. It was as if something had happened that gave her new resolve, a new purpose in life. She would take revenge. She would hunt the killers of her husband down even if it took everything she possessed. She would not rest until justice was served.

The first step she took in this direction was to fire her husband's driver. She did not want to ever, ever see him again. His job had been to protect her husband. He had failed miserably. She did not care that her husband had asked him to wait at the Lady Raffles Memorial.

Then she pulled the chief of police into a quiet corner of her laundry room where nobody else hung out. "Chief, I want you to get the murderers of my husband, no matter what. I want you to bring them to justice, all of them. You will not regret it."

The Chief knew that his reward would be royal if he delivered. The Lee family had always been generous.

"And I want you to offer a reward for the apprehension of these horrible people. Set the reward at one hundred million rupiahs for each killer caught and convicted."

One hundred million rupiahs were the equivalent of about eleven thousand US dollars, for most people in Indonesia an enormous amount of money by which they could live comfortably until the end of their days.

"For you, Chief, the award will be ten times!" she added as an afterthought.

She certainly had picked the magic words. They instantaneously sat the Chief in motion. He bowed deeply, his hands folded in front of his chest. "Madam, whatever you say. I will catch them for you and for your husband if it takes me the rest of my career! Please accept my apologies, but I have to attend to my duties now."

On his way to the botanic garden, he called his headquarters and ordered a K9 unit. His appearance at the crime scene changed everything. The detectives and police officers who had been loitering around—persuaded by his mere appearance—became immediately hyperactive. It was as if the Chief were simultaneously everywhere, bellowing orders and pushing officers around. It did not take long, and the detectives found the spot from which the four shots had been fired. They found the empty shells, some cigarette butts, and a lot of footprints in the soft soil. One pair of the footprints was clearly bigger than the other four. This indicated a Caucasian. The cigarette butts might deliver DNA samples; they might not. A German shepherd dog from the K9 unit struck gold. Fascinated by its find, the dog stared at a loogie. One of the assailants had hocked a loogie into the bushes, a magnet for the keen nose of the German shepherd. A detective carefully picked the thickened saliva up with a spatula and put it into a plastic bag. This was about all they found.

Since Mrs. Lee spontaneously had suspected Eric to be behind this murder and the large shoeprints supported her suspicion, the detectives looked for a DNA sample in Eric's former bathroom at Lee's house. The Lee family had thrown out everything that belonged to Eric after he went to jail. The police had hoped for a hairbrush, but no, there was none left. They were about to give up the hope for a DNA sample, when a young police officer had an idea. Why not check the trap in the drain line underneath the sink? When they opened the trap, it was full of greasy, grimy hair mixed with soap scum. What a find. They now had a ton of Eric's DNA. The samples from Eric's hair, however, did not match the DNA samples from the cigarette butts. He had been extremely careful. He had not smoked and had not touched anything that would leave fingerprints or DNA traces behind. What Eric had, however, overlooked was his loogie. He had probably not even been aware that he had coughed it up. The samples from Eric's hair matched one hundred percent the DNA taken from the loogie. The shoe prints matched his shoe size, supporting the DNA proof that Eric was at the crime scene. And he was at the scene at the time of the crime; the loogie was fresh, not more than a couple of hours old. It had been spit out when the murder had happened. Much, much faster than Eric could have anticipated in his wildest dreams, the noose was put around his neck. They only had to find him and then yank the rope.

From the findings at the botanical garden, it was very easy for an alert police force to conclude that the other four criminals had to be the prison guards who let Eric escape. Their personnel file indicated that they had roots in the area of the fish market. The immense reward for their apprehension loosened lips that otherwise might have remained tightly closed. And the police tracked the four prison guards down in lightning speed. Their closest friends and relatives had ratted on them. Yet the ace was missing. Eric had disappeared, leaving no trace of his whereabouts behind.

The four were placed in separate isolation cells at the feared Cipinang Penitentiary. Mrs. Lee made sure that they would not escape. At her directive, surveillance cameras were installed in each of their jail cells so that their movements could be watched day and night on a monitor in the warden's room. DNA samples were taken from their mouths with swabs and compared to the sparse DNA on the cigarette butts. It turned out that all four had smoked, and they had left enough of their saliva on the stubs for scientific proof that they had been hiding in the bushes from where the shots were fired. When the police searched the old Dutch warehouse, they found two Kalashnikovs. A comparison test confirmed that the deadly shots had been fired from them. Evidence against the four Indonesians was overwhelming.

The four hoped for a milder sentence by spilling out all details about the murder and by admitting being accomplices, accomplices only. Eric had been the driving force and the mastermind behind the murder. They had no—absolutely no—connection to Mr. Lee whatsoever. They had neither good nor bad feelings toward him. They had only played along with Eric. In their despair they even pretended it was only out of friendship and not for money. Nobody believed them anyhow. It was still murder, but they hoped for life imprisonment instead of the death sentence. They had one chance and one chance only to avoid a death sentence: by disclosing Eric's whereabouts. Where was he? Where could he be? They did not know as desperately as they tried to come up with an answer.

Mrs. Lee wielded all her power and influence to get a quick sentence, and a death sentence as such. Nothing less would satisfy her. The court complied, as expected.

*

All four were sentenced to death for the murder of Lee. The sentence was executed within a short four weeks by firing squad.

But the mastermind of Lee's murder had disappeared from the surface of this earth. Many locals had seen him before around the chicken and the fish market, by the Dutch drawbridge, by the warehouses, along the banks of the river. But nobody had any idea where he was now. The police had found a few worthless personal belongings of his in the warehouse but nothing that would give them any leads. Eric had disappeared into thin air.

CHAPTER IX

BRANDY'S APARTMENT

It had been a long and excruciating week for Brandy. Inspectors from the County of Los Angeles were crawling all over the school, looking into every nook and cranny, taking paint samples from the walls, scratching off samples from the ceilings and the floor tiles, and asking Brandy endless and, in her opinion, useless questions. The Los Angeles housing inspectors were aided by EPA agents searching with eagles' eyes for lead paint. Since mold had not been the culprit for the horrific accidents, maybe it was lead paint. Did not lead have an influence on the mind? If inhaled or ingested long enough, could not lead poisoning have a similar effect as some psychedelic drugs? Hadn't the school been built before 1978, when lead paint was still allowed and, as a matter of fact, quite common? There was a strong possibility of lead content in one of the paint layers. The agents paid no attention to principal Stadler's assurances that Pestalozzi School had been cleaned of any lead years ago by an environmental hazard abatement company. The mere mention of the words "lead paint" led to the same hysteria among students and parents as the young teacher's question about mold.

The parents would not allow their children to attend school and kept calling the principal's office from the moment it opened in the morning to the moment it closed in the evening. And Brandy was the one who had to answer all the irrational phone calls. If that was not enough, Brandy had to be everywhere, preferably at the same time: support her boss, show an agent the way to the basement, answer questions to an inspector, take notes, or unlock a door. She felt like Figaro in Rossini's opera, *The Barber of Seville*: "Ready for anything, night and day, always busy and around… Heavens, what mayhem! Heavens, what crowds!"

How glad was she when Friday evening arrived. She was the last person to leave the school office. She crammed all her stuff—lipstick, compact, car keys, house keys, cell phone—into her purse. She also grabbed a handful of pencils and threw them in with the other stuff. Tomorrow she wanted to attend an art class at the Los Angeles City College down on Vermont Avenue, not far from her apartment, to relax and distract her mind from the pandemonium at the school.

Brandy had rented a so-called single in an apartment building on Normandie Avenue overlooking Hollywood down below and, in the distance, downtown. Her building had been constructed during the 1920s and reminded her of a French castle with turrets and alcoves. The windows of her downstairs apartment were obscured by a rampantly growing ficus tree and the broad leaves of a banana plant. Brandy had fallen in love with her apartment at first sight. To her it had fairytale charm. When she came home that night, she threw her purse on the kitchen counter and began to undress. She was going to take a hot bath, with candles and incense placed on the floor around the bathtub.

"Duty first! Tomorrow I would probably forget, and then what?" She fed the pencils, one after the other, into her electric sharpening machine and arranged the sharpened ones neatly, one next to the other, on her kitchen counter, beside her purse. While the knives of the sharpening machine were spinning rapidly, grinding away wood shavings and fine sawdust from the pencils into the receptacle, the perfume of the wood escaped the receptacle and meandered through the air, filling her apartment with the sweet and morbid scent of the tropics. How she loved this scent! She drew it in through her nostrils, filling her lungs. This time she did not faint, and she did not reminisce either. She simply enjoyed the perfume that hovered in the air of her apartment. She decided that she needed neither candle light nor an incense stick. It would only interfere with the scent of jelutong wood.

She filled her old-fashioned cast-iron bathtub—what newer apartment offered such a luxury?—with piping hot water and submerged her tired body in the suds. Ah, this felt so good! A tiny sip of red wine after the bath, and she tucked herself in, the blanket pulled all the way up to her chin. Within seconds she was in Morpheus's arms, sleeping like a baby, breathing rhythmically in and out and in and out.

✿

At about two in the morning, Brandy shrieked out of her sleep. She could not breathe anymore. It was as if somebody heavy were sitting on her chest, squeezing the air out of her lungs. Brandy sat up in panic and gasped and gasped. A wheezing sound came out of her throat. She could not get any air. The frightening sensation of choking overcame her. She began to cough in convulsive spurts, and saliva sprayed out of her windpipe. She coughed more and more; each time saliva kept coming up. At least her windpipe cleared a little bit, and she could suck in some air. But the breathing still made a gurgling sound. She stumbled to the bathroom, bent over the toilet bowl, spit, and retched; slowly her throat began to clear. She turned around to the vanity, filled her tumbler with water, drank some of it, then some more. She felt so much better. There she stood in front of the bathroom mirror, panting heavily, her face still reddened. She began to calm down. What a horrifying experience! She had panicked, had real fear of death. It was as if she would choke. She had never had an experience like this before. She remembered that she had read about such choking sensations during sleep in one of the women's magazines. It had to do with stress and being overworked. You took the problems from your job to bed at night, where they continued to bother your subconscious and in extreme situations lead you to stop breathing, not for long but long enough to wake you, convinced that you were choking. What a terrible experience! To make things even worse, in her shock she had inhaled some saliva into her windpipe. Her chest still hurt. Nobody could have possibly sat on it. Did she develop a heart problem, or was it just a side effect of having stopped breathing? Or was this what they called sleep apnea? She did not know. She felt tired and wanted to go back to sleep. She opened the window a crack more and sucked in the fresh night air through the small opening. This helped. The night chill came in through the opening in the window and crept under her thin nightshirt. She shivered but it felt good, invigorating. She rushed back into her bed and slid under the cozy blankets. This felt good. The bed was still warm from her body. Quickly Brandy fell asleep again.

Sometime later this night, Brandy woke up a second time. She lay motionless, afraid to move, and stared into the dark. It was as if some noise had woken her. But now it was absolutely still. Her senses, however, signaled her differently. Someone was in her room. She strained her ears as hard as she could. There...to her left, the air moved, touching her cheeks. Brandy froze to stone.

"If I do not move, he might think I am sleeping and leave me alone," shot through her mind.

It was quiet for a while. Brandy made up her mind she was alone and could dare to get up. But right at this moment, there was an almost inaudible shuffle. God, was he back? What did he do? Why did he not leave? Should she scream? This might be her end. She decided to stay frozen. For what seemed an eternity to her, nothing happened, no noise and no movement, nothing. She pulled herself together and turned on the light on her nightstand. There was nobody in her room. She stood up, the second time in this night, got out of her bed, and tiptoed over to the kitchen counter. She did not dare to open a drawer; it might make a noise. In the sink she found a dirty knife, with which she armed herself. Then she sneaked to her bathroom. With a thundering noise she threw the bathroom door open, knocking a hole into the plaster. Nobody. She turned the bathroom light on. Nobody. With shaking hands she moved the shower curtain aside.

Nobody. She went back to her room and looked under the kitchen sink. The intruder had to be pretty small to hide there, but still she wanted to be sure—nobody. Cautiously she lifted the valance of her bed and dared to peek. Nobody! Well, there could not have been anybody anyhow. The clearing between the box spring and the floor was a mere five inches. She sat down on the edge of her bed, supported her chin with her right hand, and wondered. She was so convinced that somebody had been in her room. But there was nobody. The door to the outside was still locked. The deadbolt was engaged. How could anybody slip out of the door and then lock the deadbolt from the outside? The window? It was the way she had left it when she tucked in, a crack open. Nobody could get through this crack. She kept looking at the window. A light breeze had blown some of the twigs from the bushes through the crack. Could this have caused the movement, the noise? Or maybe it was a rat in the foliage outside. Rats could be noisy. But she was convinced there had been a presence inside her apartment. Maybe a daring rat came in scavenging for food and fled in a hurry outside when Brandy woke up. She did not know. At least she knew for sure that nobody was and nobody could have been in her room. She went back to bed.

$\mathscr{D}$

This time she could not fall asleep again. She struggled to no avail. Should she keep the light on and read? Then she would not sleep anymore for sure. Not good. It would be better if she could catch at least some sleep, and therefore she turned the light off. She lay still, thinking about the many things that were on her mind, hoping that would lull her into a slumber. She lay on her back, motionless, breathing rhythmically, in and out and in and out, hoping for some blissful slumber. There! There it was again. Damn it! With painful clarity she knew somebody was in her room gliding about almost noiselessly, but not completely silent. She could swear she heard light footsteps on the old hardwood floor. The door to the bathroom creaked. Is he in the bathroom now? How did he get into her apartment? The bathroom door creaked again. Did he come back? Brandy was afraid to even breathe. A very slight breeze touched her cheek as if he were right by her, bending over her.

She was not going to die without looking her murderer in the eyes. She tore her eyelids wide open and with bloodshot, panic-stricken eyes looked into...nothing. The night was not that dark anymore; it had turned into the eerie gray just before the sun rises. She stared into nobody, into nothing. She could clearly see the contours of her furniture in the twilight. If somebody was bent over her, she had to see him. But there was nobody. She turned all the lights on. She was alone. She had had enough of this night.

BRANDY CONTACTS CHARLIE WONG

Although the sun had not risen yet, she got up, showered quickly (ice cold on purpose); then she dressed and drove to the Ralphs market on the corner of Hollywood Boulevard and Western Avenue. When she had moved in, she had loved this old apartment filled with the charm of times past. Yet after that night, she felt very insecure in her apartment. That night would haunt her. She would not be able to erase it that easily from her mind. And what if a night like that would return? What if what happened last night was not her imagination but real? What if there was an intruder or a stalker or a Peeping Tom, and he was just smarter than she? Did he have a copy of her house key? Maybe he was a rapist. The thought of her apartment made her shudder.

"I will buy a *LA Times* and look for a new apartment. I will not stay there any longer. No way!" she said to herself. She was not even sure whether she would go back tonight or rent a room in a cheap hotel until she found a new apartment.

At Ralphs she bought a copy of the *Los Angeles Times* weekend edition, which was available at stores already on Saturdays, whereas home deliveries were made only on Sundays. She hauled the immense stack of paper two doors over to Starbucks. Here in Hollywood, Ralphs and Starbucks were open around the clock. Hollywood never slept, with all its nightclubs on Sunset Boulevard and frenetic movie directors filming through the night when they were on a roll.

She bought a cappuccino with a double shot of espresso and poured several bags of brown sugar at the condiment counter into her drink. She needed the caffeine and the sugar to get her system up and running and to help her think clearly. Then she sat down in one of the comfortable chairs, spread the newspaper out in front of herself on the little round table, and began to sip her sweet concoction. She did not care about the gazillion advertising inserts from drugstores, home improvement stores, computer stores, and supermarkets. She wanted to work her way through to "Apartments for Rent." As she flicked through the numerous pages, her eye caught a picture of her ex-husband, Eric, in the international section. She stopped turning the pages and looked closer. Yes, it was Eric. Eric's picture in the *LA Times*? What about him?

The headline of the article read: "Prominent Indonesian Businessman Killed by Own Son-In-Law." She devoured the article. She could hardly believe what she read. Lee had been murdered by Eric. His four accomplices had been captured and executed. Eric was a wanted fugitive on the run. Holding the page with shaking hands, she read on. Eric had embezzled from his own father-in-law. His wife had divorced him after the scandal; he had been fired as president of Ziegler Indonesia. The former president, a resident of Singapore, had been reinstated. She stopped reading. This could only be Charlie Wong. Who else! It had to mean that Charlie was back at Ziegler's.

"Oh my God! Oh my God! I must talk to Charlie!" The fate of Eric left her rather untouched. However, it gave her some satisfaction for all he had done to her. But that Charlie had resurfaced in this newspaper article got her heart beating faster. She had a strong desire to talk to him and tell him everything that had happened since they had talked on the phone some time ago. And she also wanted to know what had happened in Indonesia and what had happened to Charlie. She wanted so badly to hear from him, hear his voice.

She grabbed the paper, left the advertising flyers behind on the table, and took her purse and the half-finished Cappuccino. She went to her car, deposited her coffee cup and the paper on the car roof, and fidgeted nervously in her purse for the car keys. Once she found them, she unlocked the car and drove back home to her apartment forgetting the coffee and the paper on the roof. They flew off and made a mess on the parking lot. She did not notice. She was excited and in a hurry to get home. The horrors of the night were forgotten. The sun had risen behind the horizon, washing

Los Angeles and the Hollywood Hills in the typical glistening daylight of Southern California.

In her apartment she dialed the number of Ziegler Indonesia. She still knew it by heart. It must be already 9:00 p.m. or so in Jakarta. And wasn't it still Sunday there? Never mind, she had to try. The call went through instantaneously, and to her utter surprise Charlie answered the phone. Everybody else had gone home for the weekend. Charlie had really nobody in Jakarta to spend time with, so he stayed most of the time at the factory; what else should he do? When Brandy heard Charlie's voice at the other end of the line, her heart pounded, and a tear rolled down her cheek.

Charlie was almost ecstatic when Brandy's voice came out of his receiver. He had wanted to call her anyhow but at first, he had to admit, he was too embarrassed that after having left Ziegler he had not found a job anymore. And then when Lee hired him back the events kept spinning faster and faster and had overwhelmed him. Oh God, how glad he was, that Brandy had taken the bull by the horns and called him. Brandy told him she had read the article in the *Los Angeles Times* and was eager to learn what had happened. Charlie told her everything, every little detail, and Brandy listened in disbelief. How could anybody sink so low as her former husband? In the end it was a blessing that he had divorced her. Then it was her turn to spill her cornucopia filled with events since she had left Indonesia that were as unbelievable and hair-raising as Charlie's story. Finally, finally, she had somebody she could entrust with everything that bothered her. She opened her heart to Charlie. She told him about the arrival of the pencil shipment from Jakarta and how she fainted and her journey back to Indonesia in her dreams. She told Charlie all about the horrible accidents that had happened recently at her school— she stopped her account, wondered for a moment. Actually the accidents began to happen since the shipment from Indonesia had arrived. This was odd but probably did not mean anything. No, she saw no connection. And eventually she got to last night.

"Charlie, what do you say? Should I move? I am OK right now, but what about last night? I am afraid of the night. Or do you think it was just my imagination—you know the stress. I don't know what to do."

Charlie had listened very attentively, and the more she talked, the stronger a frightening thought crept into his mind. Could this be? "Hey, you do not believe in this hocus-pocus!" he told himself.

On the other hand, his suspicion was so overwhelming that he had to know for sure. He asked her, "Brandy, tell me, did you bring any pencils home last night and maybe even sharpen them in your apartment?"

"Oh, yes, why? What's wrong with that? Why do you ask?" Charlie's question seemed silly in view of the problems and thoughts she had spread out in front of him. "I wanted to take an arts class today, so I took a few pencils home."

"Brandy, take the pencils and take the pencil sharpener and get rid of them. No, take them to your school. Do it right after our phone call. Make sure you leave no pencil and not even any shavings behind."

"Charlie, I do not understand a thing. What is wrong with these pencils?"

Charlie told her the story about his wood-buying trip with Eric to Bukittinggi and the haunted stack of logs in the jungle.

"I do not know what to believe anymore," he said. "I never believed in ghosts or spirits. But when I left the company, Eric went back to Bukittinggi and bought this stack. When they floated it down the river, a raftsman had a horrible accident. After turning the wood into pencils, Eric became a murderer. And Eric used this very wood for his first shipment to America. Your school—what did you call it, Pesta-something?—got the first shipment. All your Indonesian pencils are from the haunted wood."

Brandy was very quiet.

Charlie continued, "A few minutes ago, you told me of the accidents that happened since that shipment arrived. You told me about your fainting and about your scary night. Brandy, there has to be a connection. Please, I pray you, get rid of those pencils. I am certain you will have a good night's sleep afterward. Are you going to do this? Promise! Do it for me, no matter what you believe."

"Charlie, you scare me. I will do it. I promise!"

"And call me again tomorrow; no, I will call you, at the same time!"

✿

Immediately after the phone call, Brandy took all the pencils, the pencil boxes, and the sharpening machine and packed them in a plastic bag. She looked around: nothing left, no pencil, no shavings. Then she washed her hands several times with soap and thoroughly rinsed the sink. This accomplished, she drove with the bag to the school. The janitor let her in without asking any questions. She put the bag in the principal's front office and left.

This night she went to bed very warily, determined not to fall asleep and be on the alert all night long. Before she knew it, she was fast asleep. Ten hours later, Charlie's phone call woke her up. She had slept blissfully like a baby!

"Brandy, there must be a connection. You must go to the principal and convince him that he has to gather all these pencils. We have to get them out of the hands of the students. Then please contact Joe Manner—I guess you remember him—at Ziegler's in Van Nuys. Tell him to exchange all the pencils with new ones. Tell him we will compensate him. He should call us. I will go to Sumatra in the meantime and try to find out more about this ghost and what we should do. After this emergency rescue action, we then can decide how to solve this problem for good."

Brandy took a big breath. Charlie asked a lot from her.

"Brandy, don't worry so much. Once I have been to Sumatra and know more, I will come to Los Angeles, I promise."

This gave Brandy strength and hope. She would take action.

CHAPTER X

THOUSAND ISLANDS

After shooting Lee dead, the five attackers had driven, crammed into their little Toyota Corolla, back to Jakarta. Once they arrived at the fish market, Eric paid the four prison guards and split. The four were glad that the American left them, hopefully for good. They had made good money off him, but from now on he would be nothing but a burden to them. Eric, on the other hand, was certain that these four would soon be caught. If he wanted to escape, he had to be on his own and far away from any place that could be connected with him. Mrs. Lee was rich. She would move heaven and earth to catch them and have them executed.

Once he had walked for a few blocks inland to hide his true intention, he took a bemo, the common means of transportation for the locals, to Jakarta Bay. The back of the tricycle was packed with travelers and their heavy packages, including chickens and even a goat. Eric climbed onto the back of this Noah's ark, stooping so his head would not hit the low canopy. He pushed some of the riders closer together and squeezed in on one of the two parallel running wooden benches. He handed a few rupiahs to the driver, and the driver revved up his scooter, which dragged its shaky and loud load behind. No better way to move around unnoticed.

When Eric arrived in the old Batavia harbor area, not far from the factory, he walked to the seashore and hired a small fishing boat. The fisherman would not own a television set or radio, and the murder was most certainly not yet in the papers. And even if it was, this boatsman certainly could not read. He probably would never learn about the murder in Bogor that had happened only hours before. And should he ever learn by word of mouth, he would not connect the murder with him. By the time the story got to the fisherman, it would be so drastically altered that any link to him would be obscured.

It took the fishing boat some three hours to carry Eric to a group of small coral islands floating in the Java Sea called The Thousand Islands. Some of the islands housed hotels for sports divers. Even the bigger islands with hotels on them could be circled on foot in not much more than an hour. Some of the islands were privately owned, some uninhabited, and on some of them dwelled a few fishermen. The perfect hideout. He got off the boat on Pulau Macan, a hangout for snorkelers who enjoyed floating on the water and watching through their goggles the underwater life of the coral reef. This place was too busy for Eric. You never knew who you might run into or who read what paper out here. But he pretended to stay on this island and therefore paid the fisherman and leisurely walked along the white beach toward the hotel, carrying nothing but a sports bag over his shoulder. Out of sight of the fisherman's boat, he hired a small sampan that took him to an even smaller island with only a few straw huts on it. In the center of the island was a small lodge where young adventurers could stay overnight and where you could buy some simple food or rent basic snorkeling equipment. Nothing fancy.

This island was an untouched tropical paradise. No tourist crowds yet. The waters were vibrant with tropical fish. You could swim in the middle of them as if you were in a giant aquarium. And only a few feet below the surface were corals of the most amazing shapes.

Eric decided to establish this island as his lair until the dust settled. While the police would be searching the airports, the international hotels, the ferries, the train stations and block all major roads, he would enjoy life, snorkel, and recharge his batteries. When enough time had passed, he would shuttle back to Jakarta and from there cross the Sunda Straits to Sumatra. On Sumatra he would hire a car with driver, ride all the way up Highway 25, and from where it was only a short distance to Singapore, he would board a Chinese junk and sail across the South China Sea to freedom and wealth. His fat bank account in Singapore was waiting for him.

When Eric arrived at the lodge, he paid cash for a week in advance. The man behind the counter pointed the way to his small room. It had no running water, no electricity, no telephone, and no TV set. Sun and moon gave light; water was supplied from time to time in red plastic cans that are commonly used to store gasoline. The coral reef was more colorful and vibrant with life than any TV show could be. And instead of talking on a phone, you communicated with nature. It was obvious that Eric was, at this time, the only guest at this lodge. The perfect hiding place!

Eric decided to dip into the crystal clear blue water to freshen up and wash off the sweat and grime that had settled on his skin during the last few days. He had been up since the very early morning hours, had taken his revenge, fled from Bogor to Jakarta, and taken two boats to this tropical island. He could not wait to jump into the water before eating a little bit and going to bed. He undressed, put on his bathing suit, and scampered down to the beach.

While running, he formed a fist and kept punching the air. "Free and rich, at last. Fuck you, Lee. May your body rot in hell. Fuck you, stupid Wendy, Papa's little princess, and fuck you, fuck you, Loro Jonggrang, you monstrous piece of rock."

Back in Lee's dimly lit office, curtains drawn, on her pedestal, the little stone statue seemed to come to life for a split second. Her beautiful features exuded intense hatred and lust for revenge this instant but returned to indifferent immobility the next moment.

Somebody had stuck into the sand a wooden pole with a crude sign attached to it. Whoever had placed this sign here had scribbled on it with a Sharpie marker: "Warning Stonefish." Eric skipped right by without noticing it.

He ran into the shallow, bathtub-warm water, enjoying the prickly feeling of the powdery coral sand between his toes. A grayish-brown rock lay in his path, half covered by the sand, half exposed in the water. Eric did not see it. He stepped on it. Something stung his naked foot sole. The pain was excruciating. Eric screamed as if branded with a white-hot branding iron. He tumbled back out of the shallow water and onto the hot sand, where he stumbled and fell down. A young Indonesian who sat in the shade under a palm-leaf booth knew instantaneously what had happened. He grabbed a box of matches from his hut and ran toward Eric to burn out the sting wound. Eric was, in the meantime, convulsing in painful cramps. The well-intended effort by the young man had no chance. The sting set too deep. Eric died right in front of the young Indonesian. He might have had a chance if the sting of the stonefish had only scratched the surface of his skin. But it had penetrated deep into Eric's flesh. Nobody could have rescued him.

There was a good reason for the warning sign on the beach. The stonefish is not only the most poisonous fish but also the most dangerous fish there is. Actually it is a lot more dangerous than the shark. It is not very big, maybe eight inches long. It is so dangerous because it looks like a rock and has the habit of digging itself into the sand in shallow water. Most of the time, you cannot see it at all. And even if it is not covered by sand, you will mistake it for a rock. The fish has four dorsal spines. Only one of the four is poisonous. It has enough toxins to kill an adult man. Experienced coral reef divers never enter the water without bathing shoes, a cheap and effective life insurance. If only Eric had known. Fate had caught up with Eric even faster than justice had with his four helpers.

In the meantime, a small crowd had gathered around the deceased Eric. They decided to take him to his hut, where they laid him on his bed and covered him with a bedsheet. To find out who he was, they opened his duffle bag and emptied his belongings on the floor. And there in the middle of all his stuff were a bundle of rupiahs and a bundle of US dollars. The eyes of the fishermen widened. To them these were riches beyond their wildest imaginations. The villagers looked up at each other. They did not need to exchange any words; they were in agreement. They split their new wealth among each other. It meant they could buy new outboard motors, new sails, fishing gear, and even a new boat or two with their find. At sunset two strong men took Eric way out into the Java Sea on a fast fishing boat and donated him to the creatures of the water. And there were many of them, all of them hungry. In the end Eric did a good deed and fed many hungry mouths. The villagers rode back and burnt his clothes.

WENDY TAKES LORO BACK

Wendy's world was shattered. She had fallen in love with Eric at first sight. She had given him all her love and devotion. Her dad had promoted him to president of his pencil company. They had accepted him into their family. She did not understand. How could somebody turn so bad, so evil, to bite the hand that fed him, steal from his own family, and not even hesitate to murder his father-in-law, the father of his wife? What had gone wrong? It was as if Eric had been two different persons. After a while and a lot of soul-searching, she came to a conclusion: it all had begun when her dad had the idea to substitute a fake statue for Loro Jonggrang and give Loro to her and Eric as a wedding gift. As much as Wendy thought about the events, she could not come up with another explanation. It had to do with Loro. Wendy knew what she had to do to end this haunting once and forever. She also knew she could not tell anybody of her plan; she had to go through with it on her own.

After having returned to Ziegler, Charlie Wong had moved the little statue out of sight to Lee's back office, where it stood in complete isolation. What had been Lee's commando bridge in better and happier days was now abandoned. Nobody ever went there.

Wendy mustered her strength for what she was determined to do. She drove to her dad's office armed with an oversized duffle bag, and she walked straight to the back office. She hesitated for a moment, took a deep breath, and then she opened the door. It was as if she were walking into a graveyard. Loro Jonggrang was still standing on her pedestal in the corner across from Wendy. This was something Wendy had to do herself. She did not want any help, no matter how hard it was. With all her strength, she lifted Loro from her pedestal and dropped her into the duffle bag. Dragging the duffle bag behind her, she left the back office with a big sigh of relief. She schlepped the heavy load down the stairs and through a small storeroom toward the parking lot. A clerk stacking some boxes onto a shelf saw her and asked her whether she needed some help. She refused. The clerk returned to his duty stacking boxes. Nobody was in the parking lot. Wendy quickly lifted Loro into the trunk of her car and drove off. But not toward home. She was heading to Yogyakarta. It was a long drive, some five hundred kilometers. Along her route she stayed overnight.

The next day the monsoon rain started pouring down on the road. The torrential rain made the drive difficult. Wendy did not give up. That one rainstorm chased the next one actually suited her fine. She could not have picked a better time. In Yogyakarta she checked into a hotel at the road to the Prambanan temple complex.

Long after midnight she got up, threw a raincoat on, and drove her load through pouring tropical rain, all the way to the center of the many Prambanan temples. Apart from her, not a living soul was outside. When she left her car, she was instantly drenched by the driving rain. The raincoat gave only little protection against the onslaught of water. She did not even notice. She walked to the back of her car, opened the trunk, and pulled the duffle bag over the rim of the trunk, dropping it in the splashing mud at her feet. She closed the trunk with a thud and dragged her duffle bag to the temple of Shiva. She entered the temple and proceeded into the northern room, to the pedestal that stood against the wall. In the beam of her strong flashlight, she saw the copy of Loro Jonggrang on the stone pedestal. For a moment Wendy paused and looked at the copy. You could not tell the difference. It was amazing. Wendy gave herself a push and proceeded with her plan. She heaved the real Loro out of the bag.

In the meantime, in addition to the torrential rain, the wind had picked up, the famous trade wind that used to carry the merchant ships across the ocean. It blew right through the wide-open structure.

"Good, so no curious onlookers!"

Wendy did not care about the fake statue. She gave it a good shove, and it fell off its pedestal, breaking in half. Then came the hardest part of her venture. She had to get Loro up there where she belonged. It took Wendy several futile trials. Then with a last superhuman effort, she managed to get Loro back up on the pedestal, a little crooked though and off-center, but who cared, Loro was up there. The wind blew Wendy in the face, her wet hair flying in all directions, her dress clinging to her body. But she was pleased with herself; she had accomplished what she had intended to do. To bring an end to this haunting.

Wendy bent down and packed the two fragments of the fake Loro into her bag. A strong gust hit Loro on the pedestal, and the statue swayed back and forth. When Wendy stood up, she hit the pedestal with her behind, and Loro toppled over and came crashing down on Wendy's head. Wendy was dead the same instant, Loro Jonggrang lying beside her, a satisfied smile on her face.

The dream that Loro Jonggrang had for centuries had come true. She had found her love in Eric. But he had betrayed her and had to pay for it. Now that all that was accomplished, her spirit could leave her counterpart of flesh and blood and return to its shell of stone.

*

Wendy was found after some days when the rain and the wind had calmed down. The authorities did not find an explanation to the weird sight, and in the end they did not care. Wendy's death was declared an accident. Probably she had come to worship Loro Jonggrang, who looked so much like Wendy. She might have picked a monsoon night because the ghosts were more active and out and about during such a night. And maybe she wanted Loro Jonggrang to bless her copy of the statue. Who knew?

CHAPTER XI

BRANDY TALKS TO JOE MANNER

"This is not going to be easy. How am I going to tell him? He must think I am nuts. I hope it will not cost me my job."

All these thoughts and doubts occupied Brandy's mind.

"If only I knew that this ghost thing is true. I've never believed in such stories. But maybe there is something to it. No matter what, I cannot allow these accidents to continue at our school. Something has to be done. They checked for mold, for lead paint, and even asbestos, with no result. The worst that can happen is that my ghost action does not show any results either. But if Charlie is right after all, it will save young lives. I will talk to Peter Stadler. No, I will talk to Joe Manner first. He cannot fire me. And he has been to the Far East. He is the easier obstacle. He will understand my reasoning. Once I have him on my side and he agrees to the exchange, it will be so much easier to convince Peter Stadler to go along with our plan.

Joe Manner remembered Brandy well. He had always enjoyed her company and gave her an appointment right away. At the meeting he was cordial and expressed how glad he was that she came by.

This gave Brandy courage, and she was confident that she would be able to win him over. Confidently, she embarked on her long saga.

She told Joe Manner in great detail about her long telephone conversation with Charlie Wong and to what conclusion he had come. They wanted to exchange all the pencils into new ones.

"Well, Brandy, he is from Indonesia. They still believe in ghosts and all that stuff. But, Brandy, you can't possibly believe in that nonsense. We are here in the United States!" countered Joe Manner.

"But what about my fainting and the night from Friday to Saturday?"

"You are overworked, stressed out; it is that simple."

Brandy felt it was time to tell Joe Manner everything, about the wall that had come down at the factory, the ghost at the plant shortly after they started production, how her ex-husband had changed in Indonesia and in the end even had murdered Lee, his father-in-law.

"Still not convinced?" she finished, looking quizzically at Joe Manner.

"No, Brandy, I am not. Not, not, not. Let me say, however, this: if word gets out what you told me now, we will have to close our factory down. Nobody would buy from us anymore. If only the slightest rumor would escape this room, we would have a catastrophe at our hands. Are you aware of this?"

She shrugged. "Yes, sure, but we will keep it a secret. We will exchange the pencils. Nobody ever needs to know that we did it. Charlie will not charge you for the new ones"

Brandy did not manage to dispel Joe Manner's concern. He ranted on. "Are you aware how many people believe in astrology, tarot card reading, horoscopes, palm reading? Look around. There is a psychic almost on every street corner. How many people don't dare to walk under a ladder, are afraid when they see a black cat cross the street? Look at you. You yourself believe in this ghost nonsense. You have to swear by the grave of your mother that you will never ever mention a word to anybody of what you told me right now."

"Yes, yes, I promise, but what if it is true? How can you possibly know that it is not true? Sir, all I am asking is to exchange the haunted pencils into clean ones, just as a safety measure. Nobody would ever find out. And we would have done what we could to protect the school children. The timing is perfect. The school year just started, and because of the paranoia, the students stayed away all the time. Most of the pencils are still in the storage shed."

When her report finally wound down, Joe Manner got up from his chair. "I am sorry, Brandy. No way! This is pure nonsense. I cannot run a business taking into account ghosts and spirits. We are not in the medieval ages anymore. It is the twenty-first century. Brandy, I cannot believe that you would allow yourself to be sucked into such nonsense. You are an educated, modern woman. Don't make me laugh out loud."

Brandy stammered, confused; she had expected anything else but not such an abrupt refusal. "But, Mr. Manner! It could be true. I am not saying it is, but it might be. Is this not reason enough for the exchange?"

"Could be; might be. Nonsense, shmonsense! I will not be part of such hocus-pocus. Our pencils from Indonesia are the finest in the world, and, Brandy, don't tarnish our reputation. It could cost you dearly. If I lose business because of such innuendo, you leave me no choice but to go after you, in civil and in criminal court, despite how much I like you. The damage could go into the millions, and you will never ever, ever be able to pay for it. You would be ruined for the rest of your life. Do not jeopardize everything you have. I am sorry; I have to do some real work now. You are always welcome here but not with such hogwash. Maybe we should do lunch some time."

That was it. Brandy had lost. After this disastrous meeting with Joe Manner, Brandy did not dare to take Peter Stadler into her confidence. If the meeting with Stadler would go the way as it did with Manner, this would be the end of her career at the school, and she would be down and out again.

Charlie was her only hope. She was at her wits' end. Maybe Charlie would know what to do. She did not.

CHAPTER XII

THE MAD SCIENTIST

Charlie decided to go back to the source, Bukittinggi. If he was to find an answer to the events in Los Angeles, it had to be here on Sumatra, where it had all started. When he arrived at Bukittinggi and stepped out into the clearing, he saw a great crowd of villagers gathered around one of the tents of the Swiss scientists. Charlie covered the short distance across the clearing and tapped one of the bystanders on the shoulder. He turned around.

Charlie asked him, "Tell me, what is going on here? Where are all the foreigners?"

"They are all inside this tent. One of them died." The villager pointed at the biggest tent that served as the dining and meeting room for the Swiss scientists.

"How did he die?"

"He hit himself on the head with a rock."

"What? Himself? How come?"

"Well, the guy came charging out of the forest, wielding a knife, threatening anybody in his path. He had foam at his mouth and screamed something in this weird language the scientists speak."

"You mean Swiss German."

"Yeah, maybe."

"And what happened then?"

"We all ran for cover. He hurtled right into this tree over there." The villager pointed to one of the tall trees. "The foreigner tumbled. When he recovered somehow, he bent down, picked up a rock—this one there, still lying there—and kept hitting himself on the head until he collapsed. It almost looked as if he tried to kill something that was in his head and causing him excruciating pain."

After having received this short briefing, Charlie pushed his way through the crowd and entered the tent. The dead body lay on a table, still frothing at the mouth. Two of the scientists examined him, while the others talked nervously with each other. Charlie greeted everybody fleetingly and stepped up to Roland Weber, who looked at him with wide eyes through his spectacles and explained, pointing at the dead body.

"Mr. Wong, sorry to meet again under such circumstances. Something must have snapped in this poor guy. He was a good scientist. He probably could not stand the hot, humid climate here in the forest. It almost looks like he had latent epilepsy that broke out. He could not control himself."

"I am not a scientist, but I have never heard of latent epilepsy that breaks out and then you commit suicide. Well, whatever," thought Charlie at this moment, not aware that he was close to the answer he had been looking for. He came to Bukittinggi to hopefully get to the bottom of the weird accidents in Los Angeles, and this uncanny death here in the forest gave him the answer.

Charlie did not even have to ask. In the evening a village elder took Charlie aside. "Mr. Wong, you are from Singapore. These Swiss people do not understand anything. The soul has its seat in the head, the brain. The head is the vessel for your *semangat*, your life force. This is why the spirits go for your head. Like the headhunters on some of the islands collect heads to accumulate *semangat*, the spirit from the forest took possession of the scientists head, his brain. This is why the scientist in despair first hit his head against the tree and in the end smashed a rock on his head. In his delirium, he was after the spirit; he wanted to destroy the evil spirit. The spirit, however, was stronger, and the scientist destroyed himself. He should have come to me for help instead."

"But how did the spirit get into his head? And why are not all of you possessed? Why only this long-nosed white guy?"

"He asked for it! He did not listen to our advice. We told the Swiss people over and over again to stay away from the haunted clearing. But he laughed at us. He kept going right back there. He crawled around on his knees. He collected soil samples, and bugs, and plants in little vials and took them all to his tent, where he dissolved some of it in strange liquids, studied his loot through a microscope, and did lots of things I do not understand."

Charlie remembered the ghost at the factory, how Eric changed, the murder of Lee, and, most recently, the death of Wendy. In conversations he liked to deny spirits and stressed his English education, but in actual fact, ghosts were very real to him.

The elder read on Charlie's face that he had doubts. He concluded that Charlie needed some explanation. "The people from Europe and America are too disconnected from nature, the world we are living in, and thus, in the end, from reality. In Indonesia we do not look at spirits as something supernatural or from a different world or what you call in your movies a so-called parallel world. For us spirits are an integral part of nature. They are as real as the trees, the animals, the rivers, the clouds, and the wind or the rain. Therefore we know that they act and behave in the most natural way; they only have different abilities from us, such as we have different abilities from animals and plants. If we could jump as high as fleas, we could jump over a longhouse. If we had the strength of ants, we would not need elephants. We could carry the tree trunks ourselves to the river. A cat can see at night. A dog can smell an epilepsy attack before it happens or knows when an earthquake is about to strike. Our government with all its seismic gadgets cannot. Look at the birds in the sky: they can fly; we cannot. The trees live hundreds and hundreds of years. We do not. I could go on and on. We humans are too self-centered; we think we are better and know it all just because we can think abstractly and have dexterity in our hands. But nature around us has so many abilities that we are lacking. And spirits are simply invisible to our senses. We lack the necessary receptors. The spirits have abilities we humans don't have. But still they are part of this world, this nature, and as such they have to follow the laws of nature or what you might call physics, chemistry, biology, and whatnot. Nature is all encompassing."

Charlie was impressed by the elder's knowledge. That he lived in a remote village on Sumatra did not mean that he was a dumb hillbilly. Charlie could not help it; he had to agree with the elder's reasoning. It all made sense, much more sense than the futile so-called scientific explanations the Americans tried to find: was it lead paint, asbestos, or mold? And what were their findings? Nothing! The Indonesians knew better. He would pursue this trail to help bring the accidents in Los Angeles to an end.

"But there is something I don't understand. This white guy bought all your haunted wood. How can the spirit be back here and get into the Swiss guy's brain?"

"A spirit is like the wind. It has no defined body. It is everywhere and nowhere. When the white guy picked up the wood, he may have picked up some of the spirit and left its remainder behind. We believe that he did exactly that. Before your friend bought the wood, the spirit was scary. Strange things happened, and we had great respect for him. But he was never vicious. Look, he is taking revenge for tearing him apart. When Eric floated the wood down the river, a floater died, and now the Swiss scientist."

Charlie had to agree, and he told the elder about the series of horrifying accidents that had happened in Los Angeles.

"There you go. We tore the ghost apart. He is taking revenge. He wants to be reunified, made whole again."

"How would we do this?"

"You have to bring him back here."

"We made pencils out of him."

"It does not matter. I told you the ghost has no shape."

"But did you not want to get rid of him?"

"No, not at first. Remember we refused to sell you this pile. But then greed possessed the village people, and they erred. Greed made them believe it would be a good idea to get rid of the spirit. It was not. We have to make amends where we did wrong."

"This means, if I can manage to get all the wood, in whatever shape, back here to the forest, the spirit would be thankful and not go after my life."

"That is correct. You would do us a great favor."

"I will see what I can do. I cannot promise anything."

Charlie had learned enough. He had found out what he wanted to know. Out of courtesy, he stayed one more day before traveling back to Jakarta.

THE HUNT FOR PENCILS

As soon as Charlie was back at the factory, he called Brandy and told her about his trip to Bukittinggi.

"And, Charlie, do you believe this?"

Oh yes, he did more than ever before. However, he was a little sheepish about admitting it to Brandy. "It does not matter. What matters is we have to do everything in our power to stop that onslaught at your school. If there is only a slight possibility that the deaths at your school have to do with a spirit from Sumatra, then we have to take it seriously and act accordingly. What alternative do we have?"

"Charlie, I met with Joe Manner but he will not play along. And after my experience with Joe I do not even dare to talk to my principal. What can I do?"

"Right now after I hang up, I will put a shipment of new pencils, clean pencils, together and airfreight them to you. I will travel on the same plane. In about two, three days, I should be in LA," and he added, "and with you."

She was as excited as she had never been in a long time. It was as if the sun had risen and her drab existence were washed in bright light. A split second later, her joy turned into concern for Charlie.

"But, Charlie, what if the ghost will kill you like all the others?" She was not concerned about herself, only about his well-being.

He teased her, "Hear, hear! You do believe in ghosts after all."

"I do not know what to believe anymore."

"Brandy, there is nothing to worry. We take the ghost home. He will be grateful and relieved. He will be on our side. He will support us in our effort."

"This does not convince me. How will the ghost know?"

"OK, OK. There are other ways to protect ourselves if the spirit should not be friendly toward us. Seriously, you do not have to be afraid.

In order to get into the head of his victim, the spirit needs a portal. A spirit can only enter your body through your mouth, your nostrils, or an open wound. Let's say you chew a pencil that is inhabited by the spirit. You clean your ears with a pencil or poke it into your nose, touch it to a wound. Something like this. Then the spirit marches right into your body. This is how it can happen. Otherwise not. Remember when you felt the presence of the ghost in your room. He was really there. You had sharpened the pencils, and the dust from the wood shavings filled the air. You liked the scent. You breathed some in. Luckily only a little bit. And it was certainly the same way when you fainted when the shipment had first arrived at the school."

"Oh my God, Charlie, just before the little boy ran into the bus, he had chewed on his pencil. Had not the counselor who poked his eye out cleaned his ear with a pencil seconds before the accident happened? And the bus driver was working on some report, using a pencil. Maybe she had a cut on her finger. Charlie, you are right." Brandy was convinced. She took the ghost for real, no doubt in her mind anymore.

"See, all we have to do is make sure not to allow him into our body. Before we even touch a pencil, we must make sure that we have no open wound or, better still, wear latex gloves, and as extra precaution we should put on a face mask. And we have to communicate with the spirit all the time, hoping that he understands we plan on taking him home."

Brandy had one afterthought. "Can't we simply burn all the pencils?"

"No! Because you are going to make things worse. You will spread the ghost into the air, make him airborne, and we lose all hope to ever catch him."

Brandy's adrenaline glands shot a massive dose of adrenaline into her bloodstream. Excitement took over, and she was ready for the ghost hunt!

REPATRIATION TO SWITZERLAND

Roland Weber held an emergency meeting with his scientists in his tent. He did not have to worry that somebody would eavesdrop since they spoke Swiss German, which even a German would have had a hard time understanding.

Under no circumstances could they report Roger's cause of death as anything else but natural. If the authorities got wind that Roger's head had been smashed in with a rock, an inquest would be opened by the Indonesian police; Roland Weber and his team would be stuck in Indonesia forever, the death penalty hovering over their heads. Would the detectives accept their explanation that Roger hit himself with the rock? A mad scientist, who committed suicide for no apparent reason? Hardly. The detectives would not be able to make any money from such an outcome. They would prefer to open up a murder case with the death penalty hovering over the heads of the foreigners. Such proceedings would earn the local police and authorities an enormous amount of money. The parent company in Switzerland and the Swiss Embassy would become involved while they would be rotting in an Indonesian jail—a frightening prospect.

Roland Weber remembered that he had been able to buy vaccination certificates for pretty much any disease. As a child Roland Weber had had meningitis. Therefore he could not be vaccinated against small pox. Singapore required small pox vaccination. At first Roland Weber saw in this requirement an insurmountable obstacle, until he learned in Bukittinggi that fifty—yes, fifty—dollars would buy him in Jambi any vaccinating certificate he wanted, even with authentic government seals. From then on he could travel to Singapore as much as he liked to recover from the immense strain of working in the jungle. The immigration officers at Changi Airport used to frown at the vaccination certificate yet had no choice but to accept the authentic certificate.

The scientists decided that they would buy a death certificate for Roger, with heat stroke as cause of death. The death certificate cost them one million rupiahs, a little more than one hundred dollars. The doctor in Jambi did not care. He would have written anything into the death certificate. He did not even bother to travel to Bukittinggi, since the dead person was a foreigner.

And since the death was natural, the authorities quickly approved the transfer of the corpse back home to Switzerland. This approval required another one hundred dollars. Money well spent.

The Swiss scientists had accomplished their mission in Indonesia anyhow and were getting ready to fly back home. The odd death of Roger led them to accelerate their retreat. They placed the dead body in a steel coffin and stored it in a separate small tent in which they ran the air-conditioning day and night. The tent quickly turned into an icebox. This way it was possible to keep the corpse from decomposing for the few more days they needed.

"Hey, Roland, will you be going to Jambi with us tomorrow?" asked one of the scientists.

"Who is going?"

"All of us. We want to buy souvenirs."

"Ah, nah. I don't know. I still have not finished my last project. I prefer to stay. Who knows when we will come back. When you find a nice Garuda, please buy it for me. That's about all I want, or maybe also bring me some batik paintings."

"You sure you do not want to come along?"

"Actually no. Don't worry, I'll be fine. I am in the middle of something. I need a day or two for my studies, that's all. It would be a pity if we left Indonesia and I had not wrapped up this last project."

The other scientists had no problem with Weber's decision. They did not care and had only asked him as a courtesy.

The next morning when the team had left riding down the river toward Jambi, Roland Weber walked over to the tent with Roger's body, asking himself the questions that had nagged him since Roger's demise: "What had led to Roger's erratic behavior? What had caused him to commit suicide and in such an idiotic way? Roger had been a quiet, down-to-earth, self-composed scientist. He was not the type to flip out.

"I know Roger had no money problems, he was not married, was happy in his job. Yes, he was a devoted scientist. I cannot see any reason why Roger became insane, and this from one moment to the next. There must be some explanation."

Roland Weber was determined to find out, and it suited him only well that he was all by himself.

"I need to study Roger's brain. Maybe I can find an explanation in his brain tissue."

He pulled to the side the entry flap to the tent where they kept Roger, and he stepped inside. It was freezing cold. He turned the air-conditioning off. Then he lifted the heavy steel lid off the coffin and put it on the ground.

He petted Roger on the cheek. "Roger, Roger. What happened to you?"

Weber had to get access to Roger's brain, but he shied away from cutting his skull open in case somebody in Switzerland might have the desire to inspect Roger's body. He had stuffed a Black & Decker drill with a half-inch drill bit in his belt. If necessary he was prepared to drill a hole in Roger's head to get access to his brain. This would be small enough to be overlooked under the thick hair of Roger.

Weber reached in his pocket for a pair of surgical gloves. He pulled them over his big hands with a snap. He protected his mouth with a disposable face mask.

"You never know. Could be infectious."

Then he bent down and studied Roger's head, moving it from side to side. A myriad of thoughts were on his mind. "Let's do some headhunting. Don't the Indonesians believe that our life force, our soul, sits in the head, which means the brain? Don't they still have headhunters for this reason somewhere on remote islands, collecting life force, *semangat*? Maybe they are not that wrong. Modern science does not really see it that much differently. A person is dead when he or she is brain dead. We can even exchange a person's heart, and it is still the same person. But if we amputate the brain, I mean if we were able to do so, it would not be the same person anymore. These indigenous people have known all along what we began to realize only in modern times. We used to believe the soul is in the heart or the chest. Other cultures put it in the stomach. In modern medicine it is located in the brain. The village people insist that a spirit took possession of Roger's brain."

A thought flashed through Weber's mind: "Maybe I will find this spirit in Roger's brain." He shuddered. "Nonsense, I do not believe in ghost stories. I am a scientist. I will find a scientifically verifiable reason for Roger's death."

The sudden change of Roger's personality had to have its origin at the grove where Roger had spent most of his time collecting soil and plant samples and animal droppings and a number of insects. Could something have been in these droppings or the plants or the soil? If so, maybe he would find something in Roger's brain.

To get access to Roger's brain, Roland Weber did not even have to drill. Hidden under Roger's thick hair, Weber found a small crack in Roger's head.

"Am I glad! I do not have to drill. Nobody will notice that I was in his head."

Roland Weber spread the crack a little wider with a screwdriver, peeped into the hole with a strong flashlight, and then reached in with long medical tweezers. He grabbed some brain tissue, pulled it out, and placed it in a petri dish.

"There you go."

He kept extracting more until he felt he had enough. When he removed the screwdriver, the opening in the skull contracted again into a small crack. Satisfied with his success, he closed the steel coffin, turned the air-conditioning back on, and rushed over to the tent with all the high-tech scientific apparatus of their field laboratory.

It did not take him long, and he was able to identify strange red-tinted cell-like structures about ten microns in size in Roger's brain tissue. He had never seen anything like this in a human brain.

He raced over to Roger's tent and grabbed all the samples that Roger had collected at the clearing. Was he beginning to believe in this ghost nonsense?

Frantically, Roland Weber analyzed all the samples that Roger had collected. The insects and animal droppings contained nothing. Nor did the soil and leaf samples. But he noticed the same reddish discoloration on the latex vessels of some of the jelutong chippings that Roger had collected.

A dense web of tiny latex vessels can be found throughout jelutong trees. The latex protects the tree from the intrusion of fungi and bacteria. Once the sticky sap comes in contact with air, it coagulates and closes the wounds of the tree. Jelutong trees are tapped like rubber trees for latex, leaving behind empty vessels. These vessels can clearly be seen on any jelutong product. Pencils made out of jelutong have tiny oval-shaped holes. The sharpened point of a jelutong pencil looks as if it has freckles. Cedar or incense cedar pencils do not have these freckles or holes.

When Roland Weber compared the jelutong chippings with the reddish vessels to the red microorganisms in Roger's brain, they matched. The reddish jelutong vessels contained microbes that were identical to the ones found in Roger's brain. Roland Weber concluded that Roger must have picked these microbes up from some of the jelutong specimens. He could have ingested them, breathed them in. They could have entered his body through a wound. The microbes must have migrated to Roger's brain and established themselves there.

Roland Weber became excited. He was on to something. Something big! Could it be that these microbes, these unknown fungi or algae, had altered Roger's behavior, his personality, had distorted his perceptions, had caused hallucinations, had triggered deep despair? This would mean they could use these microorganisms to develop a mind-altering, psychedelic drug. Administered in miniscule doses, they might offer a number of neurological benefits.

Roland Weber was convinced that these unknown fungi or algae, these unknown microbes, were the spirit of the villagers. Roland Weber's trip to Indonesia was going to turn out to be a tremendous success.

Feverishly he continued with his tests. Under a field electron microscope, he was able to watch these reddish structures budding, with little daughter cells inside the bigger mother cells. This meant they were alive. These cell-like reddish structures were living microorganisms. He cooked them, heated them up to 250 degrees Fahrenheit, the upper limit for life. The cells continued to reproduce plentifully. He raised the temperature to 600 degrees. This should kill them. It did not. They kept reproducing happily. These reddish cells were alive, very much alive, with a stronger life force than anything he had ever seen or read about before.

"I will isolate their DNA!" He envisioned himself already standing on a podium in Stockholm, receiving the Nobel Prize.

And then the surprise, the utter shock! He could not determine any DNA strands.

"This cannot be. This is not possible. I will check for carbon isotopes." He could not identify any carbon isotopes either.

No DNA meant no life. No carbon isotopes meant no life. There was no life without carbon. All living organisms contained carbon, and anything that lived had DNA.

Roland Weber screamed in disappointment, "I saw it! They were alive; they reproduced. Where is their fucking DNA? Why can't I find any carbon isotopes? Shit equipment."

To let off steam, he stepped outside the lab tent and kicked a tree until his foot hurt.

The villagers stopped whatever activity they were doing and looked and listened.

"Is this foreigner now also going crazy?"

Roland Weber did not. He only vented his anger and his disappointment. Once he had calmed down, he could think clearly again.

The organism lived; it multiplied even under the most extreme conditions. He, however, could not prove DNA strands and carbon isotopes. This could only mean one thing: his field equipment was not up to the task. He needed to run his tests with more sophisticated laboratory apparatuses.

He sealed his brain samples and the jelutong chips in dark-colored glass bottles and packed them in a small Igloo Cooler with cooling elements. At home in Zürich, he would have all the time he needed, and he had the most advanced equipment in his laboratory.

CHAPTER XIII

HOMECOMING

Charlie arrived two days later at LAX by Singapore Airlines Flight SQ 38. The plane touched down shortly before four in the afternoon. Brandy was nervous like never before in her life; she constantly shifted her weight from one leg to the other while standing by the handrail that separated the spectators from the arriving passengers. After immigration and customs, the passengers had to walk through a long tunnel. At its far end, the tunnel made a sharp right turn. At this point the passengers could be seen by the waiting family members and friends. The passengers now had to walk up a ramp that led to the level of the arriving hall. Their waiting friends could follow behind the railing above and were allowed to unite at the top of the ramp but only once the passengers had crossed a blue line. Brandy did not care about the regulations. She raced down the ramp and flung herself into Charlie's arms. Charlie, normally typically reserved, as most Asians are, had tears in his eyes. Arm in arm they walked up the ramp toward the exit, past a security officer swearing behind them for disregarding all the rules.

The ghost, the accidents, the murder, the pencils: it was all forgotten. They were together. That was all that counted.

Brandy insisted that Charlie stayed with her in her small apartment. They hugged and touched each other all evening. After some red wine for Brandy and mango juice for Charlie, they curled up together in the small bed, holding each other affectionately.

✐

The next day, while Brandy took a shower and he was waiting for his taxi to LAX, Charlie quickly rummaged through Brandy's drawers. When he found what he was looking for, he took it out and let it disappear in his pocket.

At the airport he rented a heavy-duty Ford pickup with hydraulic ramp and an electric pallet cart. He drove over the short distance to the cavernous Cargo Hall, where he retrieved his pencils. Customs was a breeze, and he was on his way back to Brandy's apartment in no time.

"Brandy, I say we should exchange the pencils tonight. The sooner the better. I take it that you have the keys."

"Sure, I am the principal's secretary. I have the keys to everything."

"It will be child's play. We drive up, do our exchange, and off we go."

"Sorry, Charlie, it is not that easy." Brandy looked concerned. "There is a gate to the school grounds that is locked at night, and we have a night guard on duty."

"Oh, no! Can't we go in from the back, you know with bolt cutters or something?"

Brandy bit the nail of her left thumb, thinking about a solution. Then her face brightened, and she smiled broadly. "Yes, there is a way. Actually it is rather easy to get in. Our school grounds border on Griffith Park. Griffith Park is the largest park and wilderness area within any city in the United States. Because the area behind our school is wilderness, nobody ever bothered to put up a fence."

"Yes, but how can we get there? Can I drive there with my Ford?"

"Yes, you can. Right behind our school runs a fire road, which is used by the fire department in case of a brushfire."

"Wonderful, then we are on."

They were both very excited now and could not wait to embark on their adventure, yet they had to wait till after midnight.

*

Their hearts pumping, their arteries full of adrenaline, they turned onto a narrow side street off Los Feliz Boulevard. After a few hundred feet uphill, Brandy pointed out a trailhead that led into the park. The truck slipped into the wilderness trail. Shaking and bobbing from side to side, it followed the trail until Brandy touched Charlie's arm and pointed to her right.

"Charlie, stop. Turn right. This is the fire road." The entrance to the fire road was hardly visible. It was overgrown with sage scrub and chaparral. "We are almost there."

While the Ford stealthily rolled down the fire road, yellow eyes from the slopes above were watching them, fluorescing in the pale light of the ascending moon. This was too much for Charlie. He pulled over and grabbed Brandy's left arm with two hands. The ghost had caught up with him and was ready to pounce on him.

"Charlie, Charlie, my hero with his British education!" Brandy teased him. She could not help laughing out loud. "Charlie. These are coyotes, not ghosts. They are very shy and harmless. It is too dark; you cannot see them, only their eyes. They look like scruffy German shepherd dogs, just a little smaller. They are everywhere here in California."

"Hmm…" It took Charlie a moment to recover, and then he drove on.

At the back of the school, they stopped, lowered the loading ramp, and pulled the pallet cart to the storage shed. It was all so easy. Brandy unlocked the heavy double door. Charlie entered with his cart, lifted the first crate up with the fork, and pushed the red button, and the electric cart rolled all by itself back to the truck. It took less than an hour to exchange the crates. Once this was accomplished, Brandy neatly locked the shed, and they moved on to the classrooms and administrative offices, where they substituted new pencils for all the pencils they could find. Brandy even remembered the pencils from her apartment that she had stashed away in her desk together with the shavings.

*

Meanwhile in the guardhouse by the main gate, Alex the night guard woke up from a blissful slumber. He was not supposed to sleep on duty, but at his age, pushing seventy, he could not help a few catnaps during the uneventful and boring nights. Nobody knew anyhow, and nothing ever happened. Alex lifted his head up from the desktop and rubbed his eyes. They were itching. Now his nose was itching. He rubbed it, moving it from side to side. And for good measure his back began to itch. He reached back to scratch it, but because of his age, he was not flexible enough anymore to reach the itch. He tried from above; he tried from below and from the side. He tried with his right hand, and he tried with his left hand. No matter what he tried, he could not reach the itch. As a result, the itch became ever more annoying. He looked around for something with which he could reach the irritating spot. A pencil caught his eye. At one end it had an eraser. No good for scratching. At the other end, a shiny black point. Alex took the pencil, pressed the point against the table top, and broke it off. Now he had a nice wooden cone, perfect for his purpose.

With the pencil he could reach the itching area on his back. Ah… this felt good, so good. He scratched his back and scratched and scratched it, wiggling and enjoying the sensation. The more he scratched, the more he had the desire to scratch even more. His skin turned pink, and here and there developed tiny hairline cracks with miniscule blood droplets oozing from them. Finally he had enough. He stood up from his swivel chair, limped over to the door of his guardhouse, and stepped outside. He stretched his arms and passed wind. This felt so good. He opened his fly to relieve himself in the bushes.

There! What was that? Alex froze. He strained his ears as hard as he could. Yes, there had been a noise. Was this the noise of an engine? He was not sure. There again. Yes, there was something going on at the back of the school. Alex rushed into his guardhouse, took his gun out of the drawer, and began to limp up the driveway to the administrative offices. He made sure that he did not walk on the gravel but stayed to the side on the grassy shoulder. He was afraid, so afraid, that his stomach began to cramp, but he moved on, ever so careful. As much as he concentrated, he could not hear anything anymore. Just when he began to regain his confidence, he heard a muted shuffle. It was frightfully near. Alex began to shake uncontrollably. And this very instant he saw a movement. Something moved by the entrance to the principal's office. In pure panic, Alex fired and fired and fired in this direction until his magazine was empty, not a single shot left in his gun. After the first two shots, he heard a shrieking noise, and then it was quiet. Alex stood motionless. No noise, no movement, no nothing. Alex waited and waited. Nothing. At first he felt like a hero; he had defended the school and killed the intruder. Then remorse grabbed him. Oh my God, he had killed a person. Why did he have to sneak up there? Why did he not stay in his guardhouse and call the police? The police! Oh God, he must call the police. He took his cell phone out of his pocket and dialed 911.

"We had a break-in at the school. I killed somebody."

He did not dare to go to his victim; instead he sloughed back to his guardhouse, and when within minutes several police cruisers appeared at the gate, he let them in. He told them what had happened and followed them at a safe distance up the driveway. The headlights of the police cars washed the area in bright light. The senior police officer got out of his car and, followed by three or four officers, carefully approached the principal's office. Other officers swarmed out to secure the area. When the lead officer came closer to the building, he noticed an awful smell, and he stood right above the victim of Alex's rampage. He pointed his powerful Maglite at a dead skunk hit by several bullets.

"Hey, get me the night guard; I want him to identify the victim," he bellowed to nobody specifically.

When Alex saw what he had done, he broke down crying with relief.

The police searched the school grounds and could not find anything out of the ordinary. No windows broken, no doors smashed in, no locks tampered with. The next day it was confirmed that nothing was missing. Alex had overreacted, understandable for his age.

✿

Having completed their mission successfully, Charlie and Brandy drove back up the fire road and turned left into the trail that led to the side street of Los Feliz Boulevard. At the moment when they left the grounds and entered the trail, they heard several shots being fired.

Brandy, the Angelino, confidently lectured Charlie. "This is nothing. Here in LA you can hear shots fired almost every night."

✿

Two days after the nighttime incident, Brandy announced over the public address system that the president of an Indonesian pencil company was visiting and would give a presentation about Indonesia at the auditorium. As a surprise, everybody would get a box of a dozen color pencils in exchange for an ordinary pencil from their factory.

"Why do they have to turn in a pencil for a box? Can't Mr. Wong just hand out boxes?" wondered Peter Stadler.

"Oh, that is only a gimmick, to make his presentation more interesting. You know when people have to do something to get something, the present is of more value to them."

Greed certainly is one of the strongest motivators, and after the presentation, Brandy and Charlie were confident that they had collected 99.99 percent of all the haunted pencils. Out of curiosity, they counted their loot in the evening, which was not so hard, since most pencils were still in their crates. They came to the conclusion that they had actually recovered all of the pencils but one. Only one pencil was missing.

"All our efforts were in vain. All this for nothing. Charlie, we failed," lamented Brandy.

"I would not say so. I think we were very, very successful. This one pencil cannot make a difference." After a short pause, Charlie had an idea how he could explain it to Brandy. "Look, Brandy, it is like our ghost is missing its little toe. I would not worry at all."

But worry she did. She still worried when she went back to work the next morning. The old night guard, Alex, was sitting in Stadler's office, telling his story of the scary night in all detail.

"No, not again. How often do we have to hear it? Well, it is the story of his life," thought Brandy, sitting down at her desk.

She had not even touched the seat cushion, when she jumped out of her seat as if it were the white-hot top of an electric stove. "What did he say? Just before he heard the intruders, he had scratched his back with a pencil."

Brandy raced to the door, then turned around, grabbed a paper cup, filled it with cappuccino from the espresso machine, and ran out of the door. Again she turned around, headed for her desk, picked up a pencil, and finally dashed down to the guardhouse where a day guard had taken over from Alex at dawn.

The day guard was leaning against a fence post, enjoying the warm rays of the morning sun.

"I brought you a cup of cappuccino!"

"Wonderful, thank you so much." With that, he took the cup from Brandy and sipped the coffee. "By the way, Brandy, would you have a pencil sharpener? The tip of the pencil in the guardhouse is broken. I could come by your office a little later after school started and I locked the gate."

He had said the magic word. On her way down to the guardhouse, Brandy was concerned that the pencil might have disappeared, after all, the incident had happened three days ago.

"I happen to have a new one in my pocket. I will put it on your desk," beamed Brandy, and she marched into the guardhouse.

There on the desk, in all its beauty, was a yellow pencil with a shiny, golden ferrule and a pink eraser and—no tip! Brandy substituted her pencil for it and headed back to the main building.

On the way back, she studied the production date on her loot. "Yes, I found the missing pencil. One hundred percent success!" With that, she scampered and skipped like a little girl up the driveway and into her office.

*

After having completed their mission, the time had come for Brandy and Charlie to say good-bye to each other.

Brandy drove the rented Ford heavy-duty pickup with the Indonesian pencils on board to the airport. Charlie sat next to her. On Century Boulevard, just before the airport, she pulled over and eased into the parking lot of a Carl's Jr. fast-food restaurant. She drove the Ford to the far end of the very big parking lot to give them some privacy.

"Charlie, thank you for coming. I will miss you…I will miss you so much." Her eyes became wet, and tears rolled down her cheeks. She turned and looked out of the window and began to cry bitterly.

Charlie turned her gently around. He held a first-class ticket on Singapore Airlines in his hand. She looked at it, his ticket.

"No, Brandy, this is your ticket, I'm taking you home."

She swallowed, looked at him; she did not understand.

"Brandy, I want to marry you. Please come with me!"

"I…I can't, I don't know…I—"

"We will leave together or we will not leave at all. I will not go without you."

"But my job…my apartment? My passport?"

"Here it is, your passport. I swiped it from your drawer. Your apartment, just forget about it. Call them and give notice; tell them to keep the deposit. About your job, I talked to Peter Stadler. He said he is so happy for you and he will visit you in Jakarta."

She was confused; she took her head in her hands and looked at him with big eyes, and then she flung herself in his arms.

Together they boarded the 747-400 and were inseparable from that time on.

❧

While Charlie reloaded his shipment onto a Garuda flight from Jakarta to Palembang and traveled on to Jambi and Bukittinggi, Brandy was busy turning Charlie's bare-bones house into a home. Charlie had nothing in his dwelling but a bed, a TV set, and some orange crates that served as bookshelves, tables, and chairs. Brandy rummaged through Jakarta's street markets, buying, piece by piece, Indonesian furniture: rattan, beautifully carved rosewood, handcrafted leather, and batik fabrics.

Charlie's trip to Bukittinggi was cumbersome and hard. He had to drag his heavy load of pencils upstream in a convoy of speedboats. At the mountain trail, the water buffalo struggled to pull the crates uphill. When he finally arrived at the village, he had to herd his small caravan of buffalo through a gauntlet of silently watching villagers. At the infamous clearing, he dug with a few courageous young men a deep hole into which they sank the load. His job was not completed yet. Together with the villagers, he erected a small temple in the center of the clearing as penance for Eric's sacrilege.

Nine months after their arrival in Jakarta, Brandy gave birth to a beautiful girl with round eyes sparkling like black diamonds. Her hair was as black as Charlie's but as curly as Brandy's.

CHAPTER XIV

LABORATORY TESTS

Back home in Zürich, Roland Weber went straight to his lab at Bärli Pharmaceuticals and deposited his treasures in the freezer. Only then did he drive home to recover from his jet lag. As soon as he woke up, he rushed over to the laboratory to continue with his tests. He took the dark bottles from the freezer and emptied their contents onto petri dishes. The reddish color had faded. He looked at his samples under the microscope: no more reddish organisms. He placed them under an electron microscope. The microorganisms had disappeared. Had they decomposed in the icebox and the freezer? Was it possible that they did not agree with cold temperatures? Did they need the hot and humid environment of the Indonesian rainforest?

Roland Weber had no explanation. He had to go back to Bukittinggi, where he hoped to find new samples of this reddish miniscule life-form.

AUTHOR'S NOTE —THE WRATH OF THE RAINFOREST

ow then, was the core of this story true, or was it nothing but the brainchild of my fantasy?

Do ghosts and spirits exist? Do the people of Indonesia know more than we do? Who can tell? As long as we do not have the receptors, each of us may come to his or her own conclusion.

But one thing cannot be denied. When we cut down a tree in the rainforest and thus disconnect it from the source of its life—the spirits of the earth—, its soul, its own spirit leaves the tree, and the tree becomes a soulless, lifeless, dead object. It stops breathing its breath of life, its breath that we all need for our well-being and our lives.

Uprooted from their natural habitat and transferred into our world, the trees of the rainforest refuse to provide us what we need the most: a clean, healthy atmosphere, moderate temperatures, fertile lands, protective clouds.

But when we recognize our wrongdoing and reverse our action and put tiny little seedlings back into the soil, the spirits of the earth, the water, and the air come together and nourish the little seedling. A new and vibrant spirit will inhabit the little sapling and make it grow and grow and grow into a majestic creature that will breathe life again into our world and make all other life, including ours, possible.

What these forces of life are, we do not know despite of all our knowledge and scientific research. From a superficial perspective, the answer seems easy: it is sulfur and nitrogen, water and oxygen. Any gardener knows this. But what is it that generates life? We can mix these chemicals and blend them together as much as we like, and they will remain dead matter. Where does life come from? What is the invisible force that breeds life?

Five hundred years have passed since Shakespeare wrote his famous sentence:

> There are more things in heaven and earth, Horatio,
> Than are dreamt of in your philosophy.

We know so much more, but we did not manage yet to open the barn door to the mystery of life. A cell phone is a dead object, yet electrical power and radio waves bring it to life. What brings us to life? What are these forces, these spirits that generate life, enable us to think and to feel? All we know is when we mess with them and deny them the respect they deserve, their wrath will come down on us.

ACKNOWLEDGEMENTS

I am fortunate that I had extraordinary people help me write and publish my book. My wife, Karin, with her sharp mind, incredible memory, and boundless knowledge, supported and advised me throughout writing it and made sure that the facts were correct. When I developed the story, I had my son, Markus, in mind as a person who does not believe in ghosts and whom I wanted to gain a different perspective of what is real and what may be fantasy. He was also a thorough, critical, and observant editor. It was he who introduced me to Julie Matthews, who was a supportive and encouraging friend although living thousands of miles away from my home in the northeast of Australia.